Sign up for our newsletter to hear
about new and upcoming releases.

www.ylva-publishing.com

OTHER BOOKS IN THE TASTE OF HER SERIES

The Taste of Her — Volume 1
The Taste of Her — Volume 2

The Taste of Her
Volumes 1 and 2 in one compendium
(paperback)

THE TASTE OF HER

A COLLECTION OF TEN EROTIC SHORT STORIES

JESS LEA

SEVERINA

Emilie blinked as Regina flicked on the lights. They illuminated the shop floor in a soft amber glow. No ghastly fluorescent bulbs lit these rooms, to make women flinch in dismay at every bulge and stretchmark revealed in the mirrors. No, at Severina the lighting was tender and tasteful. Emilie, who liked historical dramas, thought it made the store look like some venerable Art Deco club on a winter's evening. Which was no less real than a place with fluorescent lighting, Regina pointed out, and a good deal more humane.

It was decent of Regina to think about her customers' happiness, Emilie thought. Or clever, at least. If only Regina's generosity could extend to her staff once in a while.

Regina fixed each of her assistants with a cool, appraising glance. The look dared them to do anything wrong today, to even *think* about slacking off under her supervision. Then she gave a faint jerk of her chin, beckoning them closer.

"You know what to do."

Under the watchful eye of their boss, Emilie and Alonsa moved around the shop, preparing for the day. They stocked the register, poured rose oil into the infusers, tied back the red-and-white-striped curtains to the fitting rooms with tasselled ropes, and dressed the mannequins in today's display items: a delicate cream silk camisole with matching knickers, a corset in black satin decorated with aromatic strips of leather, and a full-cup plunge bra and thong that were mostly transparent save for a few scraps of white lace.

Emilie liked this part of the job. Displaying the merchandise at Severina felt like setting up an exhibit in some chic, private art gallery. Severina wasn't your typical clothes shop, where you could expect to find the merchandise crammed together on brittle plastic hangers or tossed into dump-bins for women to rifle through. In Regina's shop, each item had its own special display space and a price to match. As far as Emilie was concerned, that was just as it should be.

When they had finished their tasks, Emilie and Alonsa took their places in front of the service desk. As always, Regina waited whilst they composed themselves, then sauntered over to inspect them. Thoroughly.

Regina was impeccable in her dove-grey blouse, dark woollen skirt, seamed stockings, and leather court shoes, the silver streaks glinting in her black hair. She smelled delicious. As her boss stepped in front of her and looked her over, Emilie swallowed hard.

In her six months of working here, Emilie had learned how to conduct herself. She had become adept at product displays, dress and deportment, and creative handling of the book-keeping during lean times. She had learned how to manage the rejection of a credit card without a nasty scene, how to pitch her voice just right for a nervous or demanding customer, and how she should never, ever, under any circumstances, call them "hon" or "babe".

She'd progressed well, but somehow one little thing was always amiss, and Regina was guaranteed to find it.

"Well, well." Regina touched Emilie's hair where it hung in carefully arranged curls down to her shoulders. "I don't remember any discussion about you adopting a new style."

"Just trying something different, miss."

"I see." Regina's hand fell away. "Quite fetching, I suppose. But how will it look by the end of your shift, when you have"—she paused—"worked up a sweat? I don't tolerate slatternly girls in here, as you know." Regina's gaze moved to Emilie's face, and she made a small noise of irritation. "Too heavy on the eyeliner again. How many times must I remind you that this is a boutique establishment, not a nightclub?"

"Apologies, miss." Emilie's tone remained respectful, but she felt a faint urge to roll her painted eyes. Yes, Regina was probably right about them—

she was right about most things in here—but did her corrections always have to be *so* personal? Couldn't she, Emilie, have any say at all?

Not that she would dare ask that question out loud.

"Hm." Regina reached out to pick a loose thread off Emilie's blouse. "Show me your hands." Emilie held them out, then turned them over. They were spotless, her skin soft and moisturised, fingernails smooth, short, and perfectly clean. Just the way Regina liked them.

Regina gave a curt nod of approval. Then she raised her own manicured hands to Emilie's shoulders and ran them down the younger woman's back with a light pressure that made Emilie shiver. Regina was checking for bra straps—or, rather, the absence thereof.

Emilie's work at Severina went beyond fitting and assisting the customers. Sometimes she would be called upon to model the products. And when it came to Emilie's skin, Regina's standards were as unforgiving as ever; unsightly grooves or pink marks left by wire and elastic were out of the question. They might peep out from underneath the beautiful garments and mar the illusion of perfection.

Regina gave another nod, her hands resting below Emilie's shoulderblades. She was standing so close to her employee that their breasts almost touched. A flicker of Regina's eyelids signalled what she expected next.

Emilie kept looking straight ahead as she reached down with her right hand to hitch her skirt higher, until the hem was halfway up her thigh. Regina's stance in front of the younger woman adjusted so they were eye to eye. Then she slipped her own hand beneath the fabric.

Her fingertips trailed a hot line up Emilie's outer thigh, all the way to her hip, until Regina was satisfied Emilie had also obeyed her rule not to wear knickers.

Sometimes, when they were the only two people on shift, Regina might be more rigorous in her investigation. She might run both hands around the back to cup Emilie's bare cheeks, whilst fixing her employee with a level gaze that reminded her who was boss. But with Alonsa standing there, that might have looked like favouritism.

The older woman released her and stepped back. Emilie struggled to maintain her rigid stance, but she was breathing hard. Regina and her endless rules! This was so insulting and unfair.

It wasn't the inconvenience Emilie minded, although it was not always easy to spend her days like this—constantly aware of the bounce of her unsupported breasts, the swish of her blouse directly across that sensitive skin, and the embarrassing peaks of her nipples that rose beneath the fabric at every breeze through the shop door. Not to mention the difficulty of bending over to fetch things from low drawers or climbing the stepladder in search of stock when she had nothing on under her skirt.

No, it was the mistrust of these daily inspections that was hard to tolerate, the warm invasion of Regina's hands that caused Emilie's body to clench in equal parts anger and arousal. As if she needed to be supervised that closely—as if she were some dopey trainee who couldn't be trusted to follow a simple instruction!

Because whether her boss noticed or not, Emilie was a perfectionist too. Her modelling sessions did look better if her skin had no marks. And Emilie loved this place. She sold works of art in here—"underwear" hardly did them justice. She was willing to make sacrifices for their sake.

She kept her face to the front whilst Regina stepped across to inspect Alonsa. But from the corner of her eye, Emilie saw Regina pick a fleck of lipstick from the corner of Alonsa's dark red mouth and fasten a top button Alonsa had carelessly, or provocatively, left undone. Regina murmured a warning about the need for a decent and professional appearance at all times.

As Alonsa's inspection became more intimate, Emilie bit her lip. It was reassuring in a way to know that her colleagues received the same rigorous treatment, but at times it made Emilie's insides twist with jealousy and other forbidden emotions.

Sometimes when they were adding up the till or stocking the shelves together, Emilie would observe her co-workers' range of complexions and body shapes, from Alonsa's buxom curves to Lydia's waiflike delicacy—Regina was covering all bases—and realise her colleagues must be equally naked beneath their neat skirts and blouses. The idea of it, and the thought that the other girls might have felt Regina's hands inside their clothing too, was enough to make Emilie fumble with the invoices and drop armfuls of precious garments all over the floor.

"Very well." Regina's voice jolted Emilie out of her thoughts. The older woman stepped back, folded her arms, and glanced at each of them in turn. "Shall we, then?"

Her heels thunked softly against the polished floorboards as she strode over to unlock the front door. Emilie reached down to press the Play button on the stereo, and Rachmaninov's *All-Night Vigil* flowed softly from the speakers.

Severina was never a crowded shop; the prices and refinement took care of that. Another thing that Emilie loved about it. Her formative experiences of shopping had involved dragging her howling younger brothers through Kmart, praying the things they needed would be on special and arguing with the security guards when the boys' thieving set off the alarms. She found the atmosphere of Severina positively spiritual in comparison.

A treasure house, Emilie thought, gazing around her at the visions of velvet, lace, and leather. But why did it have to be guarded by a dragon?

The morning's customers began to arrive. They included a spoiled but insecure debutante unsure of her own bra size, an elegant widow in her seventies with a spring in her step and an adventurous taste in nightwear, and a middle-aged divorcee with a tandoori tan, a platinum credit card, and new breasts whose dimensions required Emilie to scurry out to the store room in search of something in XXL.

"Hasn't seen her feet in six months," Alonsa muttered as the customer finally left with one of Severina's beribboned carry bags in each hand.

Emilie smirked. "That might explain the giraffe-print heels."

But her timing was off. A faint throat clearing made her close her eyes in dismay.

"Emilie. The storeroom now, please." Regina stalked out, leaving Alonsa in charge of the shop floor. Emilie trailed after her.

"What was all that about?" Regina raised her perfectly tapered eyebrows. Emilie looked down at her feet. "*Well?*"

"We were just having a laugh, miss."

"And you think laughing at our customers is part of your job description?"

In her previous workplace, Emilie would not have hesitated to answer "Duh, of course." But that job had been at a Bras 4 U store in a shopping mall, where the customers let their sticky children play hide-and-seek in the racks and screamed abuse at her when she busted them smuggling G-strings out in their handbags. But here…

"No, miss." Emilie hung her head. It was true; she should have known better. Not that wealthy customers were necessarily nicer, but they were paying a premium to be treated as though they were. And at least there were fewer of them. "I just forgot where I was for a second, miss. And the customer didn't hear—"

"*I* heard, Emilie. It's not enough to 'get away' with things like some naughty schoolgirl, imagining that everything is all right as long as you don't get caught. The moment we give ourselves permission to lapse and slip up is the moment we begin to fail. I have told you that before." Regina hooked one long finger under Emilie's chin and forced her head up. "Emilie, why do you think women come to shop here?"

"Because they're having affairs, or want to pretend they are?" Emilie couldn't hold back her sarcasm. She was trying hard here, damn it. Would it kill Regina to acknowledge that once in a while? Emilie wasn't some bored student slumming it in a shop whilst looking forward to a "proper" career in a few months' time. This was her career, and someday she meant to have her own establishment, and it would be exquisite. Why did Regina only ever notice her when she did something wrong?

To Emilie's surprise, her smart remark won her a flicker of a smile.

"Sometimes. Or sometimes our customers are newly in love, or trying to get over being in love. Or they're buying themselves a treat they're not sure they deserve, or learning to accept a body that has changed from sickness or childbearing, or struggling to jump-start a twenty-year relationship, or taking revenge on an ex-husband's credit card. Or just wanting to feel a little bit special. It's therapy, and a therapist doesn't pass judgement." She paused, her dark eyes narrowing. "And you have no idea what it costs some women to get undressed in front of a pretty young thing like you."

Emilie looked down at her shoes. "I'm sorry, miss. I-I do want to do my job well."

"Prove it, then." Regina spun around and returned to the shop floor.

Emilie was left feeling mortified and more than a little frustrated. She'd been expecting—no, hoping for—a different kind of punishment, something like what had happened on her first day on the job, when Emilie had assumed Regina's "no underwear" rule was a joke.

The memory of Regina's severe lecture in the back office—Was Emilie unable to pay attention? Did she think herself above the rules? Did she take her work seriously at all?—still burned in her memory. Not to mention how Regina had then instructed her to strip naked so she could point out every place where the straps and waistband had marked Emilie's skin, and had tapped each blemish with a glossy fingernail.

She bit her lip, a treacherous heat stirring between her legs at the memory of Regina picking up her dressmaker's scissors and snipping the underwire out of Emilie's bra. *"Bend over the sofa, dear, and bite on the cushion if you feel the need."*

Regina had used the wire to whip Emilie's thighs and buttocks six times, to show her how unsightly marked skin could be. The punishment had lasted a long while, with Regina pausing between strokes to reiterate how disappointing Emilie's behaviour was. *"You'll need to lift your game if you want to achieve your true potential."* All the while, Emilie had writhed at the shock of being so exposed before her new boss, the stinging pain, and, well, the unexpected throbs of pleasure.

When had Emilie inspected the thin red stripes across her rear end afterwards, she'd learned to take her new boss at her word.

Emilie did her best to shake off the recollection and returned to the shop floor. She placed an order with their supplier, then stomped over to straighten out a gossamer nightgown the last customer had left in a heap. She didn't know what was making her more resentful: the memory of that vigorous reprimand or the fact Regina hadn't seen fit to repeat it today.

Her feelings of resentment and frustration intensified when Regina summoned Alonsa into the storeroom for her own talking-to several minutes later. She returned with a flushed face and a crooked skirt, which suggested her punishment had been more than verbal. Perhaps Regina had been harder on Alonsa for starting the joke, but Emilie could not help feeling more disgruntled—and turned on—than ever. Had Regina pinched Alonsa? Thrashed her, even? Had Alonsa enjoyed it?

"Emilie?" Regina cooed across the shop. Her manner was mild now; she was with a customer. "This lady would appreciate some assistance with a fitting."

Emilie dredged up a smile for the young woman at her boss's side. She hoped her face wasn't flushed from those unprofessional thoughts. "Of course. Come on through."

She arranged the items—scalloped lace bras in ivory, black, and dark fern green—in the fitting room. Then she excused herself and ducked into the kitchenette to wash her hands in warm water until her skin was pink with heat. A lingerie fitting must be a comfortable experience for a woman, Regina maintained, and nothing spoiled that comfort faster than a pair of icy hands.

"Have you been fitted before?" Emilie asked as she stepped into the cubicle and drew the curtain closed. The customer, a plump redhead with pale, freckled skin, blushed as she shook her head. Her nervous smile looked cute to Emilie, and she smelled pleasantly of vanilla. Her fingers fumbled with the zipper at the back of her dress. Emilie gave another encouraging smile. "Shall I…?" As she helped the woman undress, Emilie glanced up through the gap in the curtain and caught a glimpse of Regina standing by the desk, looking her way.

That sense of injustice flared up again in Emilie's chest. She knew how to assess a woman's size and shape discreetly, how to praise the customers' choices and steer them away from mistakes. There was no need for her boss to spy on her!

She must have been scowling, for the redhead was looking nervously at her now, clasping her dress in front of her body. Emilie adjusted her expression to something more supportive and murmured, "Let me help you there…" She stepped behind the young woman and gently unhooked her bra. This won a tiny gasp but no objection. Emilie reached for the fern-coloured creation first. "Shall we try this on for size?"

Fitting was a delicate business. *"Nothing is worse than having your lingerie fitted by some dreadful, brisk, ham-fisted woman who reminds you of your old school nurse,"* Regina liked to say. So Emilie had developed a light but steady touch for adjusting straps, and she wielded her measuring tape as smoothly as Regina herself. Not that her boss would ever admit it.

Before long, the redhead was giggling at Emilie's jokes about starting a new career in burlesque and gazing in wonder as her breasts were lifted and pressed together, their creamy curves accentuated by dark green lace. Her hair bobbed around her face as she laughed at Emilie's pleasantries; she was more cheerful than their earlier customers, Emilie realised, and prettier too.

"Not too tight?" Emilie slid a finger beneath the wire and felt the woman shiver despite the heat in the fitting room. Regina insisted on running the heaters on high in there, claiming customers must feel comfortable to keep trying on garments for as long as they wished.

"It's perfect, thank you," the woman whispered, still staring at her new cleavage. Her cheeks were red from shyness or the heat in the room, but beneath the fern-coloured lace, her nipples were erect. Was it the thrill of seeing herself looking so transformed, or the friction of the textured fabric as Emilie worked it into place? Emilie looked down at those little buds straining against the lace and a hot pulse stirred again between her thighs.

She blinked in alarm. What was wrong with her? She never ogled the customers; that was definitely not allowed here.

When Regina had first permitted her to start fitting women for their lingerie, she had explained that some women appreciated an atmosphere of tenderness and admiration, but that inappropriate behaviour was strictly forbidden. Was Emilie confident she could work with scantily clothed women and remain professional? Regina's narrow glare had suggested her boss doubted it, which had offended Emilie at the time. But now Emilie pictured herself cupping this stranger's breasts through her newly fitted bra, caressing them, tracing circles around those small, hard nipples until the woman cried out—

Emilie wondered if Regina had been right all along.

She cleared her throat.

"This model comes with matching underwear, of course. Would you prefer the bikini, boyleg, or thong style?"

"Um, the bikini, please." The other woman reached up behind her to touch the lace at her back. As she did, her fingertips brushed by accident against Emilie's breast. "Oh! I'm sorry…"

With nothing but the slippery fabric of her blouse between them, Emilie felt the contact with shocking intensity and her own nipples tightened. Oh God, were they visible? She didn't dare glance down. She looked at the other woman's face instead and saw that her eyes were wide, her lips parted. Perhaps that touch had not been an accident? Emilie knew she should move away; instead she found herself leaning closer…

"How is everything going in there?"

Emilie jumped at the rap on the doorframe and Regina's crisp voice. *Damn it!* Why was she having such dirty ideas—and why did Regina have to interrupt them?

"We've found a style that looks beautiful," Emilie explained, forcing a professional tone. "I was just going to fetch the rest of the set."

"Excellent." Regina had a way of twitching open a fitting room curtain just enough to allow herself to slip inside without exposing an inch of the customer's flesh to anyone in the store. Emilie had never quite worked out how she did that. "I see you've selected some other exquisite models too, madam. Why don't I fit you for those whilst Emilie finishes her little errand?"

And somehow, a moment later, Emilie found herself outside, on the wrong side of the curtain.

From inside the fitting room, she could hear Regina crooning about full cups versus half cups, strapless versus racerbacks and "this cheeky new 3-D model, which would look stunning on you—yes, the gelati-pink. I know you might have been told you can't wear pink with red hair, but that's all hidebound nonsense. Go on, you'll be amazed…" And from the customer's happy little squeaks, this appeared to be the case.

Emilie, demoted to passing pants through the curtain, felt thoroughly cheated. And although she hated to admit it, she was more turned on than ever. Not just by the thought of that very friendly customer half-exposed just a few inches away from her, but by the familiar soundtrack of Regina's deep, throaty purr—"That's it! Now turn around for me… Oh, just look at yourself!"—and her natural authority; the way Regina could order a stranger to undress with the merest twitch of her chin whilst enticing them to venture into daring shades of buttercup, violet, and hot flamingo—"Life's too short for beige, my dear…" Sometimes it got to be too much for Emilie to bear.

She thought about creeping off to the bathroom and releasing the tension a little. But that could prove disastrous if she had to do any modelling afterwards. Once, about a month before, Emilie had given in after an especially demanding morning with Regina and spent her lunch break in her car in a quiet corner of the carpark, fucking herself breathlessly beneath her coat—only to find herself in some discomfort ten minutes later when she was called upon to model some very small, very sheer knickers.

Afterwards, Regina had taken her aside to reprimand her for appearing "in such an intimate state". The customer who'd requested the viewing hadn't seemed offended, but other women might be less broad-minded, Regina said. In fact, that particular customer—a pierced and tattooed showgirl—had smirked with amusement throughout Emilie's display and ended up buying every item presented to her. Which might have been why Emilie escaped without serious punishment apart from a single brutal pinch of her bottom at the close of business when no more customers were around to see the mark.

"If you cannot control yourself," Regina told her, "you're no use to me."

The memory made Emilie squirm as she rang up the items for the redheaded customer, who'd emerged beaming from the fitting room. Regina remained in the shadows of the cubicle, her arms folded. She watched as Emilie folded the underwear sets with the care of an origami artist and handed over the bags. Each one was printed with Severina's logo: a sleeping wolf.

The customer headed for the door, which was held open for her with a courteous sweep by someone entering. Someone whose appearance made Emilie blink, her lips parting in surprise.

The stranger stood six feet tall in her black leather boots, their thick silver zips and chunky buckles gleaming under the store's lights. Her dark hair was shaved close to her head at the back and sides and spiked on top. Her black T-shirt and jeans looked like they'd been tailored just for her, and her jacket carried with it the tantalising scent of leather and cologne. A silver identity bracelet glinted on her left wrist. She wasn't Emilie's usual type at all—but Emilie couldn't deny she wore those things well.

Intrigued, Emilie hesitated—which was her downfall. Before she could approach this new arrival, Regina had already stepped forwards, her right hand outstretched, and asked in her silkiest voice, "May I help you, sir?"

Emilie opened her mouth, wondering if it would be ruder to correct her boss or let the mistake continue. Then she caught Regina's knowing gaze as the stranger shook her hand, and suspected her employer knew exactly what she was doing.

"It's my girlfriend's birthday." The stranger spoke with a slow drawl, as if confident everyone would be happy to stop and listen. Emilie was listening all right. She realised she'd forgotten to close her mouth. "I'd like to give her a treat."

"We have pieces in here to suit every woman," said Regina. "Emilie, perhaps you could show—" She paused.

"Jay," the stranger supplied.

"—our latest lines?" Regina raised her eyebrows. "Or perhaps Jay might appreciate a private viewing?"

Emilie gulped. All right, she was used to modelling, but today had already been…difficult. The thought of appearing almost naked in front of this slouching, leather-clad stranger, whose eyes were now leaving Regina's face to glide up and down Emilie's body… She blushed up to the roots of her hair.

For private sessions, they used a special cubicle. It was roomier than the others and lined with gilt-edged mirrors. One corner was taken up by a carved mahogany screen behind which Emilie could prepare. Jay settled herself in the armchair without being asked, one foot in its motorcycle boot crossed over her knee. Regina offered her coffee or cinnamon tea, which she declined.

Emilie could not help stealing glances at Jay's broad hands and her long, muscular legs in tight denim, and the way the seam pressed along the length of her crotch… She felt both relieved and nervous when Regina whipped the curtain aside and stepped in, her left arm draped with the items Emilie would be wearing soon. They all looked very small indeed.

"You didn't say much about your…companion's taste or style." Regina's voice was cool. "So I've selected a range."

"I'm still trying to figure out her style myself." Jay smiled. "But as for her taste, it is *always* perfect."

Regina placed the items on the side table, then sifted through them for her first display.

"This is an ever-popular model: our lace-edged slip in burgundy silk." She handed it to Emilie, who ducked behind the screen, kicked off her shoes, and began unbuttoning her blouse with clumsy fingers. She was all too aware of the faint sounds of the buttons squeezing through the eyes, the fabric slipping off her bare shoulders, the thump as her skirt hit the floor. She was naked now, with only a screen between her body, Regina's intense gaze, and Jay's lazy smile.

Emilie drew the slip on as quickly as she could, knocking the screen in her haste. She felt it totter and feared it would fall and reveal her wearing nothing but burgundy silk bunched above her waist. She yanked at the slip and shook her hips hard. The cool, flimsy material slithered down until the lace tickled her thighs. Then she stepped out from behind the screen.

"As you see, the effect is one of timeless elegance and sensuality," Regina explained in a voice that made Emilie's insides quiver pleasurably. In such close proximity to both women, with Regina's subtle perfume mingling with Jay's cologne, her excitement was becoming hard to suppress.

Emilie struck her usual poses—one hand on her hip, the other lifting up her hair—then paced a circle in front of their customer.

"Why, that is beautiful." Jay breathed in deeply, giving a slow nod as she took in everything. Emilie could feel the burgundy silk, so fine it was almost transparent, clinging to her curves. The lace trim gently chafed the tops of her nipples, which hardened rebelliously. The polished floorboards shone beneath her bare feet, and Emilie tried not to think about what might be reflected there for Jay and Regina to see.

"You can't go wrong with that style," Regina declared, sending Emilie back behind the screen with a subtle nod. "But perhaps you'd be interested in something more contemporary?"

The next display was a bra-and-panties set in soft cotton, printed with a design of Japanese cherry blossoms. Decorative bows adorned each strap, and the panties tied at Emilie's hips with pink ribbons. As she turned around before Jay's appreciative gaze, she saw her own reflection in the mirrors that lined the walls. Her cheeks were pink, her hips twitching restlessly. Jay leaned forwards, elbows on her parted knees, to take a closer look, and her breath fluttered against Emilie's bare stomach.

"Aren't these a little impractical?" Jay hooked one finger through the bow at Emilie's left hip. Emilie froze at the warm touch of this butch's skin; if Jay gave a gentle pull, the ribbon would unravel and the scant covering would drop away. The thought caused Emilie's clit to swell until she could almost feel it rubbing against the cotton.

"A woman manages," Regina supplied. "Emilie, my dear—the next display, please." But a full three seconds passed before Jay extricated her finger from the ribbon, leaving Emilie still dressed, but aching not to be.

Emilie retreated behind the screen again, unhooked the cherry-blossom bra, and rolled the panties down her thighs as fast as she could, fearing the scent and the sticky trails of desire she must have left there. She tried her best to wipe the fabric clean against her bare thigh.

Then she turned to see the next item Regina had supplied. It was a snakeskin bra-corset in metal grey and pearly white, with an intricate row of hook-and-eye fastenings all the way up the back.

Emilie stared at it in dismay. She couldn't possibly manage that by herself. She struggled into the matching briefs—tight satin, covering only the top half of her buttocks and rubbing between her thighs—and wondered if this whole fitting was another of Regina's punishments.

She slid her arms into the corset. Pulling it up to cover her chest and belly, she called out, "I need a little help with this..." She was adjusting her breasts inside the sculpted cups when she felt a tug at her waist, then the bodice being pulled together and fastened at the back, one fiddly little eyelet at a time.

Emilie caught her breath. Her waist was being nipped in, her body constrained into a stiff, upright hourglass. But surely the fastening was taking too long? Usually Regina's fingers were agile and merciless; she could lace up a corset so fast it left her models gasping. Emilie glanced over her shoulder and stifled a cry of alarm. The screen had been pulled to one side, and her half-fastened corset was held in Jay's large hands.

"Sorry to disturb." Jay's slow smile did not look sorry at all. "Your boss just stepped out. But I'm happy to help if you can be patient with these clumsy paws."

Without waiting for a reply, Jay resumed fastening the corset. Emilie was too breathless and excited to refuse. She leaned forwards instead to facilitate the fastenings, her hands flattening against the wall. The fleshy tops of her breasts spilled over the corset, and her hips rounded out until the rough texture of Jay's denims brushed against her barely covered arse. She had a shocking vision of what this must look like—and what it would feel like if Jay were to slide those broad, tanned hands down to her hips and pull her body in hard...

"Don't you find it difficult?" Jay asked, working at the final hook whilst Emilie kept her eyes closed. The tight satin chafed and grew slippery between her thighs. "Wearing outrageous things like this every day—parading yourself for strangers..." Jay's voice was laconic, amused. She finished her task and laid one hand on Emilie's bare shoulder. Emilie felt the other hand gliding down to her hip. She kept her own hands on the wall, her heartbeat throbbing between her legs. Jay's strong thumbs stroked her lightly. "Doesn't it get you...distracted?"

Oh God, how Emilie wanted to finish things off right then. How she wanted Jay to push one denim-clad leg up between her thighs and hump her vigorously against the wall, to yank down the expensive panties, spread her cheeks, and lick her all over...

What stopped Emilie from initiating that wasn't the thought of Jay's girlfriend, but the thought of Regina. Regina, with her stern, impossible standards, who loved these delicate garments and her orderly shop—this oasis of art and elegance and calm in an ugly world. Regina, who wanted her followers to understand how important these things were.

Emilie did understand, because Severina meant all those things to her too. And she understood that if she disgraced Severina, Regina wouldn't just be angry. She would be hurt.

"No." Emilie opened her eyes and with all her willpower shook off Jay's hands. "I don't really think about that side to it. The clothes here are special and sexy, but it's the people who matter to me. I always put them first."

To her surprise, this won a smile from Jay, a smile that looked almost triumphant. Emilie saw over Jay's shoulder that they were no longer alone. Regina was standing in the doorway, her arms crossed. Despite her boss's inscrutable expression, Emilie was certain Regina had observed the whole exchange.

Her face burning, Emilie began to stutter out some explanation, but Jay was quicker. Stepping towards Regina, she said, "Thanks so much, ma'am, for taking me through your catalogue. But much as I love this racy little number"—she nodded over her shoulder towards Emilie—"I was hoping for something else. Maybe..." She glanced down at the selection of garments laid out on the side table. "Maybe something like this?" Jay hooked her finger through one item and held it up: a skimpy midnight-blue thong with a plausible imitation sapphire that would sit at the top of the wearer's buttocks.

Emilie stared at it in dismay. She couldn't wear that now. Her wetness would trickle right through!

Regina curled her lip. "Certainly, Emilie would be happy to model that for you. Wouldn't you, Emilie?"

Colour flooded into Emilie's cheeks. She was pretty sure her boss had caught her unhappy stare and understood it. But before she could reply, Jay looked directly at Regina and said, "Ma'am, no offence to your excellent second-in-command here, but my girlfriend has rather different... measurements. I was wondering if you might be kind enough to oblige me yourself."

Emilie choked. Never in all the time she'd worked here had anyone dared... She shut her eyes in horror, afraid she would open them to see Jay's blood on the walls.

Instead, Regina said, "Very well."

Her eyes popped open. She stared from one woman to the other until Regina smiled and pulled the screen back across. From the other side, she called, "You don't need help to get out of that ensemble, do you, Emilie?"

"I—no." Emilie reached behind her, fumbling with the hooks, her fingers shaking. It took her a full minute to get the first clasp undone, and at least a dozen were left. Still, she gasped when Regina yanked the screen aside.

"Oh, for heaven's sake, Emilie! I expect greater efficiency than this."

Regina seized Emilie by the arm; for a moment, Emilie was afraid her boss would forcibly undress her in front of Jay. Instead Regina thrust a robe at her, along with her clothing, and said, "We don't keep our customers waiting. You can sort yourself out in the next cubicle."

Regina thrust Emilie, half-dressed, barefoot, and flustered, out of the fitting room. Thank goodness there were no other customers, only Alonsa standing behind the desk and gaping. At loss for explanation, Emilie could only scurry into the next fitting room, her clothes clutched to her chest, her heart hammering. She yanked the curtain closed and sat down hard on the striped satin chair.

How dare they? How bloody dare they? Emilie wrestled with the fastenings down her spine, her arms aching and her fingertips growing hot and raw. Her face burned. Jay flirting with her and then rejecting her—okay, Emilie had said no first, but still—and as for Regina...

As if on cue, the unmistakeable sound of Regina's rich caramel voice came from the next fitting room. But Regina wasn't snapping out orders this time or enthusing about the virtues of Spanish-style lace. She was... moaning.

Emilie's mouth fell open. Surely there was no way— She pressed her ear to the dividing wall and heard that sound again: a deep, muffled whimper of pleasure and a rough chuckle that could only have come from Jay.

Emilie didn't pause to think. There was a foot-high gap between the top of the dividing wall and the ceiling. As quietly as she could, she hauled the chair over against the dividing wall, popping another fastening on her corset as she did. She climbed up onto the chair and peeked over the divide.

Regina—masterful, controlled Regina—was sprawled naked in the velvet-covered armchair. Her head was thrown back, her hands massaging her breasts and twirling her large coffee-coloured nipples. Regina's long legs were spread apart, her feet up on the arms of the chair. And kneeling in front of her, holding Regina's ankles in a firm grip, the midnight-blue thong tucked into her back pocket, was Jay. Her head was buried between Regina's thighs, and she was licking rapaciously.

Emilie's knees quaked at the sight. God, she had never let herself imagine... Regina's face was flushed, her eyes shut with pleasure, and a sheen of sweat glistened across her naked breasts. She was biting her lip, but her moans came louder as her self-control gave way.

As if sensing the change in tempo, Jay thrust Regina back harder into the chair, her strong hands moving to the woman's outer lips and spreading them further apart, exposing her clit to a hard, wet tongue-lashing.

As Regina writhed and cried out, one hand clapped across her mouth, Emilie could no longer help herself. Her hand slipped down into the satin panties and she was dripping wet.

Tentatively, she fingered her own clit. It was so sensitised that a single touch made her jump. She traced a light circle around it with her middle finger, alarmed by the intensity of her body's response as she watched her cool, powerful boss thrashing and panting whilst a stranger held her back in the chair and fucked her.

Jolts of pleasure coursed through Emilie, every touch of her clit making her legs shake. Her climax was building already, and her face twisted in disappointment. Sure this was dangerous, but she didn't want it to end so fast!

But when Regina arched her back, the muscles straining in her legs, and came with a silent, ferocious rush, Emilie, as usual, had no choice but to follow her boss's lead. Her own orgasm burst like a shower of white-hot sparks beneath her belly, blasting her knees out from underneath her.

Flailing, falling, she grasped at the flimsy dividing wall for support and felt it rattle. She heard the screech of the chair skidding against the floorboards and the thump of her own body hitting the cushions and then the floor. One hand was still down her pants.

For a long time, Emilie lay there, too dazed to care about her bruises, feeling only the sweet, molten waves still flowing through her. As her breathing slowed, however, her precarious situation became clear to her again. Had they heard her next door? Worse, had they glimpsed her fall?

Gingerly, she righted herself, then straightened the chair and sat down. She was about to finish removing the corset when the curtain flew open.

Regina was impeccable. Her blouse didn't have a single wrinkle; her skirt was straight, her shoes shiny, her hair still its usual lacquered perfection. Emilie stared up at her helplessly. How did her boss manage it? How did she dress herself so quickly, as if nothing had happened? Had Jay helped her to get the seams of her stockings just right?

"Emilie." Regina raised an eyebrow. "Still not following my instructions, I see." Her lips pursed with distaste. Emilie caught a glimpse of herself in the mirror: her corset was crooked, her panties wrinkled. Her hair looked like a bird's nest, and her face was candy-pink from exertion.

Regina clicked her tongue. Her tone was impatient, but Emilie could hear a hint of amusement too.

"Honestly. Stand up, I'll remove that."

Her legs still unsteady, Emilie obeyed. Regina's fingers made quick work of the remaining hooks—but she didn't leave when the task was done. She remained standing close behind Emilie, gripping the edges of the corset and holding her employee's gaze in the mirror.

"Emilie, I'm not happy with your conduct today. I expect you know why."

"I..." Emilie's face fell. "No, miss, I didn't mean to look! Honestly..." Emilie's lips trembled. Would this be the end of her career at Severina?

But Regina just frowned. "Look at what, Emilie?"

"I..." Emilie blinked. "Nothing, miss."

"I am unhappy with you..." Regina released the corset abruptly. Emilie felt it slipping off her shoulders and grabbed at it, clasping the snakeskin fabric against her body.

Regina watched Emilie's discomfort with a hard, angular expression. "I am unhappy with you, Emilie, because of this." She reached for Emilie's hips and, without warning, yanked her panties down.

"Oh! Miss, you can't—" Emilie's protests died in her throat as Regina rolled the wet gusset between her fingers, then raised her hand to Emilie's eye level. Her fingers were streaked and glistening, scented with Emilie's juices.

"Emilie, do you know what these garments are worth?" Dumbstruck, Emilie nodded. "Do you appreciate how unique they are, how difficult to replace?" Another helpless nod. "Yet you chose to disregard your responsibilities to our beautiful creations—and your own duty to get back to work—and you defiled these garments like some cheap little hussy." Regina's tone was ruthless. "I won't have it, Emilie. We've spoken before about your lack of control."

"That's not fair! I control myself all the time!" The words burst from Emilie, and Regina smirked.

"Really?"

"Yes, really!" A furious heat rose in Emilie's cheeks. "That customer—that *Jay*—she was hitting on me back there. And I really, really wanted her, and I said no! Because I...because I respect this place. And I respect you."

Silence fell. Emilie's anger dwindled and embarrassment took over. She was all too conscious of the fact she was now wearing nothing but the front of a corset, her panties tangled around her knees. She reached for them with one hand, but a glare from Regina stopped her.

When Emilie obediently withdrew her hand, Regina's expression softened a little.

"Very well." A smile played across the older woman's lips. "I suppose that must have taken some willpower, Emilie. I will give you credit for that."

Emilie blinked in surprise. Then a renewed pulse of desire washed over her as her boss's smile widened and grew predatory.

Regina turned Emilie around to face her own reflection in the mirror. She flattened Emilie's left hand against the glass, then took Emilie's right hand and guided it down the snakeskin corset, letting Emilie feel the rippled surface and then her own warm, bare belly beneath it.

"As a little reward, my dear"—Regina took Emilie's hand lower and placed it firmly between her thighs—"you can leave this here whilst you take your punishment."

"My…?" Emilie stared into her own wide eyes in the mirror. The lips of her sex were swollen, a slick heat gathering anew under her fingers. Behind her, Regina smiled.

"Just bend over for me, dear."

The first blow hit Emilie's right buttock with a resounding crack, making her jolt forwards with a gasp, her forehead bumping the mirror. There was a moment's shocked numbness, then a smarting that spread and bloomed beneath Emilie's skin. Another resounding slap to the same spot caused a sharper sting and a heat that throbbed deliciously inside her.

In the mirror's reflection, Regina flexed her fingers, then shifted her attention to the other cheek. Emilie felt four swift smacks doled out at different points on the soft curvature. She bit her lip, struggling to stay quiet and fearing how the sound of flesh hitting flesh must sound in the shop.

The corset had fallen away from her body and hung from her shoulders. Her breasts swayed, her neat pink nipples standing out. Regina pressed her into a deeper bend, adjusting Emilie's stance as though she was fitting her for a new garment. Then she smacked her again.

Emilie leaned her head against the mirror, her eyes half-closed, her breath misting the glass. Regina had found her rhythm now and was spanking Emilie's buttocks alternately and steadily, ignoring what must have been a growing soreness in her own fingers. Each blow caused Emilie's hips to jerk with hard, involuntary movements and her clit to bump against her hand.

"You've made such progress, Emilie." Regina's voice was sultry now. Emilie struggled to hold back her cries. Her bottom was hot and tingling, her hips churning in time with the swings of Regina's hand. "You mustn't think I haven't noticed." Regina punctuated each sentence with a fresh slap that made Emilie's flesh ripple and bolts of sensation shoot down to her toes.

"Perhaps you think I've been harsh with you. But if you can learn to control your own impulses—your resentment, your doubts, your desires…" Regina concentrated her slaps on the underswell of Emilie's backside, where the impact would drive Emilie's clit most forcefully against her fingers. "If you can master all of that, *then* you will understand how to turn the world around you into your own little kingdom."

Liquid pleasure was coursing down Emilie's fingers. Regina leaned forwards until her lips nuzzled the plump lobe of Emilie's ear. She whispered, "There's so much more I could teach you, Emilie. Are you willing to learn?"

"Yes…" Emilie's back arched, her answer a ragged breath—"yes, yes!"—as her orgasm crashed through her, reducing her to helpless sighs and hot, sweet foam.

Regina guided her over to the armchair and helped her to sit. Emilie winced at the pressure on her overheated skin.

"I'll leave you to…compose yourself," Regina murmured. She touched Emilie's face gently with the same hand that had inflicted such harshness only moments before. Emilie felt the heat that throbbed in Regina's fingers and wondered how her boss had endured the punishment herself. As Regina moved back, Emilie saw her fingers were pink from the exertion. But setting the right example had always mattered more to Regina than her own comfort.

The rest of the afternoon passed in a daze. Alonsa kept her distance, shooting Emilie glances that were alternately suspicious and envious. Regina was quiet, issuing only the mildest of instructions now. From time to time, a smile flickered across her face.

That evening, Emilie left the shop in silence. She was unlocking her car when an engine roared to a halt behind her.

The car was glossy black, with modest fins and a huge silver stencil across the bonnet. Jay leaned out the window.

"Long day?" The butch flashed Emilie an angelic smile. Emilie narrowed her eyes in return.

"I would have thought you'd be giving your girlfriend her present by now."

"Already done it." Jay's smile widened.

"And did she like the garments you chose?"

"Oh, she already has plenty of...garments," said Jay. "What she really needs is to feel special. She drives herself too hard, does too much for other people. She deserves a treat for herself. And making every lady feel like a queen is what you do here, right?"

"We do." Emilie folded her arms. "So did you make her feel...special?"

Jay's smile grew softer, more thoughtful.

"I sure hope so. My girl already knows I adore her. But I thought it might cheer her up to show her I'm not the only one."

Emilie's gaze slid away from Jay's face down to the gleaming black bonnet. Now she could identify the large silver image stencilled there. It was a wolf, and it looked just like the one on Severina's logo. Except this wolf was howling.

Behind them, Emilie heard the clang of the shop's security screens closing and the click of the lock, then the rhythmic tap of Regina's heels.

As Regina passed the big black car, Jay leaned out the window and caught her arm. Emilie stared as her boss allowed herself to be pulled closer. Regina leaned down and kissed her butch on the mouth. Then she rounded the car, opened the passenger door, and slid gracefully inside.

When she saw Emilie staring, Regina wound down her window.

"Mouth closed, Emilie. No gawping. You did well today, on the whole. We must speak some more about your...professional development."

Jay craned over Regina's shoulder for a moment and caught Emilie's eye.

"She talks about you all the time." Jay winked. "Said you had promise. I knew you wouldn't let her down."

She tooted the horn and revved the engine. The car swung around out of the carpark and onto the road. As it passed her, Emilie could see Regina watching her.

Her boss gave her a smile that was unexpectedly tender. Above the growl of the engine, Emilie heard her say, "I'll see you tomorrow."

ILLUMINATION

The shutters slammed and rattled as a gust of wind hit the building, flinging itself against the layers of bluestone and oak. Constantia's fingers ached from the cold. The hairs prickled along her arms, and her breath lingered silvery in the air. Beneath the rough black fabric of her robe, her nipples were tight and throbbing.

It would take more than a storm to breach the defences of this place, which had served as a fortress during the last war. Still, the winter found its own way in, snaking through each tiny crack in the wood and chink in the mortar.

Beside Constantia's head, a candle flickered, sputtered, and shrank down to the wick. She encircled it with her palm, squeezed, and felt the flare and scorch as the flame leapt back into life.

She drew her hand away, refusing to wince or examine the stinging patch of skin. For a moment, she fancied she could smell it—sizzling meat, a sacrificial offering, purification by fire...

But that was nonsense. Her flesh would right itself soon enough, if it were God's will.

In fact, the room smelled of damp straw and woodsmoke. The women at the tables flexed their fingers and blew on them to ward off the cold, and Constantia could hear that wretched Dorcas sniffling again. Proper roaring fires were an expense their little order could rarely afford. The bishop was a tight-fisted old miser, although generous enough with his own household budget.

Still, the room was bright with the glow of many candles; Constantia would brook no objection from her superiors on that matter. The days were short this time of year, and her women must have light if they were to carry on doing the Lord's work.

She glanced over Maria's shoulder at the illustration taking shape under the novice's quill: a he-goat, the most lustful of creatures. Its blood was said to be so hot it could dissolve diamonds.

The women were hard at work on a new bestiary, a change from their usual handiwork of trumpeting angels and naked, decapitated saints. Calligraphy and illumination were supposed to be a monk's prerogative, but Constantia had trained her novices well. And she knew a secret or two about the local abbot that had persuaded him to let her women undertake this work, provided no one outside knew about it. As far as the official record was concerned, these illustrated texts were the work of his own male pupils.

Constantia's face tightened at the thought. She locked her hands behind her back and drew herself up to her considerable height. During her thirty years in this place, she had learned to make her physique work for her. Her firm jaw and broad shoulders, the muscular power in her limbs, her silver hair, and the glint of steel in her black eyes, these qualities that made her so unacceptable in the outside world, here gave her a sense of presence and power. Beneath her long black robe, her well-padded hips and breasts were only just discernible, held firmly in shape with no jiggling permitted. Her rosary on its woven strap swung from her hip as she walked, with a rhythmic swishing sound and a faint whiff of leather.

Slowly, she paced the room, patrolling up and down the rows of women. They worked in silence, their implements lined up like well-trained soldiers: the quills, pen knives, rulers, linen threads, pots of ink, gum, and vegetable dye. Disorder was not permitted on Constantia's watch.

In this room, Constantia never raised her voice. She never needed to. The air crackled with nervous anticipation each time she leaned over a pupil's shoulder and cleared her throat:

"Well done, Isobel."

"Sophia, what did I tell you?"

Her followers were old enough to have been wives and mothers had they stayed in the outside world, but they had not lost their awe of Constantia—or their fear.

Their book of beasts was made up of the writings of pagan philosophers, but Constantia explained to her students that it offered valuable lessons in God's wise and mysterious ways. Consider the salamander, which Isidora was etching in lampblack right now. This strange, cold serpent could live unharmed inside a fire, and if dropped into boiling water, turned it cold. Constantia explained this represented righteous people who were strong in their faith, just as Shadrach, Meshach, and Abednego had emerged unscathed from the fiery furnace.

And then there was the hydrus, the outline of which lay on Constantia's desk, waiting for the gum to dry before it could be illuminated in gold. This wondrous beast, with its coiled red tail and head like a dog, dwelled beneath the slime of the river Nile. Its prey was the crocodile, which it killed by swimming into the monster's mouth and down into its belly, where the hydrus devoured it from the inside. This muddy bloodbath, Constantia said, signified Christ descending into hell to rescue lost souls.

"Do you think it's true?" Theodora, their newest novice asked her as she walked by. "Do you think anyone has really seen these creatures with their own eyes?"

Constantia should have beaten her for that, both for questioning a task and for speaking during work time, which the women were supposed to spend in silent contemplation, communicating when necessary in gestures.

But Theodora's green eyes were so wide and bright, her voice so genuinely curious, that Constantia found herself answering instead. "How could I know? I've never travelled further than three days' ride from here. But I have faith there are countless wonders upon this earth which I will never witness. You just have to believe."

Although Theodora was Constantia's newest student, she craned again over her work with utter discipline, seemingly absorbed right back into it. Constantia watched the figure coming to life on the parchment under Theodora's already-expert fingers. An eagle taking flight.

Theodora's head was a perfect, slender oval, covered in dark stubble as soft as down. Her white scalp shone beneath it, the blue veins fluttering at her temples. Constantia had shaved this novice herself.

Some new girls trembled or wept beneath the remorseless scrape of the razor as their hair fell in clumps all around. But Theodora had sat up straight, her palms open to catch the drifting black strands. When Constantia finished, the young woman ran a hand over the denuded skin, exploring the elegant contours of her own skull, now visible for the first time since infancy. On her face was a radiant smile.

Constantia had said nothing, and the cool composure on her face never changed. Still, she had been impressed. Not many novices took so easily to life inside these walls. And Constantia's regime was stern and rigorous. Unyielding.

Her women would not be afraid of hard work, as she told each group of new arrivals, for this community must feed itself or starve. So they all took turns, labouring from dawn to sunset, hauling water, scrubbing laundry, chopping wood, mucking out the animals, bringing in the harvest. Along with the plain diet and rising at midnight for the first of eight daily prayers, it should have been enough to ensure these women were too weary to sin.

But Constantia remained ever vigilant. Her followers could be expected to be chaperoned during their rare family visits, and personal valuables and secrets were not permitted. Nothing in this world came without a price, and this was what Constantia's followers paid in return for freedom from hunger and filth, from the dangers of childbearing and the petty tyrannies of marriage. In return for a measure of respect and reverence as devotees of God denied to ordinary women. In return for calligraphy and illumination, the rare gift of literacy, and a life spent amongst bright pictures and gold leaf. This was the life that awaited Theodora, in all its harshness and beauty.

Sometimes she wondered how much her pupils really appreciated what she offered them here. Not Theodora, though. She seemed to understand. Right from the first day, when Constantia had instructed her on how to sketch her very first illumination: the bear cub, which is born without form, shapeless and eyeless until it is licked into living shape by its mother.

A whisper rippled behind her. Constantia swung around, her eyes narrowing to cold slits. Dorcas and Isabella sat up with a jolt, their giggling conversation halting at once. Constantia stared at them without blinking. She could not afford to be indulgent, as she often reminded people. The danger of insubordination, of loss of control, was everywhere. She called it sin. It was easier to explain that way.

"Isabella?" Constantia barked. "You have something to confess?"

The woman's mouth opened and closed foolishly. She shook her head.

"Come now." Constantia sauntered over to where the two friends sat. The silence in the room seemed to stretch almost to breaking point. Constantia could sense everyone watching her. Theodora especially. She ran her fingertips lazily down the side of Isabella's face. "You know the rules."

Each day, she would summon two or three of her followers in front of the others to make public admission of their sins. It was essential to make an example of their wickedness in order to remind the women that Constantia was always watching.

"I…I have been distracted," Isabella stammered. "I have neglected my work."

"So I see." Constantia raised an eyebrow. "Continue."

"I have been disobedient." Isabella dropped her head, but Constantia seized her chin and forced her to look up.

"How did you disobey me? Tell the others."

"I let the porridge boil over in the kitchen when you told me to watch it." Isabella faltered. The other women were frowning, nudging each other, or suppressing giggles at her misfortune. "And…and I spoiled the first batch of ink!"

"Shameful!" Constantia's deep, melodic voice filled the room. She released Isabella's chin and wiped her fingers on her robe. "On your knees."

As Isabella dropped from the bench to the floor and began praying the Rosary in a frantic whisper, Constantia caught Theodora's eye. Her newest novice was watching the scene with a steady gaze. She showed no sign of fear.

Unsettled by this, Constantia turned her attention to her other disobedient student.

"And what about you, Dorcas? Don't think you can deceive me; I know you're the one who leads your friend in wickedness."

"I've had impure thoughts, Reverend Mother." Dorcas positively breathed the words, and not for the first time. Constantia often suspected the woman enjoyed the attention and made up sins on the spot to keep Constantia happy—although this was not so very bad. At least it showed Dorcas was learning to follow orders.

"Again?" Constantia looked down her nose in disgust. "Last time, I thought confinement in a punishment cell would cure you of that."

Dorcas's breasts rose and fell beneath her robe. Constantia could sense Theodora's eyes boring into her, but she refused to look around. Instead, she pinched Dorcas's ear and lifted her, wincing, to her feet and then higher onto her tiptoes until Dorcas squeaked, "It was in the punishment cell that I…I…"

"I see." Constantia released her abruptly, then thrust her to her knees. "And tell us what you did in that punishment cell, Dorcas. Do not imagine you can hide your shame here."

She towered over them both as Dorcas blushed and stuttered out her confession about picturing lecherous scenes from the Scriptures and fingering herself in her devilish places. Constantia interrupted her several times, prompting, "And what happened then? What did you imagine yourself doing, you disgraceful creature? Did you not know how shameful that was?"

Only when the two women had demonstrated sufficient penitence—their faces flushed and sweating, their knees wobbling against the stones—did she relent, declaring, "Not one woman is to speak to you or look at you for the rest of this month." This won whimpers of "yes, Reverend Mother" and "thank you, Reverend Mother" from her two errant charges. Constantia added, "And you will take your fellow pupils' turns at mucking out the pigs."

This time, the thanks were less enthusiastic. She released them both with a gesture and watched them stagger to their feet and resume their work. Most days, those sorts of punishments were sufficient.

Some days she went further. Some days, when her authority had been truly flouted, Constantia would instruct a wrongdoer to bend over and lift her robe whilst Constantia took down the thin wooden switch.

She permitted the others to watch these punishments. The echoing *thwack* of slender, flexible wood against wobbling, reddening flesh; the heat that emanated from the wrongdoer's skin; her gasps and stifled cries; the pale determination on Constantia's face… It was one way to get a lesson across. Performing before an audience also helped Constantia identify the most pious members of her little band—or the ones who took rather too much pleasure in a companion's chastisement. Or the ones who hoped they might be next.

She was tempted to do that today, if only to see Theodora's response. But Theodora's head was down again; she had returned to her work. Was she not impressed by Constantia's authority? Had she seen through her somehow?

Theodora must have sensed Constantia's presence looming above her, but she did not lift her head. All her concentration was fixed upon the page, and as she examined her own handiwork, she smiled. That tender curve of her pale pink lips filled Constantia with such strange urges: to capture those lips between her own, to nibble their ripe flesh, sip the hitching breaths that escaped them, trace them with her tongue.

Theodora was wearing the hairshirt today, a measure of mortification that made Constantia uneasy. She had not ordered it. She was not sure she was pleased to see a follower choosing her own punishment without permission. Still, several times in the past, Theodora had insisted on repenting this way.

"I've broken the rules," she would say in her quiet, even voice. "I've earned this."

Every now and then, Theodora would stiffen or utter a tiny intake of breath as the coarse sackcloth chafed the sensitive skin around her neckline, her shoulders, her small, pointed breasts. Most of the time, though, she was forced to sit upright, to move with slow grace and deliberation lest any careless slouching or wriggling cause further torment to her over-disciplined flesh.

Did she know that every faint sound and minute twitch, every sign of itchiness and pain, caused forbidden feelings to throb between Constantia's legs? Did she sense how much Constantia longed to tear the punishing garment from Theodora's body and soothe the raw, smarting patches with the butterfly touch of her lips and the moist trail of her tongue?

Constantia bit down on her bottom lip instead until the pain seared. She must not give in to this. She must remain in control.

As she watched, Theodora began to outline the scalloped patterns of the eagle's feathers in dark ink made from the gall nuts of an oak tree. The book of beasts was ambivalent about the moral significance of the eagle. Some described the creature as holy; strong and virtuous enough to stare without flinching into the face of God. Others called it a predator, a ravisher of souls.

"Isn't this a monk's task?" Theodora asked barely two days later. Her voice was hushed, but it seemed to reverberate around the silent room. The other women stiffened.

Constantia wheeled around. The question had caused her fists to clench and her shoulders to tighten painfully. She stepped closer until she was glaring directly down at her newest pupil. She observed the short, fuzzy hair that sat like a fine cap over Theodora's skull, tapering down to the slope of her slender neck.

"My students," Constantia replied, her own voice as chilly as the jagged stones that surrounded the abbey, "do not speak whilst I am instructing them."

"Forgive me." Theodora ducked her head, her translucent eyelids fluttering, the neck of her smock gaping. Constantia could see her fine collarbones, her snowy skin, and the shadowy cleft between her breasts. "But I never heard tell of books being made in this place."

"Am I to blame for your ignorance?" Constantia sneered. She felt obliged to add, "But it's true. We never speak of the holy works we are privileged to perform here. The greatest acts of piety are not performed ostentatiously, but modestly and by stealth."

"The monastery near my village kept a library of the wonders they had created." Was Theodora *arguing* with her? "The monks did not hide their skill from the world."

Constantia's lip trembled. How dare this new girl challenge her in front of the others? How dare she give voice to the frustration that simmered inside Constantia herself, shut away from view—the knowledge that all the beauty and learning that came to light under her quill and those of her students would never be recognised, would be claimed by some greasy, self-serving liar as his own?

Without pausing to think, Constantia raised the wooden ruler in her right hand and brought it with a swipe across Theodora's narrow thigh. The sharp crack ricocheted around the stone walls; the other pupils jumped. Theodora gave a shocked squeak, her hand flying to cover the scorching flesh.

Constantia snarled. "Do not question my instructions again."

But inwardly, she was quivering as much as Theodora's poor punished thigh—in dismay that such a simple question had troubled her so, and in anger at the knowledge that Theodora was right.

Theodora raised her head. Her large eyes glittered with tears, and with something else too. Recognition? Her breath caught and released as she said, "I will obey your instructions, my lady."

And so she did, up to a point. Constantia could never fault Theodora's diligence or attention to detail, or the meticulous neatness and cleanliness the young woman showed about her person. Theodora never complained about hard labour, and she joined in the hymns and psalms with the voice of an angel.

But she would not stop asking questions, and each one infuriated and intrigued Constantia more than it should. Why were the words of God written in a language most people could not understand? Why were their quarters here so bare when the bishop was known to live in splendour? If the world respected them for doing God's work, why did they need guard dogs and high walls?

Worse than the young woman's impudence was Constantia's own response; she felt such an awful temptation to reply truthfully at times, before holding herself back and landing harsh words and admonitory slaps on Theodora instead. None of which seemed to dampen Theodora's spirits in the slightest. The wretched girl hummed to herself as she carried out the worst household tasks, and she settled into a week in the punishment cell as if into a feather bed. And there was no use correcting her by denying her visitors, since she had none.

Neither did Constantia.

At night, Constantia found herself poring over Theodora's half-finished parchment, where the eagle was taking shape, its mighty claws like scimitars, its eyes round and glistening. She read in the text details she already knew—how the eagle tests the worthiness of its young by forcing the fledglings to gaze directly into the blinding whiteness of the sun.

Theodora was not popular with everyone here. The other sisters murmured stories about this new girl—not to Constantia, for no one dared make idle conversation with her, but she heard the whispers anyway. That

Theodora had been beaten and cast out of her home, chased from her village for some unmentionable offence worse than the secret pregnancies, adulterous love affairs, and runaway husbands that landed some other women in this place. That she was a bad woman, and that if not for the mistaken kindness of a priest who'd brought her here, she might have suffered an unspeakable fate at the hands of the mob, and serve her right too.

Constantia did not permit gossip. It weakened the unity of their order. She had the offending women sketch her a picture of the aspis, the huge winged snake that presses one ear to the ground and covers the other with its tail, symbolising foolish people whose hearing is blocked by worldly matters and sinful nonsense. Then she put them on a gruel diet and sent them to scrub out the latrines.

She thought about what they'd said, though. She couldn't help it.

That night, she punished Theodora for talking again, requiring the young woman to lie prostrate at the door of the choir at the Hours so the other women would step over her like a pile of dirt on their way in. The exercise was supposed to promote humility.

But when Constantia lifted her own skirts and raised her right foot, Theodora turned over beneath her, looked upwards, and flashed a smile of pure devilry. Then she landed a swift, taunting kiss on Constantia's ankle.

Constantia shook all over at the touch of the other woman's mouth. It lingered on her skin like a brand.

God, what had she done to deserve this? Had she not kept a tight rein on this place, and on herself? Had she not given her life to this righteous work, been steadfast in the face of temptation? Constantia shivered and for some reason was reminded of earlier that day, when she had observed Maria colouring in a sketch of a unicorn. According to the text, this mystical creature was cunning and shy, and could only be captured by a virgin. In the illustration, the white horse was suckling from the girl's breast, whilst a knight crept up and speared it through the heart.

Constantia stared down at Theodora's positively sinful gaze and thought of the fountain of blood as Maria had painted it in crimson. Was that what came of trust?

Later that night, Constantia was unable to rest. She prowled the darkened corridors instead, her ears alert to every sleepy murmur, every twitch of slumbering bodies. Her footsteps were silent. She breathed in the damp chill that rose from the stones. Faint chinks of moonlight shone through the high slit windows, but otherwise she had to navigate this place by darkness, which she did with ease, knowing it all too well. Her fortress, her little kingdom, her prison.

She'd been so careful in here. She'd never weakened, never indulged herself in pity or greed. Never permitted anyone a glimpse of the storms that swirled, crackled and howled inside her in flashes of purple and black.

Yes, she'd longed for release sometimes, an escape from this world where she was feared and respected to her face, reviled and sneered at behind her back. *An abnormal excuse for a woman—ambitious, rigid, and cruel—a monster pretending to do the Lord's work. An unnatural creature...*

She'd never blinked. Never given in to it. She'd kept her methods within the rules, her impulses under control. And for what?

She made her way to Theodora's cell.

The cell lay in darkness. Theodora in her smock was a dim white shape at Constantia's feet. She was kneeling.

"It's not time for prayers," Constantia told her, keeping her voice low.

In the darkness, she could not see Theodora's face, but she caught a hint of laughter in the young woman's voice as Theodora replied, "I know."

Theodora reached forwards and hooked her fingers in Constantia's embroidered leather belt. Then she wriggled herself closer until Constantia, frozen to the spot, could feel the weight of Theodora's knees touching Constantia's feet, the maddening press of Theodora's breasts against Constantia's thighs, the hot vapour of Theodora's breath through Constantia's clothing, warming her most private and forbidden self.

Constantia's eyes fluttered shut. Her fingers tingled. A tremor ran the length of her arm. Her hand reached out to cup Theodora's bared skull, to caress the exquisitely soft stubble, to draw that ethereal face closer.

"There you are..." Theodora's voice was thick with longing, muffled in Constantia's robe. Constantia could feel the pressure of kisses, of lips, jaw, and nuzzling nose working against her. It made her sway helplessly. All her senses, her awareness, seemed to be concentrated in that hot and hidden place beneath her belly, each puff of Theodora's breath causing her to throb with pleasure. She felt a scrabbling at her ankles as Theodora reached for the hem of her robe and began to raise it.

"That's enough!" Constantia stepped back. This was not how it was supposed to go. She had not come here to lose control. "On your feet."

Theodora made no complaint as Constantia marched her down the abandoned corridor. Constantia heard a whistling of wind through a crack in one of the roof tiles, a distant scratching of mice. Constantia's hand fell, leaden, on Theodora's shoulder as she propelled the younger woman ahead of her, towards the infirmary.

It was empty, of course. Sickness was a moral failing, not permitted under Constantia's roof. She nodded Theodora towards the far cell.

"In there." It was as bare as the punishment cells. The only furniture was a mattress, lying on an old bedframe made of iron. Leather shackles were attached.

"Sometimes the sick and mad can display unnatural strength," Constantia explained. She kept her voice even; she controlled the longing that flickered in her fingers, demanding to touch Theodora's velvety scalp again, to rend the rough white fabric from her novice's body. "Undress."

Theodora did so with slowness that had to be intentional, her narrow chest heaving, her neat little teeth pinching her bottom lip. Stripped naked, her pearly skin shone in the gloom. Constantia could discern the shadows beneath Theodora's breasts and chin, the dark thatch of hair at the juncture of her thighs. The only sound in the room was their breathing: her own slow and rigorously controlled, Theodora's fast and shallow.

"Lie down."

Theodora scrambled to obey. Her fingertips skimmed over herself as she gazed up at Constantia, lightly touching her belly, her collarbones, her erect nipples. Her gaze was direct, boring into Constantia until the older woman could no longer bear it.

"Not like that. Turn over."

Theodora hesitated only a moment before obeying, turning that eager, knowing face mercifully away from Constantia's gaze, and exposing instead the span of her shoulders, the triangular blades sticking straight up, the length of her spine, the quiver of her small, shapely buttocks.

"Extend your arms." Constantia cursed the huskiness in her own voice. She had no business debasing herself here. Theodora obeyed instantly, stretching her arms as wide as they would go, her ribcage straining with each shallow breath as Constantia stepped closer.

Constantia rubbed the worn leather strap between her thumb and forefinger, her nostrils twitching at the earthy scent. The holy texts they worked on each day had started life the same way: as goat skins, stretched, treated, and cut to size, to be decorated with the words of God. But underneath, that old aroma lingered: of life and death, of flesh and hide. Violence. Preservation.

"You have the potential for brilliance, Theodora," she whispered. "But you cannot or will not exercise caution. I've no choice but to teach you a lesson."

Theodora nodded rapidly, her face turned to the side to watch as Constantia lingered over the straps and buckles, wrapping her wrists in leather and binding them fast.

Constantia moved back to relish the spectacle. Theodora's naked form made a pale cross in the darkness. Constantia's hand shook as she extended it to rest upon Theodora's head. She trailed her fingertips along her pupil's neck, tracing the silken hollow at the base of her skull, then down the knobbly ridge of Theodora's spine. When she reached the sensitive cleft of Theodora's buttocks, Constantia paused, letting her fingers linger there, warm and ticklish. Verging on indecency.

"Open your legs," she murmured. "I won't have you wriggling around instead of concentrating."

Theodora drew a deep breath, then did as she was told, her bare feet curling and flexing as they inched towards the edges of the mattress. Constantia swallowed hard but kept her movements controlled as she ran her hand over one pert buttock and down the twitching length of Theodora's thigh. She squeezed the small, hard calf muscle and encircled Theodora's ankle before sliding the leather thong around it and pulling the buckle tight.

"Tell me if it pinches," she said. "I don't want you to be distracted."

"I couldn't be" was Theodora's panting reply. As Constantia bent to fasten the other ankle, she caught a whiff of wet animal lust from between the woman's parted thighs. Constantia had never been to the borders of this land she had lived in for the last thirty years, let alone beyond, but she had often wondered if this was what the ocean smelled like.

The sight of Theodora stripped and secured almost undid Constantia, but she would not give in to her own frailties. Instead she leaned down and breathed hot in Theodora's ear. "You think to play games with me, my dear? You have no notion of the danger." As she spoke, she ran her short, smooth nails down Theodora's back, lightly at first, raising pleasurable goose bumps, then harder and deeper until they left pale grooves in their wake and Theodora groaned and arched at the biting pressure.

Taking care not to hurry, Constantia moved further down the bed, seized the plush skin of Theodora's inner thigh, and subjected it to a slow, hard pinch, her strong fingers like pliers pulling the skin as far as it would go and holding it there before a gradual, sliding release that made Theodora stifle a cry, her fists clenching helplessly.

"You treat this place as if it were a joke." Constantia repeated the action on the back of Theodora's other thigh. "A whim that can be taken up or discarded at will. But this is for the rest of your life, Theodora. Do you really have the strength for it?"

"Yes." Theodora was breathing hard as the cruel pinches travelled up to the swell of her buttocks. "Yes..."

"I am not convinced." Constantia moved her attentions to the thin layer of padding over Theodora's right hip, almost feeling the squeeze and burn in her own body. "It is not only the mortification of the flesh that you must subject yourself to. It is a lifetime of dedication." She nipped the most tender skin near the apex of Theodora's thighs. It felt heated and slippery. "A lifetime," Constantia said, "of obedience."

"I have the strength for it," Theodora insisted, her voice high and straining.

"I'm not sure you do." Constantia released her, then dipped her head low until she was almost kissing the suffering flesh. She blew across it instead, cooling it for one kindly moment, before landing half a dozen sharp slaps. Theodora burrowed her face into the mattress, but her hips were rocking, her moans audible.

Constantia's own body surged with heat, but she disregarded that. She would prove her own strength tonight. She said, "Show me some discipline, then. I don't want to hear a sound until I'm done. If you fail me, if you speak a word, I will walk away and leave you here. You can explain your punishment to whomever discovers you tomorrow. Do you understand?"

A pause the length of a single breath. Then Theodora nodded.

"Good." Constantia reached inside her cloak and drew out her implement for tonight's lesson: a quill pen made from a large brown-and-white feather, taken from some great bird of prey.

"Within these walls," she intoned, drawing the sharpened point teasingly down Theodora's spine, "you will find protection. Nurturance. Opportunity." She traced the line back up again to Theodora's nape, pressing down harder this time until Theodora twitched in mute discomfort, the muscles jumping on either side of her backbone. "But you will also encounter temptations." Constantia dragged the quill's point in firm yet lazy circles over Theodora's sensitive ribs, imagining the puncturing sharpness, the stinging red tracks invisible in the shadows. "Perhaps the worst danger of all is complacency. The belief that you are safe." Constantia paused, then flipped the quill between her fingers so the brown-and-white plume whisked over Theodora's smarting skin. "You will not be so foolish, will you, Theodora?" she crooned, retracing the harsh scratches she had left on her follower's body, this time with the feather's filaments, soft as air. "You will not imagine you have nothing to fear?"

Theodora shook her head and murmured some incoherent assurance. She pushed herself backwards towards the feather's touch; it appeared she was desperate to please. Constantia wafted the feather up one side of her ribcage until it tickled the side of Theodora's flattened breast, provoking wriggles of pleasure. She longed to turn Theodora over and repeat these caresses all over her pretty body—but deep down Constantia was still afraid to meet the younger woman's eye.

She flicked a light circle around the entrance to Theodora's ear instead, then teased the back of her neck for several long, blissful moments. From the tensing of Theodora's body and the way the young woman forced her face deeper into the mattress, Constantia realised this spot must be very susceptible indeed. Theodora was doing an impressive job of keeping silent, though. Constantia was pleased to see that. Perhaps her lessons had not been in vain.

With some reluctance, Constantia abandoned this pleasant interlude and moved further down the bed, turning the feather over again and pressing its sharpened end deep into Theodora's flesh. Moving with as much care as she would exercise when drawing borders on a manuscript,

Constantia scraped the head of the quill back and forth over Theodora's bare bottom, inflicting a crosshatch pattern of scratches that stood out even in the shadows. Revenge, perhaps, for the way Theodora had left her questions, her playfulness, her unsettling presence imprinted across Constantia's mind.

Constantia had always prided herself on her ability to draw a perfectly straight line without the aid of a ruler. She did so now, over and over, taking the time to admire her handiwork, until even Theodora's willing limbs began to jerk and struggle inside their leather bonds.

"Yes, you see it's hard," Constantia explained. "But this is what you must remember. Whenever you feel tempted to let your guard down in here, to assume the world holds no further dangers for you and that everyone can be trusted—remember how hurtful and duplicitous people can be."

Constantia straightened up, breathing hard. She had not broken the skin, but she could see the lines of her punishment clearly in the darkness, standing out like calligraphy against Theodora's poor tenderised skin. The younger woman's breath came in silent sobs.

With something like remorse, Constantia reversed the quill and took her time caressing the marks left by her own hand. Her tone was soothing now as she prompted Theodora. "You will be careful, won't you? There are things in this world far more dangerous than I. You've been very silly, provoking me like this, but you won't be so reckless with anyone else, will you?"

Theodora jerked her head with a sound of muffled agreement, her body loosening and relaxing under Constantia's touch. Constantia let out a long breath. She had done the right thing here. She had been hard, yes, but she had imprinted her will on Theodora and tested her own control to its limits.

And she had won. She had not given in to temptation, to the urge to touch and fondle and penetrate. To kiss…

"I'm going to release you now," she murmured in Theodora's ear. "You will go back to your cell and think hard about your conduct. I will be watching you, do you understand? You may lie on your stomach tonight, but if I catch a single glimpse of you giving in to the carnal weakness of the flesh, I will sit you on a hard wooden stool for the rest of this week. Do you hear me?"

Theodora nodded, her groan of disappointment faint but unmistakeable. Constantia ought to count that as a victory and let her pupil up. But instead she found herself dallying, trailing the soft end of the feather up and down the crease of Constantia's buttocks, relishing the squirming this provoked and startled by how quickly the young woman recovered her stamina.

Constantia realised she and Theodora were both holding their breath. The only sound in the room was the creak of the mattress as Theodora's hips lifted and fell. Constantia experimented with different touches: prolonged drags of the feather, tantalising flicks. With Theodora's ankles wide apart, the shadowy opening between her cheeks was all too obvious. Constantia could see the glint of moisture in Theodora's dark curls. She slid the feather lower.

"Oh, my love—" The young woman's words were indistinct, buried deep in the mattress, but there was no mistaking them. Constantia reared back in horror. The feather fell from her fingers.

She ought to slap Theodora for real this time. Ought to send her back to her cell in disgrace.

But that time had passed. Already Constantia could feel it starting, and she was powerless to intervene. She staggered back and watched in dread and fascination as the feather twitched and quivered in its resting place on the mattress between Theodora's thighs. Then, all by itself, with no need for her guiding hand, it rose an inch and hovered in mid-air.

Dear God, she must not do this, must not let her demons out again. Not after so long, after so many years of stifling but necessary discipline.

But it was too late.

Of its own accord, the feather swooped and swirled out of sight between Theodora's open legs and parted lips. It caressed her moist folds, traced obscene patterns around her fundament; it tickled and dipped and danced. Theodora was crying out loud now, wriggling her knees deeper into the mattress, thrusting her hips back. Offering herself.

Constantia gripped the iron bedstead until her knuckles felt fit to burst; she squeezed her eyes shut, screaming silently at herself to stop this, this mistake, this show of weakness—and worse. If Theodora should turn her head, if she should see the unnatural devilry that was giving her such pleasure…

The feather circled Theodora's throbbing bud now, firmer and faster. Constantia could smell salty, slippery flesh, Theodora's or her own, she could not say, and her ears were filled with such delectable moans and whimpering and pleas of "more" and "yes".

The leather straps stretched and yanked, their edges fraying against the iron as Theodora jolted and tensed in desperation. The bed legs juddered, screeching against the stones. Constantia clamped her hand over her mouth, biting deep into her palm as Theodora let out a wail of pure delight, and the knowledge of what she had just done burst between Constantia's shaking thighs until her face contorted with pleasure, until she clutched the bedframe, toppled, then fell.

It was too much. She dared not stay. She hauled herself up and rushed on trembling legs from the room, feeling her way blindly along the stone walls, her vision full of swirling black spots and memories of Theodora's naked, willing flesh. Finding herself in the hallway of the punishment cells, she flung herself into the nearest one and sank onto the bench, shaking with dismay and illicit, guilty pleasure.

She had never let it out before. Not since the day she had entered this place, thirty years earlier. As her own teacher had pushed her onto a stool and pulled out the razor, Constantia had watched her hair raining down around her and knew she'd been given a second chance. A reprieve.

She'd vowed never to take her safety for granted in here. She would never again risk releasing those impulses that had seethed inside her and caused trouble her whole life, the tremors in her hands that had caused the milk to spoil and the pots to bubble over in torrents when she was angry, toiling in her parents' dark, dingy cottage all day long. The force that had surged in hot pulses down the length of her arms and out the tips of her fingers that time she brought the drowned kitten back to life.

And the deep rumble in the soles of her feet that shook the earth beneath the stone fence and had sent rocks tumbling down around the heads of the boys who had tormented her, until she fled from her own wild joy at their screams and blood.

No, she would never risk letting that out again. It was only luck and quick thinking that had got Constantia away from that village and behind the security of these abbey walls before local suspicions and mistrust could shape themselves into accusations—of failed crops, sick cattle, storms, stillbirths, impotent husbands—and then into the most terrible actions.

She had saved herself, and it had been worth the price. Surely.

The cell door creaked open. The darkness thinned. Constantia raised her head, feeling the tears drying on her flushed cheeks. Theodora stood in the doorway: slender, nude, and perilously beautiful. She stepped closer, and Constantia saw she was smiling.

"Why did you leave?" Theodora asked. "That was not very polite."

Constantia gaped at her. She had left the younger woman shackled tight to the bed. From the echoing silence in the corridor, it was clear that not another soul was awake in the building. And yet here Theodora stood, her wrists and ankles unmarked and at liberty. An impossible thing.

"Why do you stare?" Theodora asked, her tone one of genuine surprise. "Surely we both know…"

"Know what?" Constantia rasped. She shook her head. The answer was there in front of her, and it was terrifying. Theodora stepped closer, then hesitated at the glimpse of tears on her teacher's skin.

"Whatever's the matter?" Theodora asked. "Does this not please you? There are two of us now."

She reached out to touch Constantia's hot, appalled face, but Constantia thrust past her and fled the cell without looking back.

All of that had happened a week before. Constantia had scarcely dared look at Theodora since.

Yet the terrible consequences she had expected had not occurred. So far, she had not been exposed or punished at all. The realisation made her bite her lip until it burned. How could this be?

Constantia drew herself up taller and looked around at the chilly schoolroom filled with illustrations and bright with candles. Her hands were clasped tight behind her back, and her chin was high. Her eyes prickled with tears.

Theodora was putting the finishing touches on her eagle. The gold leaf, stuck to the page with Theodora's own moist breath, gleamed in the candlelight. The young woman was shading the sky behind it a pale, flawless blue above the deeper indigo and frothing white of the ocean.

At last, Theodora looked up. She betrayed no surprise at the sight of Constantia standing over her.

"Is *this* pleasing to you?" she asked.

The eagle lay between them, its talons wide open, its mighty wings outstretched. It was exquisite. As beautiful as anything Constantia could have drawn herself. She should feel doubly threatened by this pupil of hers, who not only knew Constantia's worst secret but who would shortly surpass her in talent too.

Instead, with a great effort of will, she forced her eyes back to Theodora's face. Theodora's green gaze was as direct and unafraid as it had ever been. It held no horror or disgust, no threat, not even the faintest hint of surprise.

Constantia's voice came out in a whisper. "It's perfect."

Theodora smiled.

"You told me the story of this creature, from the bestiary. Remember?" Theodora's tone was conversational. Her voice made Constantia wish she need never listen to anything else.

Struck dumb, Constantia shook her head. The crowded classroom had vanished. The world had shrunk to one table, one illuminated manuscript, and the artist who sat above it, explaining.

"The sages tell us the eagle can make itself live forever. Don't you remember now?"

Constantia felt herself nodding. Her upright stance, the pride in her bearing, did not change. But her voice quavered a little as she recited, "When the eagle has grown old and heavy and blind, it knows the time has come. It takes flight and soars upward, directly into the sun's fire."

"A painful action," Theodora prompted. "Requiring great courage."

Constantia went on. "It was burns off its old feathers and sears away the mist that clouds its ancient eyes."

"Then it plunges all the way down into the sea," Theodora finished. "Three times it repeats the action, and its youth and health are restored. It can begin afresh."

Constantia met her pupil's fearless gaze and nodded. For a moment, she saw this room a dozen or more years into the future, as clearly as she saw it now. A library of scrolls all around, containing a king's ransom in beauty and knowledge, and Theodora sitting where she sat now, her cropped hair spangled with silver, faint lines around her eyes. They would be the same emerald, though, and lit by the same spark.

Was it a true vision or a dangerous folly? Or an idea that the two of them might just possibly bring to life?

A fresh breeze shook the shutters and darted around the room, fluttering Constantia's black robes out behind her and stinging her eyes until they watered.

And although it was impossible—although they were so far inland and she had never seen a white-pebbled beach or a clifftop where the eagles nested—when Constantia sniffed the breeze, she would have sworn to the God she must pretend to believe in that it smelled of the ocean.

A LITERARY LESSON

Danny Maxwell braced her hands on the podium and gazed down at her audience.

The old bluestone building—once a nineteenth-century convent, now turned into an artists' retreat—rang with the noise of metal chairs scraping the flagstones, clinking wine glasses, cash registers, and happy shrieks. The hall was hot from stage lights and human bodies. From here, she could see poets handing out business cards, and novelists sneering at their rivals. There were students laughing together, Christians and socialists clutching their long pre-prepared questions, and sharp-eyed old ladies with their husbands dozing beside them.

Her first gig at a writers' festival.

Danny tugged at the starched cuffs of her new shirt. Were they sitting okay? The shirt had looked fine in the mirror this morning, but now it felt too tight. Had she been right to leave the collar open, showing her leather necklace, or would a tie have been better? She ran a hand over her cropped hair; they never cut it as short as she wanted, but at least it was neat. She hoped she didn't look nervous.

She was here to read from her debut collection of poetry, and she had been scheduled to speak directly after a popular novelist on tour from the US. Which was both good and bad, she decided. It meant she was guaranteed a large audience but also guaranteed that virtually none of them were here to see her.

Now that the popular novelist had finished speaking, some audience members were already excusing themselves, scrambling over each other's legs to leave early. And Danny hadn't even started talking yet! She shrugged, tried to stay cool, and wished them all a grisly death.

It wasn't easy being a lesbian poet starting out these days, not with bookshops and publishing houses struggling to survive and most poetry events still dominated by straight men raging about their ex-girlfriends, and the market populated with readers who didn't see why they should pay for their literature when there was always the Internet. Not that anyone wanted to read poetry anyway…

Danny tried not to get discouraged, but it was hard sometimes.

At least the festival organiser looked displeased with the people who were leaving. Standing in the doorway with her arms folded, Charlotte lowered her spectacles and fixed the errant audience members with a glare like a Roman empress about to turn her thumb down in the arena. Some people actually quailed under her gaze and tiptoed, shamefaced, back to their seats. Danny grinned.

Charlotte was the owner of the only successful independent bookshop in town, and she had been running this festival for ten years. Impeccable in her white silk blouse, pencil skirt, and pearl earrings, she moved with a click of tastefully high heels and a cloud of the sort of perfume that didn't need pop stars to endorse it.

Danny had also spotted pretty quickly upon meeting her how much Charlotte was a stickler for protocol. She had delivered her warning about time limits for the speakers—"ten minutes only for a reading, and no more than one minute per audience question"— with a soft hand on Danny's forearm and a gaze like a cobra.

Danny glanced down nervously at her watch. It was a chunky leather-and-steel model, and this morning she'd thought it looked quite suave. Now she had a terrible sense that everyone here could tell she'd bought it off a market stall in Bali.

She began to read.

"Sometimes my appetites consume me.
Gluttony and decadence drive me to my knees."

Another audience member was leaving. *Come on!* she wanted to shout after them. *Two lines in*? Instead she cleared her throat and continued.

"Your forbidden hue
That tells of teenage lip-glossed kisses,
Frozen daiquiris on a summer's day,
Towering trifles,
Red swirls through whipped cream.
I look both ways
And pop your seal."

It was a poem about eating raspberries.

"Your peaks rise, jostling, to greet me.
I finger
The fine filaments…"

One young woman sitting by the side of the stage was actually talking on her phone! Giggling and gesticulating as though she was in a café instead of *ten fucking feet* away from a poet who was trying to give a live performance. Danny blinked and tried to look elsewhere, but her eyes were drawn back to the woman, a buxom honey-blonde in strappy shoes and a crisp new business suit. Rather formal for a writers' festival—then Danny realised why she looked familiar. She was Charlotte's assistant—Babette, that was her name. Danny had seen her earlier, arranging a book display. The bloody woman *worked* here, and she still couldn't be bothered to listen! Danny scarcely knew whether to slump over the podium or start throwing things.

She forced herself back to her poem.

"Your springy flesh
That begs to be crushed,
Probed, lapped from dripping fingers…"

When Danny risked another glance across the hall, she saw Charlotte directing an Arctic glare towards her employee. But Babette, still tittering into her phone, didn't seem to notice.

"One touch, and
Your vivid stain,
That biting sweetness
Leaves its red tattoo across my skin."

There was polite applause. Someone even asked a question, but Danny scarcely heard her own reply. She was smouldering inside, sick of being ignored and dismissed even by the people who'd invited her here.

As the session drew to a close and the audience began to rise, she made up her mind to confront Charlotte about it. Danny might be new to the festival and scarcely a headliner, but damn it, she was still entitled to expect better! She climbed down from the stage and elbowed her way through the crowd.

Charlotte had vanished. Danny couldn't see her at the bookstall, by the bar, or amongst the noisy throng, but she recalled that Charlotte had set up an office across the courtyard for the duration of the festival. The thought of confronting that imposing woman in her inner sanctum made Danny's mouth turn dry—but no, she would not back down. She marched across the courtyard, down the corridor, and towards Charlotte's closed office door.

From where she stood in the hall, Danny could hear Charlotte's deep, velvety voice raised in a tone of admonition. No one seemed to be replying, however. Was she on the phone? Danny could make out a few words: "*disgrace*" and "*ashamed*". The thought of disturbing Charlotte in a bad mood was daunting, but Danny would not weaken. She pushed open the door, just in time to hear a crisp, resonant crack and a muffled cry.

Charlotte sat in an armless chair of walnut wood and red leather, surrounded by boxes and neat towers of books. The room was alive with the scent of fresh ink and paper. And lying across Charlotte's lap, with her skirt hoisted above her waist and her honey curls in disarray, was Babette.

Babette's face was flushed, her lips swollen, her small hands wrapped around the chair legs to keep herself in place. Clearly visible below her bunched skirt, her full buttocks— framed by a black lace thong—blushed pink from a vigorous spanking.

Stunned, Danny could not help calculating; the reading had finished barely ten minutes ago. Charlotte must have summoned her underling here and put Babette across her knee straightaway!

For a long moment, Danny stood there. Her lips parted in amazement, the heat rising in her face, and an unmistakeable tingling between her thighs. Then Babette lifted her head, caught sight of the intruder, and gasped. And Charlotte, with a neat little smile and satisfaction thrumming in her voice, said, "Ah, Ms Maxwell. I'm so pleased you could join us."

Babette gave a squeak of dismay, gazing over Danny's shoulder and into the corridor outside. It was deserted, but from the courtyard nearby they could hear the rumble of footsteps, raucous conversation, and the hiss of the coffee machine. The other sessions were ending, and the crowds were pouring out. Any moment now, the three women might have company.

Babette wriggled against Charlotte's restraining hand, trying to rise. When she found this impossible, she reached behind with flailing movements to pull down her skirt.

"Now don't be silly, dear," Charlotte crooned, tugging the rumpled fabric even higher. "Put those fingers back where they were, unless you want me to restrain them." Still, she laid her free hand over Babette's rosy bottom, her flingers splayed across the young woman's twitching flesh as though to offer some rudimentary coverage.

Charlotte lifted her head.

"Ms Maxwell, if you would be so good as to close that door behind you?" Her tone was brisk. "I know this young lady has behaved abominably, but I prefer to save public punishment for the *truly* heinous offences." Charlotte's eyes narrowed as if at some disagreeable memory, and her grip tightened around Babette's chubby cheek. "Like those people who read half a book in the shop, then buy it online."

At the thought of such rudeness, Charlotte's expression darkened, and her tapered fingers dug into Babette's flesh, leaving little white dints. Danny drew in a breath, imagining how that pressure would sting against skin still smarting from being repeatedly slapped.

"Ms Maxwell?" Charlotte prompted. Her gaze grew steely. "*Ms Maxwell*?"

Afraid to argue, Danny stumbled forwards and pushed the door shut behind her.

"That's the way." Charlotte composed herself and gave that catlike smile once more. She released Babette's inflamed flesh and beckoned Danny closer.

Babette had ceased struggling after the door closed and now lay panting across Charlotte's knees, stealing wary glances up at their visitor. Danny tried not to stare at the younger woman's skimpy underwear and the hot-pink curves of her bottom, but it was hard to look anywhere else. Especially when Babette kept wriggling her hips like that... She seemed to be rubbing her pubic bone against Charlotte's thigh. The sight made Danny's clit throb so hard it hurt.

Charlotte cleared her throat, and Danny dragged her gaze upward.

"I'm glad you decided to drop by, Ms Maxwell, because my assistant has something she'd like to say to you." Charlotte smiled down at her captive and ran a tantalising finger along the black lace trim that separated Babette's buttocks. "She was going to seek you out and say sorry later at the book signing and give you a thank-you present for your reading too, but I think it's better here, don't you? It'll drive the message...home." Charlotte's hand slid all the way down Babette's thigh, and closed around it in an iron grip. "Well, my dear? What would you like to say to Ms Maxwell?"

Babette shut her eyes, her golden-brown hair falling across her face.

"I'm very, very sorry I talked during your reading," Babette mumbled. A fresh shade of pink lit the tips of her ears, matching her rear end. Charlotte tweaked Babette's thigh in warning, and Babette spoke louder. "It was rude of me." Charlotte gave another pinch, this time higher up, making the younger woman gasp and add in a breathless babble, "This event is the cultural highlight of the year, not a January sale, and I'm very lucky to be part of our city's literary heritage here. And I promise I'll never disrupt a poetry reading ever again!"

"That's the way." Charlotte beamed, then drew back her hand and delivered a single hard slap to Babette's left cheek, as if to punctuate the apology. Babette cried out, her body jolting and her flesh jiggling at the impact. Danny stared, transfixed, as the white stripes of Charlotte's fingers glowed briefly against Babette's aggravated skin before a darker colour flooded in.

"Ms Maxwell?" Charlotte cleared her throat. "Danny?" Danny started and forced herself to look away from the sight of Babette's mortification, up to Charlotte's face. "Do you have anything you'd like to say in reply?"

"Uh..." Danny's throat grated. All the moisture in her body seemed to have headed for destinations south. Her nipples tingled beneath her shirt and her underwear was growing damp. "I, uh, appreciate the apology, Babette. It...means a lot."

"Mm." Charlotte nodded in approval. "I always tell people: when you interrupt a piece of literature, you don't just show rudeness to the author and the audience, you also shortchange yourself. Every piece of writing has something to teach us, however pretentious and undergraduate it may be."

Danny blinked. She might have taken offence at that. But if she leaned a little to the left, she realised, she could catch a glimpse of the tops of Babette's breasts hanging forwards and straining against her tightly buttoned shirt. That view was enough to distract her from any insult.

"That's, um, very true," Danny managed.

"Of course it is." Charlotte ran fingertips across Babette's backside, tracing patterns against the chastised flesh. Babette squirmed and let out a whimper, as if this light touch were the cruellest punishment of all. "And to that end, Danny, why don't you share your poem with us again now?"

"I—I beg your pardon?"

Charlotte's smile broadened.

"As I said, I hate the thought that Babette missed out on your reading. Who knows what impressions it might have made on this naughty girl, if she'd only paid attention?" Charlotte slid a single finger beneath the lace to stroke the sensitive crease between Babette's cheeks. The young woman quivered and stifled a moan. "She's listening now, aren't you, my dear?"

Charlotte's voice took on an edge that made Babette stiffen and then nod in frantic agreement. "Come along, Danny. You're not due back onstage yet. Indulge us."

Danny's mind whirled. Was this really happening? An insistent pulse hammered between her thighs. She ached to touch both women right now, and instead Charlotte wanted a damn poetry reading? But the older woman's air of command made refusing seem impossible.

Her voice trembling, Danny began, "*Sometimes my appetites—*"

"No, no, no. Not like that." Charlotte shook her head impatiently. "Don't stand over there. You may as well be at the North Pole." She beckoned her visitor closer until Danny stood over them both. From here, she could smell Charlotte's tasteful perfume and a sharp, inviting aroma that she realised drifted from between Babette's legs.

"*...consume me...*"

"Oh, for heaven's sake, Danny." Charlotte's tone had grown dangerous. "What are you doing? Come closer and make a real impression." So saying, Charlotte hooked her fingers beneath the waistband of Babette's underwear and slowly peeled it down.

Babette gasped out a protest at the loss of her last vestige of modesty. Her gusset was moist and streaked silver, and a telltale string of sticky secretion clung, glistening, between the black fabric and the shadowy juncture of her thighs. Charlotte caught Danny's eye and gave a curt nod, ordering her down on her knees.

"The poem, Danny. If you please."

"*Sometimes...*" Danny sucked in her breath as her knees flattened against the stone floor. Charlotte gestured once more, and Danny shuffled nearer until she was touching Babette's feet, which were flexing and jittering inside their strappy shoes. The points of Babette's heels tapped and scraped against the floor, the muscles of her shapely calves lengthening as she sought a more comfortable position across Charlotte's lap. Danny shut her eyes and inhaled, breathing in the harsh scent of Babette's sweat, which shone in the pink creases of her knees, and the more pungent aroma that wafted from between her thighs.

"*My appetites consume me...*"

"Closer, Danny." Charlotte's voice sounded above her, echoed by a moan from Babette, who gave one more wriggle, this time edging her plump thighs apart.

This wordless invitation sent a surge of heat through Danny. In her kneeling position, her swollen clit was pressed up hard against the seam of her jeans. She wanted to reach down and touch herself, but she wanted to do something else even more, which was to take hold of Babette's underwear, now hanging tangled around her thighs, and work it all the way down.

At the tickle of the wet fabric and the warmth of Danny's fingers, Babette twitched and choked back a cry. Danny watched transfixed as Babette's hips pushed back towards her, her arse rounding out. The sight caused Danny a jolt of desire. All shyness forgotten, she cupped the younger woman's curves, relishing the softness of Babette's skin and the heat that lingered there from her spanking. She spread Babette's thighs.

"*Gluttony and decadence...*" Danny licked her lips, staring at the wisps of golden-brown hair, twisted and glinting with moisture, and Babette's inner lips, thick and glossy like the flesh of a ripe peach. Danny let out a breath against the sensitised flesh and Babette gasped.

"*Drive me to my knees...*" Danny paused between each whispered phrase, blowing gently. She could feel the muscles working with surprising strength in Babette's thighs as the young woman jerked and strained in response. She must have enjoyed being punished by Charlotte, but perhaps she didn't find Danny's poem quite so boring now either?

Keeping her touch light, Danny stroked Babette's swollen lips. God, they were hot and unbelievably slippery. How easy it would be to push inside her right now, but Danny sensed that would be overstepping her role here. Instead, she drew back her fingers to paint Babette's inner thighs and the cleft between her buttocks with her own hot juices, so the young woman would feel more acutely the brush of Danny's breath, a teasing coolness against the heat.

"*Your forbidden hue...*"

A cry above her indicated her technique was working. Danny tugged Babette's thighs as far apart as she could in this position. Babette's feet teetered as she fought to keep her balance, her ankles still tethered by her underwear. Danny bent her head and parted Babette's lips with a lingering sweep of her tongue.

A loud groan showed Babette's appreciation, but Danny was stopped by a yank of her short hair. Charlotte's voice rang commandingly above her. "The *poem*, Danny."

Never had Danny hated her own bloody writing more. With a growl of frustration, she drew back a little to mutter scraps of her stanzas, breathing hard and working her lips with exaggerated movements to make whatever contact she could with Babette's salty flesh.

Babette's hips were thrusting backwards and forwards now with serious intent. Danny nuzzled closer, her nose at Babette's entrance. Her eyes were closed. Liquid arousal trickled down her face, and the smell of sex was overwhelming. Dismissing Charlotte and her ridiculous lessons at last, Danny extended her tongue to flick Babette's exposed clit.

She heard some kind of scolding from above her, but it was muffled by Babette's thighs and the sound of Danny's own pulse ringing in her ears. She hummed a few more fragments of verse—"*probed, lapped, sweetness*"—reverberating them against Babette's tender sex before capturing Babette's clit between her lips and working it to and fro with her tongue.

Babette tensed and quivered. Danny felt herself buffeted by some new impact and realised Charlotte had begun spanking her subordinate once more, landing quick, sharp blows with each outwards surge of Babette's hips, until a deep cry sounded and Babette slumped across Charlotte's knees, all the tension in her body melting away through Danny's clutching hands.

"There." Charlotte chuckled above them. "Let that be a lesson to you."

How Danny made it through the afternoon panel session on poetry, social media, and youth entrepreneurism, she would never know.

Her short hair was rumpled, one knee of her new jeans frayed right through from the stone floor—which at least had been clean, she reflected; Charlotte would have tolerated nothing less. Her face was warm and, she feared, still sticky in places from Babette's juices. A residual heat pulsed beneath her belly. She touched her tongue to the corner of her mouth and tasted salt.

The facilitator had posed a question about which hashtags would Emily Dickinson have used, and Danny was midway through a garbled response when she caught sight of Babette again.

The young woman's composure was breathtaking. Babette's clothing was impeccable, her makeup freshly applied, and if she was still sore from her spanking, she showed no sign of it as she strutted up to the tech panel beside the stage to converse in whispers with the sound crew.

Danny cleared her throat.

"It's, ah, amusing to reflect on how the solipsism, celebrity culture, and anonymity of social media resonates with a history of nineteenth-century gossip pages, with their breathless tone and use of nom de plumes..." Danny heard herself droning on. She did not feel especially amusing right now. Her eyes were drawn again to Babette, who was gesturing towards some problem on the soundboard with one coral-coloured fingernail. How the hell did that young woman stay so coolly professional when only half an hour earlier she had been over Charlotte's lap with her bare bottom in the air and Danny's face buried greedily between her thighs? Perhaps Babette was more like her tough-minded employer than Danny had realised.

As she pondered this, Danny's mic cut out.

The crowd grumbled and shifted about in their chairs. The other writers on the panel flapped around and offered to swap seats. Then Babette trotted onto the stage, her heels beating a staccato rhythm on the boards, and her breasts bouncing beneath her jacket, to pass Danny a handheld mic.

"Something's come unplugged," she whispered as she handed it over, her glossy hair brushing Danny's wrist. "Don't worry, I've got this."

Before Danny could reply, Babette had ducked under the table.

The table was covered all the way around with a thick, floor-length cloth. Danny could no longer see Babette, but she could hear the click of electrical cords and switches and feel the bump of Babette's movements by her feet. Danny fumbled with the new mic and shuffled her papers—what had she been talking about? Then she let out a gasp that caused the mic to screech horribly and the audience to wince and mutter to each other. Beneath the table, Babette had grasped Danny's knees with unexpected strength and forced them wide apart.

In an instant, Babette had scooted forwards on her knees, inserting her curvy body snugly into the vee of Danny's open legs so there could be no possibility of closing them. Praying the other panellists weren't looking, Danny lifted the tablecloth from across her lap and caught a glimpse of Babette's teeth flashing in a devilish grin as she ran the ball of her thumb along the seam of Danny's jeans from her arsehole all the way up to her swelling clit.

Danny dropped the cloth, her heart clanging. She had never been at a greater disadvantage in her life—and she had never been so turned on either. The rhythmic movements of a single finger massaging her clit through the tough, abrasive denim, now soaked through with her own arousal, made her breath catch and her hips jerk helplessly. Tonguing Babette earlier had been all the foreplay Danny had needed, and now the briefest touch set her body raging.

Positioned as she was, she could not wrestle Babette away without attracting the attention of the three earnest writers seated beside her, and probably a whole hall full of readers too. All Danny could do was adjust the tablecloth covertly across her lap to ensure she was fully covered…and open her legs wider.

"Now," the facilitator was saying, peering around through her owlish glasses, "in this age of the visual imperative, it has to be asked whether poetry can only survive by melding with photography and graphic design—and at the most democratic level, through the creation of viral memes and GIFs." She raised her eyebrows. "Danny, your thoughts?"

Danny's main thought was that Charlotte had not spanked Babette nearly hard enough. The young woman's hand was pumping between Danny's thighs now, the friction of wet, heated fabric between them intensifying the physical thrill. Meanwhile, Babette's free hand grasped the muscle of Danny's right thigh, squeezing and pinching until it burned. Danny could smell her body's excitement drifting upwards. She felt Babette's head nudging between her legs, the bump of a cute button nose against her clit, and then the furnace of the young woman's breath against her throbbing cunt.

"Ah—well…" Danny's cheeks were ablaze, her voice husky. She swallowed and stared around helplessly, wishing for something to distract the crowd—a fire alarm at the very least! Some people must have started to wonder if her red-faced stammering was more than just stage fright, and what was taking Babette so long to fix the mic. And what if Babette's spiky heels or luscious backside were poking out from beneath the tablecloth? The thought made Danny's hips rock harder with excitement.

"I think, uh, it's important to remember that poetry as a written medium, divorced from music and dance, is a relatively new historical phenomenon…" Danny's voice veered from hoarse to squeaky, like a teenage boy busted with his first porno magazine. Turning to her left, she added desperately, "Fenella, wouldn't you agree?"

Thank heavens for other writers; they loved the sound of their own voices so much. The slam poet beside launched into her own theories about how poetry was actually everywhere, all the time—in advertising jingles, T-shirt slogans, death threats on Twitter… As she burbled on, Danny shut her eyes and bit her bottom lip hard, fighting to slow her breathing, to keep from cursing and growling and moaning. Lava waves of pleasure coursed through her. She was so close, it was terrifying. Babette's free hand had crept higher, plucking at Danny's fly. Danny glanced down and saw coral-tipped fingers stealing out from beneath the tablecloth; Babette was working at the stud of Danny's jeans.

Saucer-eyed with alarm, Danny skidded forwards and hunched over, terrified of what her fellow panellists might see if they glanced towards her. But Babette seemed to have no such worries. Her right hand was thrusting between Danny's legs now, her palm cupped tight around Danny's arse and aching cunt, the ball of her thumb riding Danny's clit. And with her left hand… Danny felt the stud of her jeans pop open and those mischievous fingers close around her zipper and give it a tug. Jesus, Babette was going to drag her pants off her right here! Unless she just—just…

Danny lifted her notes to her face just in time as she came with a clenched and silent fury, molten sensations cascading through her, her hips writhing, her face twisting.

She recovered in time to hear Fenella explaining how the collapse of publishing houses and the defunding of university arts departments were the best things that had ever happened to poetry.

Under other circumstances, Danny could have strangled her for that. Right now, though, with the warm tingling of her orgasm washing through her, all she could do was lower her papers with shaky hands, nod along, and try to look normal. From the yawning, stupefied faces in the audience, apparently no one else had noticed Danny's odd behaviour.

No one except Charlotte. At the back of the hall, the older woman leaned against the doorframe, folded her arms, and smirked.

Danny took her time rising from the table, fumbling surreptitiously with the fastening on her jeans whilst the other writers hurried towards the bar. When the stage was deserted and the audience lining up at the exits, Babette emerged, brushing dust from her knees.

"Sorry about the, ah, power disruption." She flicked back her hair, which, Danny noticed, was still neat and gleaming. Had Babette taken a compact and hairspray down there with her?

Danny shook her head. All she could think of to say was "Don't think I'm not grateful… But if that was my thank-you present, you didn't have to give it to me onstage."

"Oh, no." Babette blinked. She pointed to the back of the hall, where a row of wine bottles were lined up with cards attached. "Your thank-you present is over there. *Chateau ordinaire*, our red ink writers' special. *That*"—she cast a mocking glance below the waistband of Danny's jeans—"that was your punishment."

"My…?" Danny stared. "My punishment for what?"

"For taking more than a minute to answer your audience question in the last session." Babette beamed and gave Charlotte a little wave. "The boss did warn you, Danny. We have strict standards around here."

THE WORLD TURNED UPSIDE DOWN

Naomi frowned at her reflection, examining herself from head to toe. On the table, the gramophone spun, Lotte Lenya's voice growling above the muffled din from the nightclub floor. The bulbs flickered, casting shadows over the picture postcards pinned up around the mirror: Marlene Dietrich, Hedy Lamarr, Gertrude Lawrence. Naomi wondered if any of them had ever had a dressing room that so closely resembled a broom cupboard. Amazing how much space the chorus girls' costumes took up in here, when one considered how little those naughty garments actually covered. Performers would never get away with dressing like that in London, or even in Paris, but here in Berlin, who would stop them?

She patted her nose with a large, fluffy powder puff, rouged her cheekbones, and screwed the monocle into her left eye. Then she adjusted the large chocolate-coloured cock that protruded from her furry haunches.

"Anna? Be a dear and straighten this horn, will you?"

The younger woman rose from her own dressing table. She was wearing a gown made from flimsy cheesecloth, cinched between her small, perky breasts with a scarab brooch and only just covering her shapely buttocks. A wide collar made of plausible paste jewels extended from her delicate throat to the tips of her shoulders. An Egyptian crook and flail lay on her dressing table; they had seen some vigorous service already.

Anna turned Naomi around and fiddled with the goat's horn that poked up from her mentor's left temple. The effect was realistic; the thin headband that held the horns was concealed beneath Naomi's thick, cropped brown curls. It was Pagans' Bacchanal Night here at the Topsy-Turvy Tavern, and Naomi was determined to look the part.

"I'm not sure the satyr act is really *you*, though." Anna hummed to herself as she adjusted the headband.

"Whyever not?" Naomi frowned in suspicion. She jammed a cigar between her lips and lit it with a flick of her wrist. Then she scowled into the mirror again, scrutinising her sturdy, well-fed body.

Her top half was almost naked, her breasts flattened against her ribcage by wide, tight braces covered with dense brown fur. The adhesive on the inside would be the devil to soak off, no doubt, but for now the strips of pelt clung just right to Naomi's plump breasts, yanking them this way and that in a manner that didn't feel bad at all. From the waist down, she was clad in specially made jodhpurs covered in long, shaggy hair. They flared out around Naomi's stocky hips and large behind, then clung to her knees and calves before vanishing into a highly polished pair of Prussian officer's boots.

Naomi chewed her cigar.

"Hmph. Let me guess—too short, too fat?" Her voice was gruff. Three quick puffs of smoke escaped from her lips.

"No." Anna's smile was tender and tolerant. "I was just thinking you don't make a very plausible predator." She ran her hands down Naomi's braces, stroking the fur over the older woman's breasts until it lay flat and sleek, and Naomi nipples strained beneath it. Anna added, "Not to anyone who knows you. The stories I could tell…"

"Well then, I'd better stop that pretty mouth of yours quick-smart, hadn't I?" Naomi touched Anna's reddened lips and gave an affectionate leer.

Anna's hands slipped further down, her fingertips skittering over Naomi's belly before combing through the rough pelt below her hips.

"Don't worry; you're still a randy old billygoat in your own way," she assured Naomi, wrapping one dainty hand around Naomi's cock and giving it a good, firm tug. Naomi choked on her cigar.

"Look out, my girl!"

"Well, look at the state of you!" Anna scolded, shaking her head. Her straight black hair flew out around her heart-shaped face for a moment.

Then it settled back as usual into a sleek little cap. "You can't go onstage like this. Why, I can still see lipstick on it!"

Tutting to herself, Anna reached over to the pot of cold cream on the dressing table. She scooped some out on a cleansing pad, then wiped the cock with leisurely, circular movements from base to bulbous head. All the while, she looked deep into her mentor's eyes.

Naomi leaned back against the dressing table and took a long draw on her cigar. She did her best to ignore the flare of heat that ran the length of the leather harness and sparked like a match-head between her thighs. No need to start panting like some pimply schoolboy, Naomi scolded herself, struggling to calm her breathing and still the roll of her hips. She had a jaded and cynical reputation to keep up, damn it!

Naomi "Natty" Isaacs, master of ceremonies here at the Topsy-Turvy Tavern. Naomi the barrel-bodied bullhorn—the cross-dressing corrupter of innocents—the dirty old soft-shoe Sapphic with her chorus line of syncopated sinners!

Well, that was certainly what she *hoped* people said about her.

"Are you decent, ladies?" called a breathy voice, accompanied by a knock at the door. The two women edged apart, with Anna mouthing, "Later."

"Anna, *Liebchen*, have you seen my brow pencil?" In strutted Lola, resplendent in crimson artificial silk. Her wig was a towering pile of honey-coloured curls; her face was made up into a very plausible Gloria Swanson. A feather boa was draped around the broad shoulders that had served her well as a machine gunner at Pozières. Thick powder and orange rouge covered up the shrapnel scars.

Finding what she was looking for, Lola leaned in between them to fix her eyes.

"Everything all right out there?" asked Naomi.

"No sign of troublemakers." Lola studied herself before turning to leave. "And André's nearly got that hammer and sickle scrubbed off the front door. Oh!" Pausing in the doorway, she reached into her corset and pulled out some envelopes. "Natty, I stopped by the boarding house on the way here, and I found some mail for you. Looks like Fräulein Weber has started hiding it in the bread bin."

"Mad old bat!" Naomi snorted. "Just because I was a few weeks late with the rent..." She shuffled through the envelopes. "Eighteenth of July, twentieth, twenty-first—she's been archiving them for days!"

Not that there was anything here Naomi wanted to open. She glanced at the past-due bills and tossed them aside. Really, you would think her laundryman and her dentist would have better things to do than pester her, just because things were a little lean this month! Well, for the past couple of months.

Then she turned the last envelope over and read the address on the back. Her face tightened.

"Everything okay?" Anna was watching her. Naomi forced a smile and tucked the letter into her boot.

"Everything's perfectly splendid," she said. "Now, do you want to run those new dance steps past me one last time?"

The only thing Naomi enjoyed almost as much as being Anna's lover was training Anna as a performer. Over the past two years, she had watched Anna go from strength to strength. Naomi had helped the young woman to polish up her tap dancing, snake-hips, and shimmy technique. She'd taught Anna everything she knew about vocal control and putting a song across in English, French, and German. Neither of their voices were fit for Covent Garden, but who cared? When dealing with the rowdy mob of tourists, sailors, and working girls in here, what mattered was panache, comic timing, and above all, *volume*. And nowadays, Anna could bring the ceiling plaster down with the best of them.

Naomi had helped Anna develop her own ideas for acts too, and had bullied the club's manager into putting them onstage. There was Anna's now-famous cigarette girl routine—pink tiara, fluffy clogs, cigarette tray, and not much in between—and her sword dance in a tiny leather jerkin and Douglas Fairbanks pirate boots. Not to mention her Brides of Dracula burlesque number: Anna looking spookier and sexier than Bela Lugosi had ever managed, in correct evening dress and a swirling cape, with a chorus of blondes in see-through shrouds and strategically placed toy bats.

The memory made Naomi smile. How the audience had shrieked when Anna had whipped out her wooden stake!

Right now, however, Anna was frowning as she adjusted her cobra crown.

"I don't like this Cleopatra routine André is insisting on," she said. "It's such a cliché."

"Oh, I don't know." Naomi dropped a kiss on her bare shoulder and butted the cock playfully against Anna's behind. "You certainly know your way around an asp."

Anna swatted her away, grumbling, "Do I look like Theda Bara to you?"

"Of course not; you'd leave that poor girl for dead. You're more like Louise Brooks, my darling—if she'd been born in a palace in Shanghai."

"It was a laundry in San Francisco," said Anna. "As you know perfectly well. Anyway, I'm bored with this act. It's worse than André's Fu Manchu striptease."

"Oh, come now—that moustache suited you!"

"Don't you get sick of these fools running the show?"

"Now and then." Naomi hesitated. Could this be the opening she had been waiting for? "Anna? Have you ever thought of going away? Finding ourselves a different city?"

"Hm." Anna picked up a kohl pencil and went to work on her eyes. "Well, I wouldn't mind a vacation, I guess. But I've done Paris, and Vienna is too expensive—"

"I was thinking about England. And perhaps a little more than a holiday." Naomi cleared her throat and turned away to tidy the mess of costumes behind her. She felt oddly furtive, as though she was tricking Anna into something, and it was not a feeling she enjoyed. But she daren't speak fully just yet. Not until she could read the contents of that letter.

"London?" Anna sounded surprised. "Well, I'd follow you to the moon, darling, you know that. But—"

"Actually, Manchester might be easier to organise." Naomi buried her face in the wardrobe, rifling through the hangers so she wouldn't have to see Anna's incredulous expression.

"Natty, why the heck would anyone want to go *there*?"

"It's not as bad as that." Naomi coughed. "Think of it—new sights, new faces! No chance of our debtors catching up with us, or some big lout of a Brownshirt chasing us down the street and clobbering us over the head. And my family is there."

"Natty, you haven't spoken to them in years." Anna sounded like she was on the verge of calling for a nerve specialist. "Darling, what's this about?"

"Nothing at all." Naomi swung around and summoned up a smile. So the time wasn't quite right yet. Once she'd read that letter, maybe… "I was only asking," she said. "You told me you were tired of things around here. Perhaps it's time for a change." She pinched the remains of her cigar, took one last drag, then stubbed it out in a soldier's tin helmet that someone had left behind.

She watched Anna turning the idea over in her mind. Lately, things had not been so friendly out there. They'd had disturbing pamphlets distributed in the street outside, slogans painted on the wall, beatings in the alleyway. And Lola's cancan routine featuring Comrade Stalin in red frilly knickers had not been well received at all.

Was it possible they might lose their garish little refuge here? And might it be better to jump before they were pushed?

But Anna was already smiling and evidently shrugging the thought away, with all the resilience of the young.

"It's sweet when you worry about things, Natty." Anna leaned in to trail soft kisses up the side of Naomi's neck. Naomi shut her eyes, relishing the aroma of Anna's Jicky perfume and the silky texture of her lips. Anna flicked Naomi's earlobe with her tongue, making her gasp. "But don't fuss so much. We'll be fine here. There's nothing we can't handle."

That knot of anxiety still twisted inside Naomi's belly. But it loosened as Anna pressed the length of her warm body up against her and nibbled the curve of Naomi's ear. Naomi's breath released in a soft groan of longing.

"Well, I could certainly handle a little more of that."

"Not now, darling. I've got to finish getting ready." Anna gave a teasing smirk as she turned away to scrutinise herself in the mirror. But her smile widened and she twitched pleasurably as Naomi slipped her broad, tobacco-stained hands around to fondle Anna's breasts through the skimpy cheesecloth.

"I suspect you're thoroughly ready, my dear," Naomi crooned. Her heartbeat pumped between her legs when she felt Anna's nipples prickling through the cloth. It was hard to keep worrying about anything much at this moment.

Naomi caught the hot little buttons between each forefinger and thumb, pinched them out to full length and rolled them round and round.

"God, Natty…" Anna's hands dropped to the edge of the dressing table. She clung on tight, her eyes squeezing shut, her bottom lip caught between her teeth. Her hips were stirring, tilting backwards in search of the warmth of Naomi's body.

"Why, Your Majesty…" Naomi licked a hot, moist path along Anna's neck again and bit down firmly just above her collarbone. "Is Cleopatra trying to take me up her Nile?"

"You are such a pest sometimes…" Anna's cross voice gave way to a moan as Naomi slid one hand down over the younger woman's warm, toned belly and began to rub her through the cheesecloth, slow and hard.

"Hush, my dear." Naomi blew lightly in her ear. "The great god Pan wants to catch you in your olive grove…"

"I swear you only keep me around to practice your terrible stage jokes on." But Anna was sighing now with sweet frustration as Naomi's cock nuzzled teasingly between her buttocks.

"I assure you"—Naomi tongued the inside of Anna's ear, causing her to stifle a shriek—"that is merely a side benefit." She lifted the cheesecloth, plunged her hand into Anna's knickers, and found her swollen and sensitised, sweet syrup trickling through Naomi's fingers. "Bloody hell! How long do we have?"

"Not long enough," Anna panted. She dropped her head and gasped as the rough fur of Naomi's costume chafed the backs of her thighs and Naomi moved impatiently to tug her knickers down.

Outside, the band burst into life with a drumroll and a blare of trombones. Naomi swore breathlessly.

"It sounds like the great god Pan is due onstage," Anna sighed, wriggling reluctantly away. "Hurry up, they're expecting you out there."

"Bloody perverts," Naomi growled. "Spoiling my debauchery."

"Go on." Anna adjusted her costume. "They can't start without you."

"I know, I know." Naomi groaned and stepped away. "The show must go on." She reached for her top hat and settled it on the back of her head, making sure her horns were still on display. "I am nothing if not a professional."

She checked the shine of her soldier's boots, straightened her enormous cock, and hurried out onstage.

"Ladies and gentlemen, *willkommen, benvenuto, bienvenue*!" Naomi hollered from her spotlight. "Welcome to the inaugural Pagans' Bacchanal!" The fur braces stretched and creaked across her ribs; her cock bobbed a cheerfully obscene greeting to the crowd, who hooted and shouted back.

Inside her boot, the envelope scratched against her skin.

"Welcome, all you devotees of Dionysus, all you followers of the poet Sappho, all you practitioners of the Greek vice!" The band broke into a jaunty ragtime rhythm. Naomi jittered, shuffled, and spun her short, round body from stage right to stage left, pausing here and there to shake a hand, steal a glass of sherry, and take a quick draw on a pretty woman's cigarette. "Have we got a treat in store for you tonight! First onstage, please make welcome our syncopated slave girls, our naughty nymphs—ladies and gentlemen, the Topsy-Turvy Tavern's incomparable cabaret girls!"

The spotlight shifted, illuminating the half dozen young women now tripping onto the stage in miniature versions of the costumes from *The Last Days of Pompeii*. As they whooped and shimmied to the jangling music, Naomi stood alone in the darkened wings.

She had handled herself all right out there; she always did. But she couldn't concentrate. All she could think about was the paper inside her boot, now growing crumpled and damp. She could wait no longer; as the dancers finished their opening routine, she dug it out, flattened it, and ripped the envelope open.

It was from her sister, Deborah.

Dearest Podge, I was so glad to get your letter…

Naomi blinked. So glad—really? And her sister hadn't called her Podge, her old boarding-school nickname, for thirty years. Affection, nostalgia… Naomi had not expected that.

The band gave a familiar drum roll; damn it, she was due back out there! She hid the letter behind the curtain and dashed onstage.

"Aren't our girls divine, ladies and gentlemen? Wouldn't you just love to join them in a Roman bath one of these days?" Naomi waited for the applause to recede. She was sweating, she realised, her skin scorching beneath the stage lights. Her heart beat faster. *Get this over with fast!* She had to read the rest of Deborah's letter.

"Now, ladies and gentlemen, please make welcome to the stage those stars of the arena, those colossi of the colosseum, the death-defying gladiators Marius the Miniature and Horatio the Huge! Duelling for the favours of the deadly Empress Lola, the real reason Rome fell!"

The band struck up a tune of comical buffoonery, preparing for a mock fight between the dwarf acrobat and the circus giant. Naomi hurried backstage as fast as she could and fished out her letter.

She skimmed through the first page, through news of growing children and aging relatives. Naomi knew that was a rotten thing to do, but there was no point in lying to herself. After years of silence, she had not contacted Deborah to ask for news of the family.

It was late at night when she'd written to Deborah three months ago. After a bad evening at the club and an alarming walk home at midnight. Her head had been swirling with known and unknown fears: of debtors, eviction, police raids, and darker possibilities still... Seeing her options vanishing before her eyes, Naomi had swallowed her pride and written to ask a favour. And for the first time in thirty years, to ask her sister's advice.

In her neat handwriting, Deborah continued.

> *I've spoken to Max, as you asked me to, and he thinks he can organise a job for you here. Isn't that good news? It's a company that makes the parts for sewing machines; they have a space in their typing pool. Of course they usually employ the pretty young things, but Max thinks he can persuade them. I don't suppose the pay is much, but you know how it is these days.*

Naomi looked up and reminded herself to take a breath. Her eyes hurt from squinting in the shadows.

> *And you should be able to live frugally. Mrs Starks told me they've got a spare room they would rent for very little, if you're willing to help with the children and her grandmother. Now, you will wear a skirt, won't you, dear? And don't swear. And don't smoke those horrible cigars.*

Naomi mopped her brow. Could she do it? Go back to an England that had made clear it had no use for women like her—back to a life she'd sworn she would never lead again? Would that be the price of safety?

She began to read on, but the band gave a blast of trumpets and a clash of cymbals, beckoning her back onstage.

As she introduced the last of the warm-up acts—a comedian who played political anthems on a rubber pig's bladder—Naomi felt her palms growing wet with nerves, her voice sliding off-key. She had done the right thing by writing to Deborah, hadn't she? The thought of being dragged back to her old life was appalling; it would make her feel like a bear being thrust into a cage at the zoo.

The comedian bolted out onstage with a grin and a raspberry. Naomi hastened back to her hiding place and leaned against the wall. From the nightclub floor came the sounds of laughter, corks popping, glasses clinking together. Suddenly it seemed very far away. She glanced down again at the paper.

> *Now, dear, you mustn't be cross with me, but I've told Max to organise your tickets. I know you'll call me bossy, but really I think it's best you come home as soon as we can arrange it. Your letter sounded so worried, and you did say you wanted to show your friend around England. I'll wire you as soon as we have the details.*

Naomi realised she was breathing hard; her chest hurt. The letter quivered in her hands. The music clanged inside her skull; all at once, it seemed hellishly loud. How she longed to leave, to sink down into a chair somewhere and think about this.

Well, said a flat voice in her head. *It's a way out.* It was a rotten bargain, but she and Anna would manage and at least this way they would be safe. Anna's safety was worth any price.

> *Podge, you will come home, won't you? We read such alarming things in the newspapers, and Max says there's bound to be a war. I miss you, dear, and I don't like to think of you over there on your own.*

Naomi traced her sister's farewell with one gentle fingertip. Then she looked up and caught a glimpse of Anna in the opposite wing, perched on a stool, still in her skimpy costume, but with her reading glasses on her nose. She was flicking through an old copy of *The Woman Worker*. She caught Naomi looking at her and gave a little wave. Naomi's heart clenched with love. *Well,* she repeated to herself. *It's a way out.*

She tucked the letter out of sight again and straightened her shoulders. Time for a change of costume, a quick cup of coffee, and one last cigar.

She had a show to put on.

Evenings didn't always go smoothly at the Topsy-Turvy Tavern. Sometimes there were fistfights, political quarrels, tearful lovers, and people slipping over in their own sick—and that was just the band members. Other nights, the place was dead, and the performers found themselves serenading two drunken old queens and the bartender's cat.

But by some strange alchemy of cabaret, the Pagans' Bacchanal Night was magnificent.

Lola made an excellent sea witch Circe, doing obscene things to Odysseus behind the cover of his cardboard boat, then dancing the Charleston with his sailors—now wearing pig snouts and curly tails. The ventriloquist's act with Cerberus the three-headed dog puppet got a good laugh. The Leda and the Swan tableaux, accompanied by the weird, plaintive whine of the musical saw, was mournfully filthy. And Naomi's tap-dancing number as the Emperor Nero—toga, laurel wreath, violin, chorus line of lions, and Christians doing the Lindy Hop—brought the house down.

When Naomi catapulted offstage at interval, she was sweating and grinning from ear to ear. Her clothing reeked of greasepaint, cigarette smoke, and the dancers' perfume, and the applause, howls of laughter, and final trills of the band still reverberated behind her. If this was to be her last performance ever, at least she could say she'd gone out with a bang. No drug on earth could equal this: the feeling of a live show that had just gone really, perfectly, bloody *fucking* well.

She slammed the dressing room door shut, seized hold of a laughing Anna, heaved her up onto the table, and yanked her knickers down.

"So you didn't get the bird out there, then?" Anna giggled in between kisses. Naomi bit her bottom lip until she squealed, then hauled her cheesecloth dress up around her armpits. "Ooh—who knew Mr Nero would be such a dirty boy?"

"It's the togas," Naomi muttered. "You get a good healthy breeze under there." She clutched Anna's buttocks, lifting and squeezing her closer, and took Anna's entire left breast in her mouth.

The jerking of the younger woman's hips, the taste of her salty skin, the hot, lithe legs wrapped around Naomi's waist, and the muffled yelps above her were intoxicating. Naomi tightened her mouth on Anna's breast, letting her beloved feel the crooked ridge of her teeth. Then she swirled her tongue in slow, lascivious spirals, pausing to strum the taut little tip until Anna let out a cry, her fingers twisting in Naomi's hair.

"Oh, that's..." Anna was shuddering when Naomi released her. She turned her attentions to Anna's other breast, sucking her with firm movements of her lips and jaw until Anna grabbed her mentor's hand and jammed it between her legs.

"Good Lord." Naomi panted as slippery heat coated her fingers and dripped into her palm. "That's the routine I forgot to write for tonight: Mt Vesuvius!"

"I swear, Natty, one more joke..."

"Well, it's positively molten down here! What have you been doing whilst I was onstage? Playing with yourself the whole time?"

"Not the whole time..." Anna was grimacing with need, rotating her hips to catch every brush of Naomi's fingers. Desire radiated from Anna's body, that illicit scent filling the cramped little room. Naomi's chest was heaving, her pulse galloping. She spread Anna's lower lips and entered her with two thick fingers, then three.

If only this never had to end, she thought as Anna's ankles locked behind her back, the young woman's breathing coming fast and hoarse. If only she could keep the sweet smell of Anna's soap and perfume and sweat and cunt, the wet grip of her body around Naomi's fingers, its texture rough and spongy by turns.

If only they could stay so carefree, so full of joy.

She was almost sorry when Anna's rhythm changed. The younger woman's hips thrust frantically now as she pounded her clit against the fleshy heel of Naomi's hand. Naomi twisted her wrist, angling her curled fingers to hit the right spot, loving the clenching and pumping of Anna's hidden muscles and the proof of her pleasure that was pooling on the tabletop, slipping and sliding beneath her bare thighs. Naomi's free hand gripped Anna's bottom, digging deep into the plush skin. Anna flung her head back, perspiration glistening along the curve of her throat, and let out a wail of such operatic power that they must have heard it on the dance floor.

Anna collapsed back onto the table. Her bare breasts were heaving, still marked with the red-and-white indentations of Naomi's teeth. Naomi grabbed the edge of the wood to steady herself. Her heart was thundering, a fire was raging below her belly. *If only we could stay like this.*

She scarcely knew why, but she was conscious of something like anguish when Anna slid to her knees in front of her.

"Darling, don't, you'll spoil your makeup..." Anna ignored that. She looked up at Naomi with a smile that chimed painfully in the older woman's heart. Then she knocked her mentor's knees apart and slithered up underneath her toga.

The stinging pressure of Anna's nails as she gripped Naomi's thighs made Naomi's body clench with anticipation. She drew in a startled breath when she felt another sensation, the smooth head of her discarded cock circling her entrance. Where had Anna pulled that from?

Anna increased the pressure with each lazy rotation, coating the cock's thick length in Naomi's juices and coaxing it past her fluttering muscles until her knees bent under the delicious strain and her defences gave way. Soon Naomi's breaths came fast and shallow in time with the burning friction between her legs, her body jolting at each hidden, intimate touch. And when she felt the glide of a hot, flat tongue along her clit, it was too much to bear.

Naomi came, shaking and almost weeping, the waves of pleasure rising behind her eyes. She held on to the table until her knuckles stood out white, as if some terrible force might prise her grip loose and send her tumbling down and down.

They dressed hastily. Anna was fixing her smeared cosmetics in front of the mirror as Naomi slipped out. Naomi couldn't wait until they got back to the boarding house; she needed to know what was going to happen as soon as she possibly could. If she and Anna were indeed destined to leave this city, they needed to start making plans.

The telephone in André's empty office was strictly off limits to performers. So naturally she used it.

"Fräulein Weber?" She waited for the indignant twittering to die down. "Yes, I know it's late. But I gather you've been hiding my mail, and I need to know whether any telegrams arrived for me."

Naomi squeezed her eyes shut with frustration as her landlady launched instead into a litany of complaints about her rudeness, her crazy comings and goings, her rent being late yet again...

"Fräulein Weber, listen to me." Naomi interrupted, using the booming tones she generally employed for dealing with hecklers and ordering troublemakers out of the club. "Now, I'm going to be leaving your premises very soon. When I go, there's a chance I might decide to be very generous, in spite of your ghastly cooking, and not ask for my deposit back. I might even leave you with a little something extra." There was an expectant silence on the other end of the line; the landlady was listening at last. "Now, can you please go and check whether any telegrams have arrived?"

There was a clump as the phone was put down and a silence that stretched on and on. Naomi ran her free hand through her hair until her curls stood on end. Her guts were twisting with anticipation. If it had all been arranged, if they were really, truly going... The thought was like swallowing cod-liver oil—but even so, she found her mind beginning to adjust, to formulate plans. The typist job and the spare room in Manchester sounded perfectly ghastly, but they would do for a month or two. Once she was there, she would phone David's agency, see if they could sort Anna out with a part of some kind—good Lord, they should feel lucky to have her! She would call in on Micky, who knew everyone, and ask about cheap flats. She would catch up with Topper and the girls. She would—

"Fräulein Isaacs? Are you there?" The old woman's voice quavered.

"Yes, yes! Was there something?"

"There was a telegram under the sofa cushion. I don't know who put it there. You visitors, you make so much mess—"

"Fräulein Weber, read it, please!" Naomi's voice burst out loud enough to make the old lady yelp.

"It says, *Passage booked. Leave on the twelfth. Arriving at Folkestone Tuesday. Please wire confirm.*"

Naomi let out a long breath. This was it, then. She stood up taller; she even straightened her ridiculous toga.

"Well, thank you, Fräulein Weber. I'll give you my notice in writing tomorrow—"

"Wait, wait," grumbled the voice at the other end. "You never let me finish. You English, you are very impatient, very rude..."

Naomi closed her eyes. Suddenly, leaving this city seemed rather appealing.

"Fräulein, did you want to say something more?"

"Not me, your telegram! It says, *Max asked about visa for your friend, but no luck. Too many foreigners coming here already and not enough jobs, I suppose. And it's not like she has family here. Sorry, Podge, but we did try. See you soon. Love.*"

Naomi looked down at her fingers wrapped around the handset. They flexed and tightened; they felt strangely numb. She put the handset down quietly. *Well, then*, said that quiet, flat voice inside her. *Well, then.*

"What's this?" asked Anna when Naomi opened the dressing room door. Deborah's letter had tumbled out of Naomi's boot.

Anna picked it up and perused the stamps, looking at Naomi's address written in her sister's careful, anxious hand. Naomi hesitated. Emotions swirled inside her: rage, shame, despair. Defiance.

"Nothing." She took the letter and dropped it into a drawer full of hairpins, newspaper clippings, old lipsticks, and other abandoned junk.

"Just an offer of a job," said Naomi. "But I've decided I don't much fancy it after all."

For all her complaints about the part, Anna made an unforgettable Queen of the Nile. Her entrance, carried on the shoulders of six oiled-up strongmen in leopard-skin loincloths, drew cheers so loud that passers-by jostled each other in the nightclub's doorway to see what they were missing. And her musical number, "If You Could Taste My Asses' Milk," had the audience yelping and stamping along to the Arabic jazz.

When the belly dancers wobbled into the spotlight, Anna flung herself offstage and flopped down beside Naomi in the wings. Her bare skin glistened from exertion and the heat of the stage lights. Her fingers found Naomi's and squeezed.

"Penny for your thoughts?" Naomi prompted. She watched the younger woman's face in fascination. Had she, Naomi, ever looked like that? Not so beautiful, of course, but so hopeful, so impervious to fear? So certain the future was hers for the taking?

"I was just thinking," said Anna, "about what might have happened if I'd stayed home and kept trying to make it in Hollywood. I might be making a film with Mr DeMille right now." She raised an eyebrow. "Playing 'Fourth Slave Girl from the Left.'"

Naomi looked at her closely.

"You really think you're better off here, don't you?"

"I've made a life here, Natty." Anna's jaw jutted out. "No one here gives my role to a white woman in eye makeup. Here I'm not a servant. I'm a star!" Her eyes implored Naomi to agree. "And I've got you here." Anna paused. "I have got you, haven't I?"

Naomi gazed back at her, feeling her eyes growing wet.

"Always."

"The hard times will pass," Anna assured her. "I'm not really worried. And if things should get worse… Well, we'll just go away then, won't we?"

It took an effort for Naomi to nod. She couldn't bear to tell Anna about her correspondence with Deborah, her efforts to protect them both which had failed so pitifully. *Go away where?* she wanted to whisper. To some other Continental city teetering on the brink of bloodshed and ruin? Or to an England that would not take Anna, or an America that would not take her?

Instead she said, "To the moon, I suppose?" and Anna gave a smile that made Naomi think she would never stop loving her.

"The moon," said Anna. "Definitely."

The snake charmers were taking their bows; Anna was due back onstage. Her fresh appearance, flanked by ostrich-fan dancers, drew whistles and hollers of delight. And Naomi got a huge laugh when she made her entrance as the world's shortest, fattest Marc Antony, in a red-plumed helmet, breastplate, and strips of leather slapping against her thighs.

The crowd on the floor was reaching fever pitch now. Naomi could see couples and trios dancing together at frantic speed. She saw young footballers in the arms of fat Swiss businessmen, Lola dancing the tango with a disgraced Argentine politician, and the ventriloquist holding forth to three pudgy streetwalkers in their garter belts and feathers. Cleopatra's scantily clad serving girls were pelting grapes into the audience, who gleefully made a game of catching them with their mouths.

But when the chorus took their bows, when the stage darkened and she and Anna waltzed together in the spotlight, it seemed to Naomi that the noise of the crowd had faded away. Despite their comical differences in body shape, hours of practice had made the two women fluent and graceful dancing partners.

They dipped and swayed together, the queen and her soldier, moving in perfect time. Spinning round and round in each other's arms in the last pale circle of light.

MAKING UP

ENTERING THE WOMEN'S BATHROOM AT Hera Studios was like stumbling into a colour chart of flamingo, salmon, coral, and rose-pink. The room had been built in the eighties, when the studio was at its height and money and good taste were no objects.

On one wall hung a framed cover from *World of Soap* magazine (1981) celebrating the very first season of the studio's longest-running daytime drama, *Sunrise Parade.* The star of the show, Louisa Deverill, didn't look all that different on the old magazine cover to how she looked now: regal, tormented, and airbrushed, with truly magnificent hair. What Miss Deverill thought about her picture being hung in a bathroom, no one would have dared to ask. (The star had demanded her own private facilities years ago.) But at least the décor was on theme.

Pink porcelain fittings, flecked with gold, were screwed into the pink tiles. Little pink soaps sat in pink china dishes on the sides of the basins next to the pink fluffy towels and boxes of pink tissues. The lighting was soft.

Panning across to the cubicle doors, an observer might have glimpsed a pair of shoes poking out beneath the stall on the far left. A pair of white-and-gold snakeskin pumps, with pointed toes and eyewateringly high heels. Their owner was leaning up against the door.

"Yes, goddammit, *yes*..."

In close-up, an observer might also have noticed the tanned feet quivering and straining inside those shoes, the tendons flexing, the toes curling. And the elegant white trousers crumpled around those ankles with white lace panties twisted up inside.

Sierra's breath was coming quick and shallow. Her full bottom lip was clamped between her teeth; her eyelids were fluttering closed. Her right hand was moving between her thighs.

With two fingers, she circled her slippery little bud, feeling it stirring, growing fuller. Her nostrils flared at the musky scent. She withdrew her hand and slipped it up beneath her crisply ironed blouse, yanking the cups of her bra aside until her breasts stood straight out, framed by wire and lace. She stroked her nipples with sticky fingers, enjoying how the lubrication cooled across them, making the wide brown disks tighten into crinkled peaks. Then she pinched each one in turn, hard, until silvery jolts of pleasure zigzagged through her body.

This was terrible workplace behaviour. Lewd. Shameless. She sucked the salty, gooey delicacy from her fingers. Then she put them to work between her legs once more. God, her flesh down there felt like satin.

Her slick fingers swirled around and around her clit. She could feel its shape becoming more defined, its pulsing flesh sensitised, especially when she pulled back the softly furred lips and held them taut with her palm.

Her stroking turned to a rapid tapping on the very tip of her clit, causing reverberations so intense they were almost painful. Her orgasm came fast and hard. She staggered in her killer heels, her hips rocking hugely, helplessly, her face twisting in silent curses: "*Damn you, damn you…*"

She slumped, breathing hard, against the closed door.

God, what was she *doing*? Was she not Sierra Williams, the famously tough woman who practically ran this studio—the woman with a solution to every problem and a sarcastic jibe for every situation? Sierra Williams, who had seen it all and found most of it ridiculous? Sierra, who never ever lost her liquid-nitrogen cool—jerking off in the bathroom like some dopey teenage apprentice?

It was crazy. Impossible.

Sierra straightened her clothing, took several deep breaths, then stepped out into the pink bathroom. She washed the evidence of her loss of control thoroughly from her hands and pushed back her thick flounces of chestnut hair. In the mirror, she observed the residual quivering of her lips and the dilated pupils of her hazel eyes.

Control yourself, for God's sake. She drew herself up to her full height—six foot two inches in her heels—and pulled her shoulders back. *This isn't you.*

Only one person could have this effect on the great Sierra Williams. And Sierra hated her even more than Louisa Deverill hated natural lighting.

By the time Sierra left the bathroom, she was the picture of composure. As she strode down the corridor to the makeup section, she took care to keep her footsteps regular, decisive, ominous. To her colleagues, the rhythm of her high heels approaching would sound like a chisel being driven into a rock face.

The noisy, crowded room fell silent.

Sierra stepped into the doorway. She paused there, letting everyone take in her statuesque figure and enjoying the respectful hush that always greeted her arrival.

The man in the makeup chair cleared his throat. He was silver-haired and square-jawed and an arresting shade of orange. He was Grant Wixler, *Sunrise Parade*'s leading man since 1992. He played Lloyd Hamilton—hero, patriarch, mayor, brain surgeon with a troubled past. Sierra would bet good money he'd still be playing that part in another twenty years, even if he needed the help of a Ouija board by then.

"Excuse me, Miss Williams? I don't want to bother you, ma'am, but my big scene is in half an hour, and this hairline is just impossible..." He gestured with a pained expression towards his receding silver coif.

Sierra paused long enough to build anticipation. Then, with a wave of her hand, she dismissed her assistant, picked up the comb, and took her place at Grant's side. If Sierra couldn't make Grant's vanishing hair look bushy and lustrous again, no one could.

His request had broken the spell of silence, and now the other members of the *Sunrise* team were tiptoeing closer. The new costume designer came to ask Sierra's opinion on an electric-blue power suit for the show's new villain. An intern scurried off to fetch Sierra's coffee. And the director sidled over to break the news that their second male lead, Chad Major—the actor playing Lloyd's mysterious younger brother who may or may not have been an assassin—would need her help before today's shoot. He had taken a squash ball in the face late last night, and now he had eyes like a panda.

Sierra resisted the temptation to ask whether Chad's squash partner had been his cocaine dealer or his pool boy. Instead, she nodded in curt agreement and ordered the director to send Chad along in ten. The director scuttled away, murmuring his thanks. Sierra Williams was known for her discretion as well as her prodigious talent.

Never mind directors, producers, or—God forbid—writers. And forget the stars too. In the world of daytime soap opera, the mistress of hair and makeup was queen.

And no one had occupied that throne more successfully than Sierra Williams. For twenty years, she had led her team here at *Sunrise Parade*, wielding her lip pencils and eyelash curlers with an iron hand. It wasn't easy to keep actors looking the same for decades, and shooting seven episodes a week was no job for the faint-hearted. Most scenes had to be shot in one take, so the hair and cosmetics had to be as resilient as a suit of armour. The "looks" Sierra created were designed to survive passionate kisses, swimming pool scenes, drinks thrown in the actors' faces, slaps, tears, and, in one episode, an attack by a demonically possessed poodle.

When Sierra Williams did someone's makeup, it stayed done.

Sierra had seen the show through thick and thin: through nose jobs, Botox, facelifts, and skin bleaching; through experimental hair implants and accidents in the tanning salon. Sierra had dealt with botched eyebrow tattoos and forests of nasal hair. She had talked hysterical actors back from the brink when they'd woken to discover an outbreak of acne. And she had dealt ruthlessly with young starlets who turned up to a shoot with new, unauthorised piercings. Interns at Hera Studios whispered to each other about the locked drawer in Sierra Williams's cupboard, said to contain a shoebox full of facial and body jewellery she had personally ripped out of dozens of celebrities down the years.

Yes, Sierra had coped with everything. She knew her duty here on *Sunrise Parade*: to help transport the show's audience to a different world. A world where the fashions of thirty years ago never went out of style and where even people killed in helicopter crashes would always come back.

But this was shaping up to be an unusually stressful day. The makeup artists were jittering and snapping at each other, the director was chewing his nails, and the leading man had already called his sponsor twice.

Today was the final day for the show's longest serving leading lady, Louisa Deverill. After thirty-six years of onscreen adventure, romance, tragedy, and giving speeches whilst gazing out a window, Miss Deverill was retiring. Sierra wasn't sure of the star's future plans, but she gathered they involved a Scientology retreat in the Rockies and a personal trainer named Javier.

Sierra didn't care much for actors, especially the ones who threw their weight around in the makeup chair, so she wasn't sorry to see Miss Deverill go. But she'd been dreading this day nonetheless. The producers had declared that Louisa's character, Tabitha Martini, was too popular to lose. Bringing another actress into the role to replace her naturally meant a new plot involving a house fire, a coma, memory loss, and a facial transplant performed by Dr Rex Riccardo, who'd been secretly in love with Tabitha for years.

All pretty routine in itself—until some fool in publicity had persuaded the powers that be to include a shocking glimpse of Tabitha's burned-off face. Sierra grimaced at the thought. Their show might feature murder, mayhem, and incest, but since when did it show people looking *ugly*? It was a travesty!

Worse than that, a travesty that required a special effects team. Sierra, for all her skill with eyebrow brushes and colour cream, did not know how to construct a scorched face out of latex—not that she would have wanted to, for God's sake. So the job had been put out to tender.

Yesterday, with dismay and anguish, Sierra had learned the studio had contracted the task to Electric Eel Effects. And *that* meant...

Silence had fallen once more in the makeup room. Sierra glanced up from Grant's hair to find half her colleagues staring at her. The others were looking towards the doorway. In the mirror, Sierra could see a new figure standing there.

She had known this moment would come. She had steeled herself to be ready for it. And she had masturbated like a crazy woman beforehand to clear her head.

Sierra straightened up. She spun around and swept her hair back with all the regal composure of a makeup artist so skilled at her job that she could wear a pure-white pants suit without fear. She lifted her chin and faced the new arrival.

"Hello, Chelsea. How delightful to see you again." Sierra was pleased with her tone. It could have frozen a penguin.

Chelsea gazed back at her. Was Sierra imagining the faintest tremor in Chelsea's bottom lip? "Yeah. It's been way too long, Sierra." Her voice was subdued, her brown eyes... Were they sad? God, if Chelsea had come here with some insipid notion of *apologising* for her behaviour five years ago...

Sierra's mouth twisted into a sneer.

Too late, Chelsea. Far too late for that now.

The new young makeup artist Hera Studios had just hired didn't present in what Sierra considered to be a professional manner at all.

Whilst Sierra wore tailored pants suits, gold jewellery, and towering heels, Chelsea Banks wore jogging shoes, cargo pants, and singlets that showed off her wiry arms and *X-Files* tattoos. (*X-Files*? Really? It was 2012, for God's sake, and Sierra had not approved of all that nonsense even back in the nineties.) Whilst her résumé had contained promising details, Sierra would never have hired her had she met her in person first.

A stylist should be her own canvas, Sierra believed, and her own hair and makeup were always impeccable. Chelsea, on the other hand, wore her blonde hair in a no-nonsense ponytail, and her only facial decoration was a nose ring. She spent her weekends painting superheroes' faces at Comic-Con; she chewed gum, swore, and called the director "dude". It was unsatisfactory and irritating. Within ten minutes of meeting Chelsea, Sierra knew she didn't want her on the team.

There was just one thing, though. Chelsea was *good.*

Chelsea could create world-class smoky eyes and a standout pout in less time than it took most girls to find their mascara wand. She could shape a brow or conceal a blemish almost as well as Sierra herself. Chelsea didn't seem the type to work in this industry at all, but here she was, making her colleagues look like incompetent bimbos. The talent that lurked beneath that rough exterior—and the idea that she, Sierra, might be the one to bring that talent to the surface—was *intriguing*.

Because Chelsea wanted Sierra's mentoring all right. She made that plain.

Every word Sierra uttered about contouring, highlighting, and airbrushing, she caught Chelsea listening in. Chelsea was becoming bold enough to quiz her superior about colour charts, super-hydrating moisturiser, and illuminating primer. The look of avid attention on Chelsea's face when Sierra explained her position on eyeball-whitening drops and dentine fluid was...flattering. And so were the long, admiring glances Chelsea kept casting up and down Sierra's imposing figure.

God, Sierra, romance is the last thing that should be on your mind.

Ever since her cruel long-term lover, Valentina, had broken Sierra's heart and then died a month later in a freak skiing accident, Sierra had sworn off relationships forever. But she was unprepared for the fluttering thrill she felt when she and Chelsea reached for the same lipliner and their fingers touched. The two women exchanged smouldering glances over the top of Chad Major's head as they worked together to attach his toupee. When Chelsea winked at her whilst dusting a starlet's cleavage with rouge, Sierra's heart skipped a beat.

During one late shoot, when they were alone together tidying their workstation, Chelsea started a teasing argument about fuchsia versus tangerine lipstick. Sierra raised the issue of durability, and Chelsea—the nerve of it!—challenged Sierra about the endurance of her own lipstick.

So what choice did Sierra have but to prove its quality by leaning forwards and kissing Chelsea hard on the mouth?

The touch of the younger woman's lips, plump and smooth, made Sierra catch her breath. This was most unprofessional—she shouldn't do this. But now Chelsea's lips were parting, and Sierra felt the moist heat of her protégé's breath and the electric tip of her tongue...

Before she knew it, Chelsea took the lead, spinning Sierra around and pressing her back against the closed door. She pulled Sierra's face down to hers, parted Sierra's lips with a flick of her tongue, and without shyness or hesitation delved inside her open mouth. The hot, wet rhythm made Sierra's heart pound. When Chelsea drew back and caught Sierra's bottom lip between her teeth, she pinched harder and harder until Sierra moaned at the pain and at the sparks of pleasure between her thighs.

"You were right, baby." Chelsea's voice was breathless as she kissed her way down Sierra's arched throat. "That mouth of yours *is* fuckin' perfect."

"Oh God…" Sierra's knees had begun to wobble. The room drifted around her like the hot, perfumed haze of a greenhouse. She had not meant to take things this far—had she?

Chelsea had no such reservations. She twisted her hand in Sierra's hair and drew the older woman's head down again for a firm, biting kiss. Then those nimble fingers of hers got to work on Sierra's clothing, popping buttons and tugging zippers. She had Sierra half-undressed and her own face buried greedily between Sierra's tanned breasts—licking and nibbling at the velvety groove between them, nosing the lacy cups aside—before Sierra collected herself enough to call a halt. This was too inappropriate for words. Sierra Williams never fooled around in the workplace! And besides, she could hear the twitter of actors approaching from down the corridor, damn them.

Chelsea's chest heaved. She leaned back against the dressing table and watched openly as Sierra adjusted her bra and rebuttoned her blouse. Had Sierra not put a stop to things, Chelsea clearly would have been happy to continue, even in front of an audience. The thought made Sierra tremble. What in God's name had she begun?

Sierra ought to have kept her distance after that. But dammit, it was hard to be strong in the face of Chelsea's knowing smiles and provocative comments about oil-free primers and moisturising balm. Not to mention those well-stacked cargo pants of hers.

Before long, the two women began gazing openly at each other across the makeup chair once more. As they teased Louisa Deverill's hair to its full volume, their fingers brushed inside that great candyfloss bouffant. When Chelsea was late back from lunch one day, Sierra could not resist waggling a hairbrush at her in warning, and Chelsea gave such a naughty wink in reply that it was all Sierra could do not to bend her over the dressing table right then.

Then Wyatt Byron, the show's tormented romantic lead, flung himself down the studio stairs in a desperate last-ditch attempt to be released from his contract and tour with some dreary Arthur Miller play. (Sierra wasn't surprised; Wyatt was always moaning about his craft and how degrading it was to be stuck in a soap opera.)

Chelsea dealt with the damage he'd done to himself so smoothly that she left Sierra speechless. Wyatt might have been bruised, battered, and more miserable than ever, but there would be no sign of it on camera. He was back on set within the hour.

"No one else could have done that," Sierra breathed, one hand pressed to her heart. "You're the heir to my throne."

That night, Sierra and Chelsea made frantic love in the studio's rose-pink bathroom, grappling with each other so wildly that they knocked Louisa Deverill's picture off the wall. Sierra gasped when Chelsea ripped the last three buttons from her blouse, quivered when Chelsea thrust a hand inside her bra to fondle each tingling breast in turn, and whimpered when Chelsea sank to her knees to deliver a scorching-red love bite to Sierra's inner thigh.

Chelsea wrenched Sierra's heels, trousers, and panties off, spread Sierra's knees, then unzipped her own cargo pants to reveal a bright magenta cock with gold accessories. It matched Sierra's favourite pants suit *exactly*.

Sierra's lip trembled with emotion. "Chelsea! You got that for me?"

Chelsea grinned, dipped her head, and ran her tongue lightly up Sierra's slit, making Sierra jolt and moan.

"I learned about complementary colours from you." She winked. "You are one classy lady, Ms Williams."

Sierra got six months of happiness with her brilliant protégé. They had spent their days blow-waving, highlighting, and lip-plumping together, and their evenings fucking blissfully up against the sink in the rose-pink bathroom. Or in the costume wardrobe—oh God, those sharkskin suits against Sierra's bare behind—those shoulder pads! Or in the back of Chelsea's panel van with the carpet chafing Sierra's knees, behind van doors spray-painted with Gillian Anderson's face. It was madness, but Sierra had never been so happy.

But every Eden has a serpent, and this time it came in the form of Adrianna Fox, special effects consultant from that damned Electric Eel company. They were shooting an episode of *Sunrise Parade* where Lloyd's granddaughter found a baby alien in the attic—it turned out to be a trick staged by her evil stepmother to frame the poor child for insanity. Someone had to construct the extraterrestrial, and Adrianna was said to be the leader in that field.

Adrianna—that conniving bitch!—with her python tattoo, blood-red dreadlocks, black lipstick, and that ridiculous eyebrow ring. At her age, honestly! If only Sierra could have got that woman into the makeup chair, her shoebox of trophies would have had one more gory addition.

Nevertheless, the woman lost no time in capturing Chelsea's imagination with her tales of designing purple tentacles for sci-fi shows and hacked-off limbs for horror movies. She gave Chelsea lessons in creating tattoo transfers for actors playing prisoners and bikers. She taught Chelsea how to make her own pair of goblin ears. And all the while, she was cooing in Chelsea's real ear: *Isn't this fun? Isn't this so much cooler than doing makeup for some silly soap opera?*

And then just like that, Adrianna wooed Chelsea away with an offer of a special effects job on a new Japanese action movie, *UltimoMan!*—due to start filming in Tokyo the very next week.

"You don't understand." Chelsea's speech was full of excuses about wanting to develop new skills and broaden her résumé. "I can't keep working in your shadow! I have to find myself…" The whine in Chelsea's voice left Sierra so stunned, her hands shook. Chelsea—her beloved, infuriating Chelsea—was choosing severed heads and radioactive lizards over her. Tears brimmed in her eyes.

But when Chelsea pulled out the demonstration piece that had won her the Tokyo job—a latex mask for UltimoMan's outer-space girlfriend, Asbestia—Sierra's eyes widened with outrage at last. The winged eyeliner and lip shaping on the alien woman's mask replicated precisely the technique Sierra had taught Chelsea here at *Sunrise Parade*!

She rocketed to her feet and flipped the table more explosively than Louisa Deverill herself could have done. Her glass of chardonnay soared across the room, and Chelsea ran out the door. In her rage, Sierra refused to notice that she was crying.

After Chelsea left, no one ever spoke her name in Sierra's presence again. Oh, everyone spoke about what had happened behind her back for sure; Sierra had no doubt about that! For weeks, she glimpsed the smirks on her colleagues' faces and heard the whispers that went silent when she approached. How they must have relished seeing the ball-breaking ice queen Sierra Williams brought low at last, and by her own star pupil!

Yes, the humiliation had clinched it for Sierra. She would never forgive Chelsea for as long as she lived.

Now, five years later, Sierra lifted her chin and glared at this new version of Chelsea with all the contempt she could muster. It wasn't easy. The woman in front of her looked virtually the same as the woman Sierra had farewelled with shrieks of rage and a glass of wine in the face.

Nowadays, Chelsea's cargo pants were black, and her jogging shoes looked new, clean, and expensive. There were tiny lines around her mouth and eyes, and two new studs in her left ear. Her arms were more toned and tanned than ever. But she was still Chelsea. Still the woman Sierra had loved and hated with something approaching madness.

She turned her back and began scraping back Louisa Deverill's hair in preparation for the application of the latex horror mask.

Behind her, Chelsea cleared her throat.

"You're looking good, Sierra." Her voice was hesitant, subdued. The rest of the crew had quickly retreated at Chelsea's approach, and Louisa Deverill had wisely put her headphones in.

Sierra's eyes narrowed. "How sweet of you to say so." She did not look up from her work.

"Yeah, um, you haven't changed a bit."

"I must have been in frozen storage, then." Sierra glanced at Chelsea in the mirror and curled her lip. Chelsea looked away, colour rising in her cheeks.

"So I brought the latex fittings along." Chelsea cleared her throat again, sounding more professional this time. "I'll just need some help to attach them to Miss Deverill's face." Sierra gave a curt nod and gestured to an empty space on the table where Chelsea could lay out her special effects paraphernalia. The mangled version of Louisa Deverill's face was skilfully done, Sierra had to admit. To herself. Not one word of praise would Chelsea get from her.

"Um, what do you think?" Chelsea's voice was nervous again.

Sierra paused for effect. "Grotesque. Overdone. Unnecessary. Much like your new boss. How is Adrianna, by the way? Too afraid to show her face around here?"

"She's away." Chelsea shrugged. "You know that action film director, Rocko de Mornay? He invited her to some party. On his yacht in the Caribbean."

Sierra's heart gave a nasty little leap. Oh, this was too perfect for words. So the treacherous Adrianna had seduced Chelsea, only to abandon her?

"What a shame," Sierra purred. "You must feel lost without her."

"Um, well, actually it's good to talk to you alone." In the mirror, Sierra saw Chelsea looking down at her running shoes. She took a deep breath, then gazed directly at Sierra as though willing the older woman to look back. "Sierra, last time we saw each other, everything happened so…so fast. I didn't say the things I needed to."

"Oh, I think you made yourself clear." Sierra's fingers didn't miss a beat as they twisted back Louisa Deverill's hair, but her insides boiled with a witches' brew of rage and triumph. So Chelsea had been dumped by Adrianna and thought she could come crawling back?

"Listen, I know it was wrong, walking out on you like that." Chelsea winced. "I tried to call you later, but you kept hanging up. I should have explained properly, but my hands were tied."

"By Adrianna? What a charming image."

"Sierra." Chelsea stepped between Sierra and her styling equipment, a dangerous move. "I never stopped thinking about you."

Slowly, Sierra turned her head. She found Chelsea watching her imploringly, tears glistening in her wide brown eyes.

How…interesting.

Her voice preternaturally calm, Sierra murmured, "I'm busy here, Chelsea. And you have a monster mask to attach to our leading lady. But once she's on set, why don't you stick around? We could…talk some more."

The look of gratitude on Chelsea's face was painful. It almost caused Sierra to falter. But she ordered herself to harden her heart. She would not be humiliated by Chelsea again.

When Louisa Deverill had been led out onto the set in her terrifying new face, Sierra ordered the rest of her staff to leave. When the last one had departed, Chelsea shut the door behind them with unsteady hands.

"Thanks for sticking around, Sierra. Listen, I don't expect you to forgive me for bailing on you five years back. But—" Chelsea caught her breath as Sierra put one manicured finger to her lips.

"Shh, darling. There's no need. You're here now, that's what matters." Chelsea's eyes widened as Sierra leaned in closer. Her breath ghosted over Chelsea's cheekbone and down the side of the younger woman's face. Sierra could smell Chelsea's sandalwood soap and feel the exquisite softness of her skin. Sierra's lips tickled the sensitive spot just beneath Chelsea's ear as she crooned, "My poor darling. Did you miss me?"

"Yeah." Chelsea's voice was ragged. "Like crazy. Sierra, I'm so sorry..." Her words faded into a sigh as Sierra pressed her lips to the curve of Chelsea's throat. Chelsea turned her head, eager to kiss Sierra's lips, but gave a muffled squeak instead when Sierra seized her by one shoulder, thrust her back against the wall, and plunged her tongue into Chelsea's ear.

Sierra restrained her former lover with one hand. With the tip of her tongue, she traced delicate whorls and fleshy spirals, pausing now and then to probe teasingly inside, each incursion winning a twitch of pleasure from the younger woman. Chelsea's skin was warm, her body quivering. Sierra sucked Chelsea's earlobe into her mouth. She flicked each stud in turn, working her tongue between metal and flesh and tugging until Chelsea gasped at the pressure and the hint of pain.

"Oh, baby, we should talk first..." But Chelsea's willpower was crumbling fast, just as Sierra had known it would. Beneath her tomboy swagger, this was a woman who took a deep pleasure from being fucked.

Sierra drew back, hooked her thumbs into the neckline of Chelsea's black singlet, and pulled down hard until the fabric stretched and Chelsea's small breasts popped out over the top.

"Why, hello there." Sierra smirked. Chelsea wore a cobalt bra with Roswell alien heads over each erect nipple. Under Sierra's determined fingers, those aliens never stood a chance.

"Oh, fuck..." Chelsea clutched at Sierra's back with shaking fingers as Sierra tongued her nipples. They were light beige, small, and perfectly round. Like cherry stones, Sierra had always thought. Sierra drew one up against the roof of her mouth and clamped it there, applying a firm, stroking pressure underneath with her tongue. She took note of the rough breathing and guttural moans that sounded above her. Oh yes, she remembered what Chelsea liked.

Her hands, meanwhile, skimmed the loose waistband of Chelsea's cargo pants, creeping inside to flick the elastic of her jockey shorts. At last, Sierra stepped back, taking a moment to appreciate the burgundy shade of her own lipstick smeared artistically across Chelsea's tanned breasts. Then she dropped to her knees and unzipped Chelsea's pants.

"Oh, Sierra..." Chelsea's voice shook as Sierra eased her underwear down over her full, firm behind. The seam was dark and wet with proof of her arousal. Sierra nuzzled a path through Chelsea's light brown curls towards her core. "Sierra, are you sure? This is kind of fast..."

"Mmm..." Strong hands held Chelsea's thighs apart, as Sierra's thumbs extended to pull back Chelsea's lips. Inside, Chelsea was the colour of a pale pink daisy. Unexpectedly innocent.

"You like it fast," Sierra whispered. Breathing in the scent of Chelsea's excitement, she dropped a kiss on her exposed clit, which made Chelsea moan in desperation. Sierra ran her tongue the length of Chelsea's inner lips, tasting the trickle that ran along between them. Then she covered Chelsea's hot clit with the flat of her tongue, flicking at the small muscles with all her skill until the young woman's body was shaking with need.

"Look at you." Sierra drew back. "Why, you're about to come already, aren't you, Chelsea?"

"Oh God, yes, Sierra, please..."

"Yes, you do like it fast." Sierra exhaled, pausing to vibrate Chelsea's clit lightly with her tongue. Chelsea was panting now, her hips thrusting in earnest. Sierra looked up at her, and her tone hardened. "Look how fast you betrayed me for Adrianna."

"Wha-what?" Chelsea's eyes flew open. The smirk Sierra had ready for her former protégé went glacially cold.

With exaggerated care, Sierra drew Chelsea's underwear up her legs and wriggled the cotton back into place over her damp inner thighs and wet curls. Then she pulled up Chelsea's cargo pants, zipped them, and fastened the stud.

"What are you doing?" Chelsea whispered. Hurt and dismay dawned on her face.

The sight caused Sierra a stab of pain. Was this really the right thing to do? Was revenge actually better than happiness? Wouldn't she rather take Chelsea in her arms and tell her to forget Adrianna, forget what had passed between them, and come home?

But no, Sierra would not give in to her own weak emotions. She got to her feet and forced herself to fix Chelsea with her most poisonous glare. "I gave you everything," she hissed. "*Everything*. Do you know what that meant for me? After the hurt Valentina caused me, I swore I would never love again. But *you*...you made me think things could be different. I'd never shared my skills or my life with anyone in that way before. And you left me. You made me a laughing stock, and why? So you could chase after some middle-aged skank who couldn't even be bothered getting her nipple rings to match!"

"Sierra, what are you talking about?" Chelsea's cheeks were wet with tears, but now her look of pain and betrayal was giving way to something else. Genuine bewilderment. "Hold up. You thought Adrianna was my *girlfriend*?"

Sierra blinked.

"She—she isn't?"

"God, no!" Chelsea's eyes were wide. "I couldn't tell you the full story at the time. She made me promise not to. Her parents were church ministers, and she said it would kill them if the truth got out, but surely you must have suspected?"

"Suspected *what*?" Sierra snapped, now utterly confounded. Chelsea shook her head.

"Sierra, Adrianna is my mother."

For the second time that day, Sierra felt the room whirl around her. She tottered in her heels, then sank into the makeup chair in a faint that would have made Louisa Deverill proud.

A sharp crack, followed by a spreading burn, revived her. She opened her eyes with a gasp. Her cheek was stinging. Chelsea was standing over her.

"Are you okay?" Chelsea sounded more concerned than Sierra would have expected. She lifted a glass of water to Sierra's lips. "Here."

"I...I'm fine." Sierra gulped, then blinked. She was both relieved and disappointed to see that Chelsea's breasts were no longer on display. "Did you just *slap* me?"

"Isn't that what you do when someone faints?"

"No, that's hysteria. And even then, I think it only works in soap operas." Sierra rubbed her tingling skin.

"Oops." Chelsea didn't look especially sorry, but Sierra supposed she couldn't really blame her.

"Chelsea... You said Adrianna was your *mother*?"

"Yeah." Chelsea perched on the edge of the dressing table. "I told you I was adopted, right?"

"You told me you were found in a shoulder bag under the makeup counter in Walmart."

"Uh-huh. Well, it turned out she'd been searching for me in secret for years, but she couldn't say anything openly because of the family shame..." Chelsea sighed. "I'm sorry I kept the truth from you, Sierra. But I had to go with her, to get to know her. I tried to contact you later, but when you kept blocking me..."

"I couldn't bear to hear from you." Sierra looked away, her eyes watering. "Too proud, I guess."

"Sierra..." Chelsea touched her arm. "Do you think—"

But whatever she was about to say was drowned out by the sudden explosive sound of a gun being fired.

Chelsea tore out of the room, heading in the direction of the noise, before Sierra could stop her. Had the stupid girl worked on so many action movies that she'd forgotten the basic principles of survival? Sierra swore in a manner most unprofessional. Then she kicked off her high heels and ran after her.

The studio was in uproar. The extras were screaming. The director was trying to shout negotiations from behind his chair. The camera crew ran for their lives. And in the middle of the *Sunrise Parade* set, with a gun waving wildly in one hand and Louisa Deverill clutched to his chest as a hostage, stood the show's ever-tormented romantic lead, Wyatt Byron.

"I am a real actor!" he was bellowing. "I played Horatio! I played Bassanio! I did my one-man kabuki production of *Death of a Salesman* at the Edinburgh Festival! The reviewers said I was destined for greatness! I once stood next to Kenneth Branagh at the urinals at the BAFTAs, you bastards!"

"What the fuck's wrong with him?" Chelsea hissed to Sierra as they peered around the doorway.

Sierra shook her head. "He's never been happy making daytime TV drama. Which is ironic, because he's really quite suited to it."

"You all kept me a prisoner here!" Wyatt wailed with a demented gleam in his eyes. He was clearly delighted to have such an audience at last. "All I wanted to do was play Stanley Kowalski off Broadway, but you used my contract to keep me here twenty-four-seven, playing this spray-tanned fool! Mouthing your horrible, wooden scripts—falling in love with my own sister, recovering miraculously from leukaemia, plotting to take over a fashion empire!" He spat in disdain. "Well, I've had enough!" A mad grin lit up his face as he brought the gun to Louisa Deverill's head. "You wanted a big final scene for Tabitha Martini? Well, try this on for size!"

"*Hey*!" To Sierra's horror, the impetuous Chelsea stormed forwards. "You mess up that latex mask and I will fuckin' smash you! Do you know long I worked to get that thing right? That burned-off face is a goddamn work of art, you asshole!"

"*Chelsea, no*!" Sierra slapped a hand over her own mouth. Oh God, this was all her fault. She had taught Chelsea that nothing mattered more than getting their work perfect—but how terribly wrong she had been.

"You..." Wyatt's boggling eyes focused with difficulty on Chelsea. "Wait, I know you! You were the one who stopped me escaping last time! You strapped me to that makeup chair and hid my suffering under ten tons of fucking foundation!"

"Neutralizer and concealer, actually."

"*You bitch*!" Wyatt hurled Louisa Deverill away. With sweat pouring down his face and a murderous gleam in his eye, he took aim at Chelsea instead.

"*No*!"

All anyone probably saw of Sierra Williams was a white blur. She flung herself through the air and hit Wyatt Byron with a rugby tackle that sent him crashing through the plywood set. The gun went off, filling the studio with screams and tumbling plaster.

Sierra grappled with the wriggling, howling Wyatt, struggling to pin down the arm still waving the gun. "If you don't let it go, Wyatt," she panted, "I will have you killed!"

He didn't seem to be paying attention. The gun jerked dangerously. Sierra raised her voice: "And I will make sure you go to your coffin viewing wearing absolutely no makeup, no facelift tape, no cosmetic dentures, and nothing but your own natural hair—or what's left of it!"

Wyatt froze. His eyes goggled in horror. And Sierra, seeing her chance, seized Louisa Deverill's ever-present glass of wine from the coffee table and hurled it in Wyatt's face.

He was still blinking, spluttering, and cursing when Sierra wrenched the gun from his fingers and Chelsea brought both jogging shoes down hard on his crotch.

Much later, when everything had quietened down at last and the police, crew, and cleaners had gone home, Sierra sat up atop the sink in the rose-pink bathroom with Chelsea standing between her knees. They gazed into each other's eyes with their hands down each other's pants.

"Come back to me," Sierra implored, her breath hitching as Chelsea painted her clit with her own abundant juices, then pressed and pulsed on either side with two forked fingers. Oh God, Sierra had forgotten how good that felt. "Keep on making your stupid alien tentacles for teenage movies if you like. But let me love you again, my darling."

"Well, that depends." Chelsea's voice was hoarse. She was massaging the hood of Sierra's clit with her dripping fingers, making satisfied sounds at each judder of Sierra's hips, every cry that escaped her. "I've got a favour to ask."

"Anything." As Chelsea entered her with one smooth movement, her thumb pumping rhythmically just below the clit, Sierra's back arched. *Seriously, anything, darling.*

Chelsea tugged Sierra's head down and breathed in her ear. "I've been contracted to do the makeup for *Wasp Women from Mars*. Would you help me with the designs?"

"Yes..." Sierra grunted and writhed, her fingers laced in Chelsea's hair. "Yes—yes!" Her orgasm burst, sending a shower of fiery hot-pink sparks cascading down to her toes.

She melted back into Chelsea's arms, burying her face in the younger woman's dishevelled hair. *This is perfection*, Sierra thought as they exchanged dreamy kisses. If this was an episode of *Sunrise Parade*, the credits should be rolling now.

Until—

"*Sierra*?" A voice from the doorway: deep, throaty, and full of cruel amusement. "Is that *you*?"

Sierra and Chelsea whirled around. The woman at the door had an excellent view of their flushed faces and messy hair. And Chelsea's muscular bare bottom, her pants around her knees. Not to mention Sierra's naked breasts and well-groomed, dewy bush.

"Get out of here!" Sierra gasped, struggling back into her tangled panties and holding her blouse together across her breasts, which were still glistening with sweat and the tracks of Chelsea's tongue. "Who are you?"

"Why, Sierra. How very hurtful." The woman tossed back her black hair and chuckled in cold amusement. The face was completely unfamiliar, but her lips...

They were painted the colour of blood.

Oh no.

Sierra had not forgotten those lips, nor that mocking laughter. But surely the woman to whom they belonged had died many years before? In a freak avalanche on a ski slope...

Sierra teetered backwards, grabbing the basin for support. "*Valentina?*"

The pink room swirled and faded to black.

A GOOD SHOW

The dressing room door slammed shut. Jacky thrust the blonde woman up against it and yanked her short white dress up over her buttocks. They were large, pale, and soft, crammed enticingly into ripped fishnet tights and pink cotton underwear. Printed across the back of her knickers, and surely visible from across the room, were the words *Handle With Care*.

The woman swivelled her head back for a second to look Jacky up and down. Her face was flushed, and she was smirking as she allowed herself to be turned firmly around again so that her brow, her spread hands, and her full breasts were all pressed against the door. Like the rest of the room, it was papered with layers of tattered bill posters: for the Clash, the Slits, Poly Styrene, Joan Jett and the Blackhearts. There were phone numbers and lewd messages scrawled in lipstick—coral, burgundy, shocking pink.

Jacky pressed her wiry body, clad in ripped denim and well-worn leather, up against her companion. She shut her eyes, relishing the feel of the other woman's pillowy flesh. The odour of exhilarated sweat and the clinging sharpness of cigarette smoke combined with the sweetness of Aqua Net hairspray and Poison perfume.

She pursed her lips and blew a teasing breath into the other woman's ear. "What's your name?"

"I'm Lana." The woman's sky-blue nails were splayed on either side of her face, half covering a glossy print of Annie Lennox. Her magnificent arse was pushing backwards, inviting Jacky's attention; Jacky gave it an appreciative squeeze.

Bit of a cliché, getting so randy after a gig. But it had been a good one. The band had been on fire; Jacky had felt each note thrumming inside her and shaking the stage under her Docs. And tonight's pub crowd had felt it too, bodies moving in time to Jacky's voice as she growled and wailed and crooned. She might have been conducting them with every jab of her finger and jerk of her narrow hips, spurring her fans to whirl and shriek with release, holler the lines back at her, or fall into a breathless silence as she paused over each word in the final refrain. They'd been with her all the way, surfing the same waves of sound and sweat.

Now Jacky's chest was straining with excitement, her skin drenched beneath the leathers, her spiked and shaggy black hair dripping. Her throat was raw and her body ached, but her head was still whirring. There would be no slowing down or sleep tonight.

She pulled back her companion's mop of teased, peroxided hair and dragged her tongue up along the tender whorl of the woman's ear, making the half-dozen silver sleepers rattle softly together. Then she worked those fishnets down to her visitor's knees, earning her an all-body quiver. "Well, that's lovely."

She slipped her hand inside Lana's knickers. Lana was already wet and jolting at every touch of Jacky's fingers. Her underwear was soaked through. Jacky wondered when this sweet deluge had started. During the show, while Jacky had strutted, spun, and howled under those pounding red and blue stage lights? During their dance beside the throbbing speakers, with a squeeze of Lana's hand as Jacky tugged her away to "somewhere more private"? During those kisses outside the dressing room, all giggles and sleaze and wandering hands, Jacky's mind already halfway on what would happen inside?

Hell, maybe Lana just liked the idea of letting her knickers down for someone who'd once opened for the Ramones. Jacky didn't mind that.

She rolled calloused guitar-player's fingers round and round Lana's straining clit, getting it good and slippery. The red bandana around Jacky's wrist was rubbing back and forth in the cleft between Lana's outer lips. Jacky wondered if the fabric would smell of her later; she hoped so. Her mouth was pressed to the stranger's ear, pulling gently at the sleepers and whispering filthy sweet nothings, while Lana wriggled and her moans reverberated around the room. She wasn't shy, this one. Good. The louder the better.

Part of Jacky would have liked nothing better than to finish it now, just like this: her hand pumping out of sight down Lana's pants, her hips grinding into Lana's lovely big arse, her body draping over Lana's from head to toe, as if shielding what was left of her modesty as Lana thrashed and groaned and came shamelessly fast.

But that wasn't enough. Jacky wanted to put on a better show than that, wanted nothing but the best for her girl.

For Rose.

She reached back with her free hand, tugging restlessly at the studded leather belt that held up her skintight jeans. The seam was cutting up between Jacky's buttocks and rubbing a hot groove down the length of her crotch.

"You okay, Jacky?" Lana panted, and turned back to catch a glimpse. At the question, Jacky deliberately glowered, took Lana by the back of her neck, and pressed her forehead to the door, just below an old signed flyer of Siouxsie and the Banshees.

"Stay there."

After a step back, she tugged down the zipper of Lana's white dress, exposing a creamy back with a scattering of freckles. Jacky took a moment to admire the extreme smoothness of Lana's generous flesh, the way it cushioned her hips and upper arms. There was a neat little tattoo behind Lana's left shoulder: a rusted padlock split open by a blooming rose.

Jacky stared. She knew the original version of that tattoo very well; it was inked over Rose's heart. No one else saw it nowadays, and the last time Rose had mentioned it was in an interview three years ago. This girl must be a genuine fan, then.

Had Lana heard the rumours about what else went on in Jacky Taylor's dressing room? Was that the real reason she was here?

The possibility sent through her a fresh surge of excitement. She popped Lana's bra hooks open and slid her hands around and beneath the fabric to squeeze and strum those gorgeous, plump treasures.

Lana's breasts flowed over her palms, the large nipples stiffening further between her fingers as they brushed against the posters. Jacky kept her movements slow, pausing now and then to draw the tiniest circles around the ridges of Lana's crinkled peaks.

Rose always enjoyed that.

She pushed the dress and bra straps off Lana's shoulders until the fabric fell around her waist. Her roughened hands caressed Lana's tender skin and again cupped and fondled her heavy breasts. She ran her palms lightly over Lana's shoulders, belly, and throat, and arousal flared up at how the spiked leather bracelets on her left wrist snagged against those erect nipples, which caught Lana's breath.

"I must be making an impression, eh?" Jacky teased. Then she dropped to her knees and tore those tights and knickers all the way down to Lana's ankles.

It would have made one hell of an album cover: Jacky Taylor kneeling on the concrete floor, guitar discarded in the corner, wearing through the frayed denim over her knees, the soles of her boots curling back on either side of her tight buttocks. And above her, Lana was grinding her tits against the door and pushing her hips back as far as she could. Her flesh rippled deliciously as Jacky squeezed her full, dimpled cheeks and spread them, then ran her tongue up the salty crevice in between.

She was sweating. Jacky shed her leather jacket with an impatient movement and flung it away. Then she manoeuvred her new lover's hips until she had Lana poised just the way she wanted her and worked her long, wriggling tongue deep into Lana's cunt.

"*Jacky, Jacky...*" Salt molasses filled Jacky's mouth, and Lana's voice sounded in a breathless chant, reminding her of the girls who'd whooped and shrieked in front of the stage tonight. Getting a woman that bloody happy was the best feeling in the world. Most boys joined a band hoping to get the girls, but for Jacky, it had been the other way around. All those women who'd whispered and screamed her praises in her shabby little bedsit flat—in parked cars, in alleyways, in darkened corners at parties—had given her the guts and drive and brass to ignore all the bullshit she'd been taught about rock-and-roll being no place for a lady. To pick up that guitar and step out onstage.

Chubby knees were vibrating on either side of Jacky's shoulders. She suspected Lana was finding staying upright difficult. Jacky's own knees were aching on the cold concrete, her clit throbbing desperately against the seam of her jeans. Unable to stand it any longer, she unzipped and shoved her hand down inside the scented denim and the cotton underwear that was soaked and sticky.

"Do it, Jacky, do it..."

Jacky's black singlet stuck to her skin, damp darkness spreading out like wings across her shoulder blades as she used her breath, her agile lips, and her rolling, probing tongue to bring Lana to ecstasy. The smell and taste and thick, clinging texture were all around, flooding Jacky's mouth and nostrils, and smearing itself across her chin. It felt scalding at first, then mercifully cool in the night air that crept in through the cracked old doors and windows.

"Oh, fuck me, fuck me." Lana's voice forced itself out of her in fast, melodic pants taking flight as Jacky's had done onstage, each breath coming quicker than the last and punctuated by the rhythmic thrusting of her hips.

It was time to take her own movements up a pace. Her right hand pumped hard inside her jeans, strumming her clit in a firm bass rhythm. Her tongue extended to its full length, flickered and swirled, and Lana came long and hard, swearing gleefully, her grappling fingers reaching high above her head, tearing the Sex Pistols right off.

Her pleasure—noisy, vulgar, unashamed—was almost as much of a turn-on as her willing body. Jacky's belly tightened, and she felt a steady, building rush of pleasure that ran the length of her legs before exploding into her twitching cunt. Coughing and gasping, she collapsed back onto the concrete floor.

Then, after a long, blissful moment, she zipped up. She stumbled to her feet and lit a cigarette, then leaned against the wall and watched with enjoyment as Lana fumbled back into her clothing. Jacky's tongue flickered into the corners of her mouth to sample that taste of cunt once again, now mingled with the acrid, crackling rush of tobacco.

"My friends are waiting." Lana looked her up and down. "But..." She pulled a black lipstick from her bag and wrote her number on the wall, across an old flyer for the Poison Girls. She moved towards the door, then paused. "What about an autograph, then?"

"Sure." Jacky chuckled. More secrets that weren't really so secret. Retrieving her jacket, she grabbed a purple marker pen from the table and tossed both of them across to Lana, who spread the jacket open and looked for a clear spot on the silky lining. She scrawled her name in large, spiky letters amongst the signatures of the many other women who had enjoyed Jacky's past performances.

"Thanks." Jacky caught the jacket and shrugged back into it. "It's been a pleasure." She opened the door for Lana, then escorted her out into the corridor. "A real pleasure."

Lana glanced back behind them as if to gaze through the crack in the dressing room door. For the first time, she looked almost shy. She lowered her voice and asked, "Do you think she liked it, though? She was watching, yeah?"

Jacky gaped. Her face then relaxed into a grin. Yes, the fans had their own ways of finding things out, their own stories swapped along with cigarettes, chewing gum, and eyeliner pencils between sets. Stories that never made it into the music magazines.

"Course." Jacky winked. "She's only human." She kissed Lana on the mouth. "I'll be calling that number."

Lana's eyebrow rose. "Who said I left it for you?"

Jacky sauntered back into the room, closed the door, and rested her back against it. She took a long draw on her cigarette and expelled the smoke upward in a blueish stream, then flicked the second light switch, illuminating the far corner of the room.

Rose sat in the shadows.

"Good show tonight."

Jacky nodded and strolled over to stand between Rose's open knees and trusty combat boots. She smiled down at her beloved, seeing her as if for the first time: the older woman's golden-brown eyes, creased in the corners; her wild mop of hair the same colour, but nowadays streaked with silver that glinted in the light. Rose's long, slim face had never been what most people would call pretty, but it was watchful, humorous, and sharp, and Jacky loved it. Her lanky body owned her well-worn jeans and homemade black T-shirt with writing scrawled across her chest: *She's beautiful when she's angry.*

Jacky plucked out the cigarette she was smoking and settled it in between Rose's lips. "Aren't you going to wish me a happy birthday?" she prompted.

Her frown, the graceful movements of Rose's long fingers adjusting the cigarette how she wanted it, and the short, smooth nails stained amber with nicotine were all a pleasure to watch. "It's not your birthday, love."

"Mm-hmm. October tenth—it's the anniversary of when I wrote my very first song eight years ago. Because of you. Remember?"

Rose's eyes creased at the corners as she smiled. She sucked thoughtfully on Jacky's cigarette and nodded.

"The last gig of yours at the Ballroom? Bloody amazing night." Jacky shut her eyes. "That punch-up at the back of the hall? And how you hustled me into your dressing room and let me hide out in there till the cops had left? I couldn't believe it—the lead singer of the Gorgons looking after a gobby little cow like me."

Rose's smile widened. "Someone had to, love."

"You told me if I had that much energy to burn, I should use it to make something besides a bloody mess. And since I was clearly into music..."

"Although you did take the time to tell me it was mostly shite."

"I went out and got my first guitar the next day. You told me I'd figure it out. 'No skill, no problem,' you said."

"Lack of skill was never a problem for you." Rose leaned back in her chair, casting a long gaze up and down Jacky's figure. The first time Rose had looked at her like that all those years ago, they'd stumbled back to Rose's motel room. They'd left the lights on while they tore off each other's clothes, patches and safety pins bouncing across the floor. Naked and straddling her new companion, Rose had leaned in, her face alight with each sigh that parted Jacky's lips, with each blissful spasm of Jacky's climax. If Jacky had had any shyness left back then, it had melted away in the golden heat of Rose's gaze.

Now Jacky lifted Rose's right hand to her lips, inhaling the familiar, erotic scent of her mentor's juices. She ran her tongue over Rose's fingertips, lapping up the sticky trails and catching that special taste, rich and salty, that Jacky would recognise anywhere. She'd never had caviar, but she'd always assumed it would taste like Rose.

"You should have joined in tonight," Jacky whispered.

"Love…" Rose's smile faded. She drew her fingers back. "We've been through this. The mastectomy…"

"I know, I know, you don't want me touching you now. Well, that's up to you, love—you know scar tissue never scared me off." Jacky shook her head. "I can wait, as long as you like. But I wasn't talking about Lana." Taking her time, Jacky picked up her discarded guitar by the head and balanced it on the floor, upright and side-on. The neck of the instrument—rosewood sprayed gleaming black—split the open vee of Rose's legs. "I meant out there." She jerked her chin towards the outside world. The stage. "You should have come on with me. Those kids would have lost their minds."

"Have they never been on a school trip to the museum?" Rose snorted. "Jacks, they wouldn't know who I was." Still, when Jacky wiggled the instrument, making the metal pegs flash, Rose took a small, sharp, audible breath. Fresh colour rushed into her cheeks. Clearly, voyeurism alone had not been enough to satisfy her.

"You *made* this scene." Jacky held the wood in a steady grip, then began rocking it to and fro, a gentle, rhythmic pressure against Rose's denim-clad mound.

With a loud whimper, Rose began moving her hips in time. "I helped make it," she mumbled. "About a million years ago." But her dismissals were fading fast as Jacky pressed the slender length of wood, with its frets and taut strings, more firmly against her covered sex.

"You're a legend," said Jacky. "There's kids out there laying down their words because of you." Her breath caught in her throat as Rose let out a soft moan, now pleasuring herself openly against the neck of Jacky's trusty instrument. Jacky imagined the denim growing hot from friction and from Rose's aroused flesh. The scent of her was rising.

"You're the one who once headbutted a National Front arsehole right into the drum kit," Jacky said. "You're the one who wrote 'Taxidermy Dildo' and used to prance around out there with electrodes on your nipples."

"Those were the days, eh?" Rose's voice was breathless. Her movements grew sharper, wilder.

"It's still your day." Jacky narrowed her eyes. She held the guitar neck fast. "Come on. I want to see you. I want to see you out there."

Rose's back arched, and she let out a cry. It could have been a sound of delight, regret, or relief. Before she could crumple, Jacky's free hand caught her, and she cradled Rose's head between her sweaty breasts. Stroking her hair, she said, "Now, are you going to show everyone what you're made of?"

Maybe Rose didn't need the fans and the applause any longer; maybe she never had. But Jacky knew she needed the sound, the stomp, and the sweat. And she needed the sight of Jacky in her element, not glimpsed from backstage, but up there beside her. She needed that look of ecstasy on Jacky's face at the sound of Rose ripping into the opening chords. She needed to see Jacky up close as she yelped and jived and watched Rose watching her.

Rose struggled for breath. "Hell, Jacks, it's been years. I'm not sure I'd even remember half the songs."

"You'll be fine." She pulled her mentor up to her feet and hummed the opening bar to her favourite of Rose's songs, "Breaking Through". Rose smiled in recognition, fingers tapping against her thigh. The strength and rhythm in those hands of hers took Jacky back to that long-ago gig. To that goddess in her boots and chains who had looked at a loudmouthed little punk and seen something more. She lifted the guitar again, this time to pass it over. It settled into Rose's weathered fingers as if she had crafted it herself.

"One last time, love." It was all Rose would promise, but Jacky would take it for now. One last time was a good start.

CANDY TOPPING

SONIA PARKED HER GLOSSY, JET-BLACK SUV across two spaces. She switched off the engine and closed her eyes to practise her yogic breathing, inhaling the fresh leather scent of the seat covers and a hint of the YSL Black Opium she'd dabbed between her breasts. Today was a big day. She needed to focus.

She opened her eyes again to gaze upon the little photograph that hung from the rear-view mirror. Not one of her irksome teenage children or preposterous ex-husbands, but her beloved Boston terrier, Maddie, who had passed away a year before. A heart attack, brought on by a savage attack on a Labor Party candidate who'd come door-knocking. Sonia took some comfort from the knowledge that it was how Maddie would have wanted to go.

The sight of Maddie's flapping bat ears and joyful, drooling smile made Sonia wipe away a tear. Then she adjusted her blow-waved ash-blonde hair, held back by her Gucci sunglasses, and sat up straighter. Her spirits lifted. Of course today would go well.

She had prepared for this venture for months—researched, financed, and designed it personally. When Sonia Fitzgerald set her mind to succeed at something, she did exactly that. And she had Enid to help her, didn't she? Enid, who was proving so very quick, keen, and pliable.

A little too keen, perhaps...?

Sonia frowned into the mirror. Yes, Enid was everything a successful businesswoman could ask for in an assistant. But there was something about her, something Sonia couldn't put her finger on, that was not quite right...

No, she mustn't get distracted. Today the launch of her newest business venture would transform the marketplace, leave the commentators gasping, and add to Sonia's already considerable fortune.

She tightened the laces on her violet Air Zoom Elites, opened the door, and then hopped nimbly down to the ground. It was quite a distance, but Sonia prided herself on keeping agile. She had no patience for people who complained about four-wheel-drive vehicles in the inner suburbs. At the end of the day, you couldn't put a price on safety, and that cyclist this morning should have looked where he was going! Anyway, she needed a roomy vehicle. It wasn't her fault she had such long legs.

Once out of the car park, she looked up at the building in front of her, an Edwardian cottage converted into a boutique shop. It had an ornamental gabled roof, elegant fretwork, decorative lead lighting, and a miniature garden off to the side with begonias, ferns, and a flowering plum. Too cute for words and guaranteed to make her rivals turn an unfashionable shade of green.

The neat, curly lettering in the front window read *Hundreds and Thousands*. And in smaller script below: *Purveyors of finest fairy bread.* When Sonia unlocked the front door and stepped inside, she found Enid there already.

A tortoiseshell clasp held back the young woman's auburn hair, and there were baby pearl studs in her dainty ears. Her tight white shirt was buttoned up to the hollow of her throat, but it skimmed the curves of her breasts in a manner most distracting. Enid was shorter and fleshier than Sonia, with a ripeness about her that Sonia had been enjoying from a distance since Enid's first day. Whenever Enid bent forward to wipe the display cabinet, Sonia's neck craned discreetly. Enid's plain, well-cut skirts somehow always made the view from behind even more sumptuous.

Seeing Sonia in the doorway, Enid's hazel eyes widened, and she gave an eager little smile. Sonia smiled back. Her smile faded, though, when she saw who was leaning against the counter, talking to Enid. Hadn't Sonia told that journalist to come at nine? It was barely eight.

"Good morning." Sonia stepped forward, lifting her sunglasses. The journalist, who looked about twelve and had been snapping pictures on her phone, hastened forward with her hand outstretched. Sonia paused before taking it, just long enough to convey her opinion of people who disregarded meeting times.

"I'm Angelica Russo from *Gourmand.* I'm sorry I'm a bit early, but I did ring, and Enid said it would be okay."

"Did she?" Sonia's chilly smile swept across to her assistant, who blushed and hung her head. "Well, young Enid is very hospitable. I'm afraid she's going to find it awfully hard to shoo all our customers out the door at the end of the day." Sonia softened her smile just a little. "That's why she employs a terrifying old ogre like me!"

The young women laughed obediently. Angelica looked suitably embarrassed, but Enid… Sonia narrowed her eyes, studying the look on her protégé's face as Enid busied herself at the cash register. The word that sprang to Sonia's mind was *busted.*

Did Enid imagine she could make a name for herself by giving quotes and cute pictures for this article in the *Herald*'s food lift-out? Sonia shook her head. The idea of being eclipsed by her assistant was ridiculous. The advertising revenue Sonia's companies supplied for that newspaper would be enough to ensure she got the final editorial rights over any piece.

Still, if Enid wanted to drape herself over the counter in Angelica's pictures, Sonia supposed her good looks wouldn't do the shop any harm. And by the time the piece went to print, it would have Sonia's name and reputation all over it. She could afford to be lenient.

"Well, ah, *Angelica*—what a darling name, by the way—I hope you won't mind chatting to Enid for a few more minutes while I go and change." Sonia gave a self-deprecating smile. "I can hardly give interviews in my dreadful old workout gear, can I?"

In fact, Sonia's activewear was of the highest quality. She was especially fond of the organic-cotton-and-bamboo compression leggings with mesh panelling, glute-shaping technology, reflector detailing, and her initials down one thigh. Well, what was the point of torturing yourself with exercise unless it boosted the self-esteem?

In the back room, Sonia unlaced her sneakers and peeled off her clothes. She had left the door open a crack to listen to the younger women's conversation.

"So," Angelica was saying in a dubious voice, "fairy bread?"

It wasn't the thrilled reaction Sonia had hoped for, but what would a teenage intern know?

Enid cleared her throat.

"Absolutely, Angelica. Fairy bread." Enid spoke in her best seductive "promotions" voice. "You're probably wondering why the corporate queen Sonia Fitzgerald decided to take such a bold step into the world of boutique foods."

"Well…"

"Of course you are," Enid interrupted sweetly. Sonia raised her eyebrows; the girl was good. "Now, the last time most of us ate fairy bread was at our own six-year-old birthday party—am I right?" Enid didn't wait for a reply. "It's such a fabulous memory, isn't it? Makes you think of hot afternoons under the sprinkler, backyard cricket games, stuffing yourself with lolly cigarettes and red cordial back before those things were bad for you…"

Sonia could hear the forceful charm in Enid's voice; it was clear Enid had been paying close attention to her boss's style. A lesser woman than Sonia Fitzgerald might have found it unnerving.

"It's so quintessentially Aussie, isn't it?" Enid went on. "The experience of fairy bread is something that absolutely everyone in Australia can relate to."

"Well, actually, I'm not sure—"

"And why should the fun have to stop just because we're grown up now? Why not relive that delicious, nostalgic taste of childhood, but with a contemporary adult twist?"

Sonia heard the tippy-tap of Enid's little heels as she led Angelica over to the display cabinet.

"This," said Enid, "is our take on fairy bread."

As she listened to her assistant's smooth patter, Sonia let herself relax. Of course this venture would go well. And she'd chosen a gem in Enid. Admittedly, the little madam was voraciously keen, but why not? Sonia had been the same at her age. A high-flying legal career, a stint as a political adviser (which had taught her where all the bodies were buried), two well-chosen marriages and *very* well-chosen divorces, a couple of decades of canny investments in property and the stock market, and a highly lucrative libel case against an obnoxious talkback radio host had all left Sonia very comfortably off. Certainly comfortable enough to amuse herself by starting up a little hobby business on the side.

A hobby business that would wipe the floor with all the hobby businesses of her old school friends and ex-husbands. Not to mention her sister Bianca, who never shut up about her bloody Mexican mosaics import business, and who had implied over their Christmas lunch that Sonia wasn't creative.

Well, Bianca would be eating those words soon. Along with Sonia's take on fairy bread.

The thought of victory always gave Sonia an agreeable little shiver.

As she stepped out of her leggings, she took a moment to straighten up and contemplate her reflection in the full-length mirror. Clad only in a lacy white bra and matching high-cut panties, she looked tanned and fit. Those spray-salon and gym sessions were paying off nicely, and she never regretted getting her underwear fitted at Severina, where they understood their customers. Yes, the flesh was loosening a little at her décolletage, and she'd never quite lost the soft puckering across her belly (it would be nice to say that the joys of motherhood made it all worthwhile, but Sonia thought of her whining children and decided to reserve judgement). Still, on the whole, she was not displeased.

She took a moment to contemplate her own success while listening to the soundtrack of Enid's voice rhapsodising about what a privilege it was to work for the great Sonia Fitzgerald.

Not bad, Sonia repeated to herself. She paused to cup her breasts through the white lace, flicking her nipples lightly until they assumed a tighter, more pleasing shape. A lazy heat stirred between her thighs. Not bad at all.

"Now, tell me," she could hear Enid saying to Angelica, "when you hear the term 'fairy bread', what do you expect?"

"Um, sliced white bread, buttered and covered with hundreds and thousands."

"Exactly. Or chocolate sprinkles, if your mum was feeling daring. So we asked ourselves, what would that concept look like if someone were to make fairy bread nowadays?"

"Well, I think people do still make it nowadays..." Angelica tried to interject, but Enid, decorative and obliging though she might be, was not easily silenced.

Sonia liked that about her. She had no use for passive women. As Enid took back control of the interview, Sonia leaned against the wall and shut her eyes. She ran her fingers down over her belly, tracing light circles around her navel. A pleasant sensation. Invigorating.

"So, over here on the left," said Enid, "we have our 'classic' range. We take a brioche base, add a thin layer of organic lemon butter, and top that with shaved dark sea salt or chilli chocolate and grated candied orange." Sonia squeezed her eyes shut tighter at the thought. Delicious. Her fingertips skittered lower, running along the waistband of her panties. "Or, as a variation, we offer a cream cheese Nutella spread, sprinkled with silver pearls and multicoloured sugar stars. Gorgeous, right?"

"Um, yeah, it looks nice." What was wrong with this dreary Angelica, Sonia huffed to herself, her self-care regime set aside a moment. Not that it mattered what the newspaper's work-experience girl thought, but her lack of enthusiasm was insulting to Sonia's products and to Enid's delivery.

Enid, however, was undeterred, and something about that inspired wonderfully dirty thoughts. "But not everyone wants something super sweet, right? So we've also developed a range of healthy fairy bread options." Sonia nodded, recalling how pleased she had felt with herself the day she came up with that idea. She plucked at the lace across her hips, then decided to treat herself. After all, she was worth it, wasn't she? She let Enid's voice fill her consciousness as she slipped her hand inside her panties.

"Over here," said Enid, "we have a light, crispy croissant base, fresh from the French patisserie next door. We add a layer of citrus-and-ginger preserve—"

"You mean marmalade?"

"Citrus-and-ginger preserve," Enid repeated firmly. "Then, in place of hundreds and thousands, we sprinkle the base with pomegranate seeds, passionfruit pulp, and halved miniature white grapes. It tastes *divine*."

Sonia shut her eyes again, relishing a mental image of the glistening fruit—the seeds like jewels, the sweet, fresh smell—and Enid's pink tongue extending to lick the juice from her bottom lip. She combed her fingers through her carefully groomed curls, in search of the damp flesh below.

"That's the healthy option?" Angelica asked.

"Well, for those customers who are on a strict health kick, we also offer a delicious savoury version. Wood-fired sourdough, spread with garlic hummus and topped with our healthy-sprinkle range: toasted pine-nuts, pumpkin seeds, and fresh pearl couscous."

Oh, yes, the girl was good. Enid's seductive, take-no-prisoners delivery and the thought of her own imminent success had already made Sonia wet. Wet enough that she slipped two fingers inside herself, curled them expertly, and exhaled hard.

"Now, that's fairy bread like you've never seen it before, right?"

"Yeah, it is." Angelica's doubtful tone was bordering on sarcastic. Sonia wished she'd given Enid permission to slap the rude little miss. That scenario alone sent a throb of enjoyment through her that made her hips sway. She'd seen Enid hefting around the boxes of ingredients and knew the young woman's arms were surprisingly strong. At the thought of them, Sonia parted her thighs wider, the heel of her hand pumping against her clit.

"And you *must* see our novelty range," Enid was saying. "Now, over here is our Christmas-in-July fairy bread. Dark rye with a cream cheese spread and scatted with currants, chopped glacé cherries, and preserved lemon rind. You see how the visual effect calls to mind a traditional Christmas pudding?"

"Does it taste like one, though?" Angelica asked. Sonia clenched her jaw in frustration. Why did people ask such stupid questions? And especially now, when she was so close...

"Next to it we have some of our funkier items. This piece features a glazed and sweetened Asian-style baguette with red velvet icing, sprinkled with the heads of jelly snakes and chocolate frogs. And over here is my absolute favourite: a thick, white marzipan base with brown fudge bordering, sprinkled with colourful dyed croutons." When Angelica stayed silent, Enid cried, "Do you get it? Confectionary topped with breadcrumbs? It's reverse fairy bread!"

The sound of Enid clapping her hands with delight made Sonia stifle a cry. Her hips were rocking fast now; it wouldn't take much more...

"But..." Angelica hesitated. "Wouldn't that taste kind of...disgusting?"

Sonia's eyes snapped open. She could imagine the look of outrage and contempt on Enid's face. It was the same expression she could see right now in the mirror.

In a tone that was poisonously polite, Enid explained, "Well, that's not really the point." Her voice was so clipped, so authoritative that it set Sonia's hand moving again between her thighs. As her body began to clench with delight, Sonia heard Enid say, "It's *ironic*."

Sonia's hand stopped moving.

With eyes wide, Sonia leaned closer to the cracked-open door to make sure she was not missing something. In an instant, shock had turned her body to stone. Did she just hear…?

"*Art*," Enid corrected herself in a trice. "What you're seeing here is on the cutting edge of finest edible art. And we're very proud of it."

Sonia stepped back from the door in a horrified daze. Her hands trembled as she dressed herself quickly in tailored black trousers and a simple cream silk blouse.

Surely she was wrong. Surely her hearing was defective, her suspicions paranoid.

An idea struck her, and she reached for Enid's handbag, which the younger woman had left hanging over the back of a chair. She took out Enid's wallet, opened it, and rifled through the cards until she came to the driver's licence. With hesitant fingers, Sonia pulled it out and held it up to the light.

What she saw there shocked her to her core.

Sonia returned to the shop, posed for photographs, and gave her own interview to Angelica. She barely noticed what she was saying, although she was confident it was witty and appealing. Her eyes kept sliding away from the reporter's scribbling pencil, back to the shop counter where Enid stood, avoiding her boss's gaze.

Was Enid capable of betraying her? Enid, who had been here from the start—setting up the shop, testing the recipes, trotting out for coffees, massaging the finances, disinfecting the phone, laughing at all her jokes, and even tactfully screening calls from Sonia's ghastly family? Could Enid have deceived her mentor so completely?

Of course she could. Sonia had been in the corporate world long enough to know the depths to which ambitious people could sink. And as her shock turned to anger, she began to contemplate what she might do about it. The thought of punishment, of revenge, caused her pulse to quicken and her skin to prickle in a way that was not unpleasant.

At last, the shop door jangled shut behind Angelica. Sonia turned to face her assistant.

"Enid. I couldn't help overhearing your conversation with Angelica earlier. You used a rather...surprising word."

Sonia stepped closer. Enid drew in a breath and shuffled backwards, her small heels clicking with a nervous air against the floorboards. Sonia followed her, her own heels hitting the polished boards with a deep, resonant beat.

Due to a certain cosmetic procedure last Thursday, Sonia couldn't move her forehead very well at the moment, so frowning was difficult. But she had no trouble fixing Enid with an unblinking stare, like a cat about to pounce.

"Enid, dear. Is there something you would like to tell me?"

"I...I don't know what you mean, Ms Fitzgerald."

Sonia trailed her manicured hand along the countertop.

"'Ironic'," she murmured. "Ring any bells?"

Enid gulped, then shook her head. Her expression of innocence was so obviously faked that Sonia couldn't believe she hadn't sniffed out the young woman's treachery weeks before.

"You described my exquisite creations as 'ironic'." Sonia's mouth twisted around the word as if tasting something nasty. "That is not how we talk about the things we value. Not on this side of town."

"I don't know what you mean, Ms Fitzgerald."

"Don't you? Then I'll make it clear." Sonia reached into her pocket, drew out Enid's licence, and sent it skidding across the counter. "That's you, isn't it, dear? Although I must say I barely recognised you at first."

"You had no right to touch my things!"

Sonia gave a sniff of contempt. "In my place of business, I will touch anything I please. And this is you, isn't it?" She pointed to the little plasticised card from a distance, making her disdain quite clear. "Look at you in that photograph! It was only taken a year ago. Fire-engine red hair in a faux-fifties beehive. Cat's eye spectacles which you clearly do not need. Polka dot rockabilly dress. Diamond dimple stud. And just a hint of ink..."

Without warning, Sonia surged forward, seized Enid by her tight white blouse, and wrenched open the buttons to reveal flushed, heaving breasts in a strapless satin bra and a positive gallery of tattoos.

"Get your hands off me, you crazy bitch!" Enid hissed—although she made no effort to wriggle away.

"Now, now, don't be shy. It looks like you paid rather a lot of money for these decorations. You may as well show them off." Sonia ran one fingertip along Enid's collarbone, then slowly down the crevice between her breasts. "Look at them all! Salvador Dali's elephants, Betty Boop on a unicycle, quotes from the sutras of Patanjali..."

Sonia traced the shimmering edge of the fabric that held up Enid's breasts. It cut straight across, just above her nipples. If Enid breathed any harder, one of those taut little treasures might pop right out. Sonia could feel the illustrated skin tightening beneath her caressing touch, rippling with goosebumps.

"Got any more under here?" she whispered. "Shall we take a look?"

"You've seen enough." Enid smacked Sonia's wandering fingers, hard.

"Oh, yes, I've seen enough, my dear. Enough to know what you've been up to. Enough to know what you are." Sonia leaned in closer until her breath tickled Enid's parted lips. "You're a *hipster*."

A moment of unmistakable alarm and guilt spread over Enid's face. Then she collected herself, sniffed contemptuously, and drew back from Sonia's grasp.

"No one calls themselves *that* any more." She rolled her eyes. "You elites are so out of touch."

"Well, forgive me if I'm not fluent in the latest fashionable language to describe how I don't care about being fashionable." Sonia rolled her eyes. "But I think you know what I mean. According to this licence, you live on the *other* side of town, Enid. In one of those suburbs where people drink beetroot coffees and raw hemp smoothies and ride expensive bicycles distressed to look old and conserve water by not showering. Ironically, of course."

"Well, *I'm* sorry if my parents didn't buy me a Porsche and a boob job for my eighteenth birthday," Enid sneered right back. "I'm sorry if there are some people on this planet who didn't go to the same snotty private school as you."

"That's down to parental choice." Sonia shrugged. "And I won't be called snotty. I worked hard to get where I am today."

"You lied, cheated, bribed, blackmailed, stole, flirted, and slaughtered your way to the top!"

"And it was *very* hard work." Sonia leaned back and regarded Enid through hooded eyes. "So, are you going to confess to me why you're really here? Since your original pretext of loving gourmet foods and personalised service was obviously a lie."

"It wasn't a lie." Enid tossed her head. She braced her hands behind her on the counter and inflated her chest. "I saw an opportunity to build up my resume, even if it did mean travelling an hour each way and dodging your horrible monster truck every morning. I'm a hard worker—what's wrong with that?"

"Nothing at all. But I don't believe you." Sonia craned in closer. She tucked a strand of hair behind Enid's ear, then traced the line of her jaw. The skin was soft, like rose petals. "Your qualifications were already strong. You didn't need to work for someone you despised. And you've been a very busy bee, haven't you? Rifling through my finances, sucking up my business knowledge, pumping me for information..." Sonia gave each verb a dirty little emphasis. Then she drew her forefinger lightly across Enid's pale, pink lips, feeling them open under her touch. She whispered, "I know when I'm being played, Enid. But what's your game?"

"I don't know what you're talking about." Her lips pushed forward slightly. Her hips quivered.

"Right." Sonia's jaw tightened. She reached for the reel of decorative purple ribbon they planned to use to tie up the gift boxes of fairy bread for special customers. "We'll do this the hard way."

She spun Enid around, thrusting her up against the counter. All Enid had to do to escape was step sideways—but somehow this did not happen. Instead, Enid's full, firm arse wriggled backwards into Sonia's belly, causing Sonia a deep throb of pleasure.

Sonia loosened a length of purple ribbon with a theatrical whoosh (she had been practising this move all week to impress the customers) and used it to secure Enid's wrists behind her. Enid protested and tugged at her bonds—but only after Sonia had finished tying them. And after she had added a decorative butterfly bow.

"Now." Sonia exhaled against Enid's ear, filling the delicate pink cavity with her hot breath. "Why are you really here?"

"Honestly," Enid panted. "I love selling croutons on marzipan."

Sonia gave a soft snarl of annoyance. Without warning, she plunged her tongue into Enid's ear, then licked a trail along the velvety outer rim before biting down on Enid's earlobe. Hard. Enid let out a squeal, her hips juddering. Sonia repeated, "What are you doing here?"

"I knew you'd turn out to be a pervert." Enid gave a breathless laugh. Sonia could smell her Bulgari shampoo—dammit, the little undercover agent had even taken the trouble to smell the part! Enid added, "Posh people are such freaks."

"Is that a fact?" With her hips pinning Enid against the edge of the counter, Sonia pulled the younger woman's blouse free from her skirt and slipped her hands up underneath, caressing Enid's smooth, warm skin and receiving a shiver for her efforts. She snuck one finger beneath the tight elastic and wire that held Enid's bra across her ribcage. Snapping it playfully, Sonia whispered, "Why are you here?"

"Because I couldn't get a barista job on the funky side of town, all right?"

"No. That sounds all wrong to me." One-handed, she squeezed the clasp of Enid's bra and popped it open, letting the stiff, satiny scaffolding fall away. Enid's breasts swung free, with large pink nipples and a merciful absence of any more tattoos.

Sonia asked her again: "Why are you here?"

"Because I thought it would broaden my horizons to hang around with entitled blonde people and their vicious designer dogs."

"Right." Sonia was in no mood for this sort of backchat. She reached sideways over to where the ingredients were lined up for the next round of fairy bread, grabbed a large mixing bowl full of red velvet icing, and slammed it down in front of Enid. Then she pressed hard between Enid's shoulder blades, bending her forward.

A muffled shriek arose as Enid's erect nipples touched the cold icing, creamy and gritty with sugar. She gasped and swore, but Sonia pushed her down remorselessly until Enid's naked breasts were submerged in the sweet mixture and squished against the cold glass sides of the bowl.

"What a mess," Sonia murmured. "Now, I could help you up and clean this off, making sure none of it gets on your nice clean blouse...or I could just leave you here. Which is it to be, Enid?"

Enid struggled fruitlessly with the ribbon around her wrists. Then her shoulders slumped, and she mumbled "Help me up" in a petulant tone.

"First tell me why you're here."

"For fuck's sake!"

Sonia dipped one finger into the bowl, scooped out a dollop of whipped red confectionary, and dabbed it onto Enid's lips, working her fingertip between them.

"The shop will be opening soon, Enid. If you really want to draw this out..."

"All right, all right!" Enid strained to keep her head up even as her chest was pushed deeper towards the marble bench top. "If you must know, I'm writing a book. About the businesses in this shopping village. I came here to work undercover, to supplement my research. Okay?"

"A book?" Moving with care, she drew Enid upright by her shoulders and turned her around. In her curiosity, it took Sonia a moment to fully appreciate the sight before her. Slathers of decadent red velvet topping clung to Enid's generous breasts. "What sort of book?"

"Get this stuff off me before it melts onto my skirt," Enid demanded, "and I'll tell you."

Sonia paused. Then she picked up a metal spatula from beside the bowl. Moving unhurriedly, she ran it underneath Enid's left breast, catching a sweet blob of icing as it began to drip. Sonia licked the spatula, assessing the mixture—a little too buttery, maybe? Then she applied the spatula again, scraping the chilly edge of the metal up the underside of the same breast, gathering up a thick layer of red and exposing the pale skin beneath. Enid quivered, her breath coming fast.

She plied the spatula again. Each time, she pressed the edge of the implement harder into the soft sphere, making the delicate flesh dint and wobble in her wake. She moved from the outside in, catching some of the icing on the spatula and working the rest carefully inward.

When all the remaining topping was gathered in the centre, caked around Enid's protruding nipple, Sonia drew back at last. She scraped the spatula on the side of the bowl, then bent her head and took Enid's breast into her mouth.

Holding Enid's hips in a tight grasp, Sonia sucked off the icing with a forceful tug of her lips and a circular motion of her tongue. Above her, Enid began to moan.

It was a full minute before Sonia lifted her head. With her face still brushing against Enid's breast, she took out a compact mirror to check her lipstick and flicked a droplet of icing from the corner of her mouth. Then she asked in a casual tone, "What sort of book are you writing?"

"Do the other one." Enid's voice came out in a growl.

"Tell me about your book."

A glance upward treated her to Enid's frustrated grimace. "It's about the 'specialised' shops in this neighbourhood—all the weird, expensive shit that's sold around here, the stuff no normal person could ever afford. I've been talking with staff and customers, observing the prices and the people who shop there. You know, like that French fromagerie and foot spa next door. And the place on the corner that sells hundred-dollar pet toys. And the shop across the road with the hand-carved children's mobiles, spice racks, and antique walking sticks."

Sonia frowned.

"What's wrong with that?"

"They cost more than my car! And some of the other stores are even worse. What about that place behind the gallery? It pretends to be a ritzy cigar shop, but everyone knows they have a room out the back where they supply pathetic old rich men with—"

"There's no need to go into that," Sonia warned.

"—top-dollar toupees!"

"It's called *discretion.*" Sonia glared.

"And don't even start me on that so-called antique bookshop next to the florist." Enid rolled her eyes. "I doubt any of their customers have read a book in fifty years. They sell them in beautiful old leather covers by the square foot!"

"Well, Enid." Sonia drew herself up and slapped the spatula against her palm. "I gather this book of yours won't say very nice things about my neighbours and associates. No doubt you'd prefer it if their shops sold crocheted vulvas or Tibetan cushions stuffed with organically grown beard clippings. Well, that's their lookout. But I'd be interested to hear what your book will have to say about me." Sonia pulled the spatula back until it curved ominously, light reflecting off the thin, flexible metal. Then she let it thwack sharply against the side of her thigh. "My solicitors might be interested in that too."

Enid tossed her head.

"Actually, I haven't said anything much about you."

"Oh, Enid." Sonia shook her head. She bent the cold, flat metal of the spatula between her hands, then drew it warningly over Enid's right breast. A tiny groan escaped Enid's lips. Then her whole body jolted as Sonia gave her nipple a sharp little flick.

Sonia was quick this time, almost businesslike. She cleaned Enid's right breast with five firm strokes. Then she bent the spatula back and landed several spanks against Enid's aroused nipple. Enid gritted her teeth and yet also writhed sinuously under Sonia's devilish attentions.

Slowing down, Sonia circled the reddened bud with the ball of her thumb, wiping away the last of traces of butter, sugar, and colour. She gave her thumb to Enid to lick clean, then whispered, "Tell the truth."

"Honestly." Enid was panting now. "I barely mentioned you. See for yourself: the book's coming out next week."

"Next week?" Sonia felt a flicker of worry. The wretched thing had better not draw attention away from her own publicity for the shop. "Who are you publishing with?"

"You won't have heard of them." Enid was still breathing heavily, but her tone had turned condescending again. The self-possession of the young woman was rather remarkable, Sonia had to admit. "My work is being launched at the Cherry Pop First Time Writers' Festival. And it won't be an actual physical book. No one's buying those any more. We're publishing it entirely in tweet form."

"I see." Sonia didn't really. In her corporate career, she had employed teenage interns to take care of the social media for her. Privately, she'd never really understood why it was so compulsory to do all that nonsense nowadays.

Still, Sonia did know how important it was to secure any information that might be relevant to her commercial interests. "Come on, you didn't spend weeks working for me just so you'd have a pretext to spy on the other shops in the street. There must have been more to it than that. For the last time, Enid, *why are you here*?"

Enid held her boss's gaze. Despite being bound and half-naked, a smirk played across her lips. In an innocent tone, she asked, "What will you do for me if I tell you the full story now?" She paused. "Otherwise you'll be reading about it in the papers next week at the same time as everyone else."

"You little..." With a growl of rage, Sonia lifted Enid's skirt and delivered half a dozen sharp smacks to her plump inner thighs until Enid cried out at the stinging heat. Sonia watched in satisfaction as the firm skin turned pink above Enid's stocking tops. A nice little novelty, that. "Don't try power plays with me, my dear. You know what I'm capable of." Sonia hoisted Enid's skirt higher and, without warning, yanked her cream lace knickers down around her knees.

Enid squeaked, but she recovered quickly and gave another teasing smirk.

"I told you," she said. "I have no problem with your fairy bread concept, Ms Fitzgerald. No problem at all."

Sonia studied her hard. Enid's cheeks were flushed, her eyes wide, her exposed chest rising and falling fast. Such an impudent little tease! Still, whatever nonsense Enid was planning—books in tweet form, scathing toupee exposés?—it shouldn't be difficult to get the rest of the story out of her now. Enid was desperately aroused; Sonia could smell her excitement from here. It was...tantalising.

Her movements unusually lithe for a woman of her age, Sonia sank to her knees.

"I see you're a slave to ridiculous fashions even down here," she murmured, running one lazy finger up the cleft between Enid's hairless outer lips. They were pink and puffy, parting a little as Enid squirmed under her mentor's touch. Sonia hooked her thumbs into the plump flesh and pulled gently outwards, exposing a hardened clit and long inner lips alive with a tell-tale glistening.

"You girls are so silly nowadays." Sonia leaned in closer so that Enid would feel the warm puffs of air brushing her most intimate self. "Women should look like women, my dear. I've always said so. We'll have to do something about this."

She reached up to the ingredients counter and took the can of whipped cream, shook it, then with quick, deft movements sprayed a triangle of white fluffy peaks across Enid's bare mound.

Enid yelped. "Oh, that's weird!" She giggled, visibly struggling to hold still. "Quick, it's going to melt on my stockings!"

"Then you'd better answer my questions, hadn't you?" Sonia gave a low chuckle. "I warn you, this product is pure dairy—none of your trendy almond and soy alternatives! So come clean, Enid: Why are you really hanging around my shop? It's not just for your silly book, is it?"

"Oh, lick it off, please..."

"I don't know why you imagine that I would do a vulgar thing like that." Sonia flashed a smug grin and reached for the can again. "All I care about, as always, is bringing a little classical elegance to an unsatisfactory situation." She added fresh squirts of cream to Enid's upper thighs before aiming the can up between them. Enid let out a hoarse cry as her clit and inner lips were subjected to a long, firm spray.

"Delicious," said Sonia. "Now tell the truth."

Enid's body was jerking and arching now, so clearly yearning for release. "If I tell you, will you lick this off?"

Sonia cocked an eyebrow. "I might."

"All right." Enid struggled to catch her breath, her face twisting with a mix of emotions that, to Sonia, wavered between humiliation and triumph. "If you must know, I'm starting my own business. I'll be selling fairy bread too."

"You?" The muscles in Sonia's face went taut. "But that's...that's preposterous."

Still, it was important to keep the younger woman talking. Sonia lowered her head and licked up the trickles of cream that were melting rapidly down Enid's thighs, the sweetened dairy mingling with the briny streaks of Enid's pleasure. She licked her lips, then drew back. "There's no room for two such operations around here," she warned. "And if you think you can stand against me on my own turf, you must be even sillier than you look right now."

"I won't be doing that." Enid panted. Her hips were rocking forwards, as if to recapture the touch of Sonia's tongue. "I'll be starting up my business in my own part of town."

"Over *there*?" Sonia let her voice turn pointedly incredulous.

"Why not?" Enid shot back. "If doughnuts and burgers and fries and coffee scrolls can be reinvented as trendy quality foods, why not fairy bread? I reckon hipsters—*interesting* people, I mean—will be queuing around the block."

"You're an ignorant, callow, arrogant young fool." Sonia punctuated each adjective with an angry stroke of her tongue up Enid's pudenda, tasting air-filled confectionary and sweaty flesh with a hint of stubble. "Do you really want a spanking from my lawyers? I should warn you they play rough."

"They'll have nothing to play with." Enid's tone was dripping with a sense of its own victory even as her knees began to wobble beneath her. "Fairy bread is a traditional recipe; you don't own it, Ms Fitzgerald. Especially since I've been remaking all of your lovely creations at home and posting them to my Instagram account for weeks. I've got ten thousand followers already."

Sonia glowered up at her.

"You had better be lying, my dear." When Enid didn't reply, Sonia worked her long, hot tongue between the younger woman's lips, catching trails of pleasure and oozing cream. She drew back and watched those torturously swelled privates up close as Enid emitted a short, sharp cry and struggled to open her legs further, her knickers tangled around her feet.

Withdrawal must have made Enid very cross indeed, for she blurted out, "That's the real reason that journalist Angelica was here before. Oh, she'll publish your boring interview in that old broadsheet that no one reads any more. But her personal blog will feature her interview with *me*. I'll be talking about innovative new business models and how entrepreneurs like me are making the old guard like you totally irrelevant, *Ms* Fitzgerald."

"What rubbish!" Sonia spat the words out. "Even if you imagine you can steal my intellectual property—and, my dear, you have no idea how I will make you pay for that—what's new about what you're doing? Opening an identical shop in a different suburb? The only original thing is the postcode!"

"I won't be opening a shop." Enid was thrashing in earnest now, trickles of arousal seeping down her thighs. With an impressive display of strength, she popped her hands free at last and shook the purple ribbon away.

Her naked breasts were heaving. "My business will be an online ordering model. People nowadays don't want to waste time driving to another part of town during business hours and queuing up in some dusty old shop to look at things they might not like. With my model, they'll be able to jump online at their convenience and choose the products themselves. They can click on their preferred style of bread, toppings, designs—everything."

"But that's appalling!" How could anyone prefer some ghastly mobile phone app over her beautiful, one-of-a-kind shop?

Still, the scent of the younger woman was so very inviting that Sonia made no objection when Enid twisted one hand in Sonia's hair and pulled her closer, back to where Enid clearly still needed her boss's touch. Licking Enid's clit with firm, lingering strokes, Sonia heard the younger woman stammering above her, as if desperate to confess the full extent of her betrayal.

"People will be able to order my fairy bread any time, twenty-four seven." Enid's voice cracked into a guttural cry as Sonia circled her clit with her tongue, then began to suck on it hard. Her hips convulsing in her boss's hands, treacherous Enid cried out, "And when it's ready, my employees will bike the fairy bread around to our customers. On—on our own authentic fair-trade rickshaws!"

Enid's gloating tone, so annoying to Sonia, cracked at last and then rose to an uninhibited wail, and she fell back limp against the counter. She lay there, twitching.

Sonia got slowly to her feet, wiped her lips, and took in what she had just heard. She made sure her gaze was ice cold, that her stance radiated danger. "*You—*"

The bell above the shop door jangled. Both women jumped in alarm.

"Excuse me?" a voice called out.

Sonia flattened her hair hastily with her hands. Enid grappled with her wrinkled blouse, jamming the buttons through the wrong holes. Thank goodness they were standing behind the counter; at least the state of disarray below Enid's waist would not be visible.

When they spun around to face the intruder, Sonia noted that Enid wore the same professional smile she was sure she had plastered on her own face—a slightly glazed one.

"Good morning." They spoke in a dead heat before Sonia silenced Enid with a glare. Turning back to their very first customer, she asked, "How may I help you?"

"Oh, it all looks so pretty!" The woman was small, elderly, and squinting through her glasses. It was clear she had no idea of what she had nearly witnessed. "Do you do bulk orders? For parties?"

"But of course." Sonia forced another smile.

"Wonderful! It's my grandson's fourth birthday on Saturday, and I—"

"*Fourth* birthday?" Sonia stared. She glanced at Enid and saw a matching astonishment on the younger woman's face. "You want my fairy bread for… for a *children's* party?"

"Well—yes." The customer blinked in surprise. "I thought—fairy bread…"

"We don't cater children's parties, I'm afraid." All embarrassment was gone now, and it was Sonia Fitzgerald at her iciest and most majestic who explained, "There's a Woolworths down the street, madam. I daresay you will find everything you need there."

The customer tried to argue, but Sonia was both charming and adamant. Enid had learned from the best. When she'd eased the woman out the door and shut it firmly behind her, Sonia swung around to face Enid. "A *children's party*? For sticky, grubby, screaming preschoolers? My God!"

"Totally gross," Enid agreed with a shudder.

"As if we were a common supermarket!"

"People don't get it," said Enid. "They'd probably complain that we didn't use margarine and Wonder white bread."

"No standards." Sonia winced. "No sense of style."

"No sense of irony," Enid added.

"Honestly," said Sonia. She shook her head, gazing around at her exquisite shop, her clever recipes, and her young protégé, who might be a treacherous little cuckoo in the nest but who did understand her. So she had a new arch rival in Enid, an enemy determined to take the fight to her. Well, at least Enid was worthy of the title.

"Good taste," said Sonia, "is so very hard to find."

A DIFFERENT VIEW

THE PROBLEM WASN'T THAT THE dress was powder-blue organza.

Nor that it was strapless, with shimmering beads accentuating the bust and a frothy, ruffled train at the back. Nor that it came with matching sequined kitten heels, and a box of pins and a roll of gaffer tape sitting ominously beside it.

The problem was that Steph was contractually obliged to wear it. For a photo shoot in *Women's Life* magazine. And Steph would rather swim the English Channel with two broken legs than be photographed in this dress.

"This is a *coveted* opportunity, love," Evie insisted. It was the same thing she'd said the last two times a miserable Steph had called her about it this morning. "The previous time they did a celebrity spread was with the prime minister's wife! And no offence, but you're just a sportswoman. It's kind of a miracle to get this."

Steph groaned. "Um, all right." Despite being described by Evie's focus group as "too threatening" (read: large, brown, and tattooed), Steph had never found it easy to say no to people. "But isn't that magazine kind of... old?"

"Course it is, love. Young people don't buy magazines." Down the phone line, Steph could hear the click and whoosh as her agent lit up a cigarette. "But who cares? *Women's Life* is on display at every checkout counter of every supermarket, newsagent, and corner store around the country. It's in your dentist's waiting room, on your grandmother's coffee table... We need that kind of exposure. We want the average person waiting to buy their milk and bread to be asking themselves: 'Should I know her?' If we can nail this and lift your profile, those sponsorship dollars will come flowing in."

"Couldn't we do another courtside shoot instead?" Steph pleaded. When she'd been chosen for the Australian national team last year, the evening news had filmed one of their training sessions, and it hadn't been so bad.

She pictured Evie's compassionate smile.

"Steph, people need to see that you're a fully rounded young woman with an exciting-but-relatable life off the basketball court. It's time to celebrate your feminine side and have some fun!"

This all sounded very sinister.

"Don't look so worried, love," Evie crooned, as if she could see her. "We're letting you keep the dreadlocks, aren't we? And it won't be some dreary old-lady shoot. I haven't told you the most exciting part. They've got Rin Takahashi working for them now."

"Who?" Steph sank down on the bench in the changing room and held the phone away from her ear to reduce the impact of Evie's outraged squawk.

"Sweetie, *everyone* knows Rin Takahashi!"

"I don't."

"Ex-punk performance artist?" Evie prompted. "Gave it up when it got too mainstream? One of the edgiest, most important photographers of our time?"

"Nope. Sorry."

"Oh, you're hopeless." Evie clicked her tongue. "Listen, Rin has photographed *everything*, okay? Paris catwalks, the Brixton riots, the last Yangtze River dolphin right before it died. Remember that iconic shot of the tribal medicine man staring down a bulldozer in the Amazon? Or the front-page picture of that tennis player punching her abusive father right there on the court? That was all Rin's work!"

"Um, okay..."

"All you need to know about Rin is that she's brilliant." Evie paused. "Basically, if Andy Warhol had been a woman with actual talent, he would be Rin."

If she's so brilliant and cutting-edge, what's she doing working for a housewife's magazine?

But the main point was clear long before Evie stopped talking: Steph was going to do this thing, regardless of her own wishes, and be grateful for the opportunity. That sort of message had been so pounded into her over the years by so many coaches, sporting federations, agents, and sponsors that she'd learned to tune it out and play video games in her head instead.

But now, as she hung up and stared again at the dress in front of her, she wished she'd fought Evie harder. Seriously, if Rin had chosen this thing for Steph to wear, how good a photographer could she really be?

"Nobody told me there was going to be ink."

The very first words uttered to Steph by the supposedly legendary Rin Takahashi were spoken with a metallic New York snarl and a crooked finger for the make-up artist, who came scurrying over. Jerking her chin towards the thick, black tattooed bands that encircled Steph's biceps, Rin snapped, "I could have worked around these if you had texted me about them even this morning. Now you'll need to cover them up."

The other women muttered their apologies to Rin and glared at Steph as if she'd got the tatts done on purpose to inconvenience them. Steph, who still hadn't received so much as a *hello*, folded her unacceptable arms and set her jaw.

Rin certainly looked the part of a cool, edgy artist: She wore a tight black velvet suit with an oversized collar and cuffs in dazzling white. There were thick silver rings on her pale fingers and thick silver bolts through each earlobe. Her glossy black hair was scraped back tight, and a single white stripe cut through it like a lightning bolt. Even in her chunky, studded heels, Rin barely came up to Steph's shoulder.

She did not look happy. "Well, let's get on with this."

For the shoot, Rin had chosen the car park of a crumbling closed-down factory. Steph glanced around at the chain-link fences, potholes, and graffiti, and didn't think they would match the dress at all. Much as she didn't want to do this, she didn't want the photographs to look ugly either.

"Couldn't we take the pictures somewhere nice?" she suggested. "Like a garden?"

The look she got from Rin could have stripped paint. The photographer didn't bother replying, instead busying herself with the lighting and snapping at the stylist and assistant to fetch this, adjust that, and "move the hell out of the way! I can see your shadow!"

Well, what did Steph know about photography? She sometimes took pictures of her lap by mistake with her phone camera. But she hadn't known she was signing on to this. An icy wind whipped through the car park, raising goosebumps over her exposed skin and making her nipples ache. Rin soon was ordering her to walk back and forth, to look over her shoulder, and to trail the hem of the dress through the rubble and muck. (The rep from the magazine squeaked in high-pitched dismay about that, but another one of Rin's glares silenced her.) Then Steph was ordered to lean for what felt like hours against a wall where someone had scrawled *Martian pussy* in giant green letters, before she was then told to crouch down and stare into a dirty puddle. As she felt the dress straining dangerously across her hips and back, Rin stalked around, a frown on her heart-shaped face, her heels kicking up mud as she barked out instructions to the stylist: "More powder—I can still see the shine! Tape that gaping neckline, it's not a porno! You gotta do something about that *hair*. It's killing me here!"

With each impatient shout, Steph felt her body—so fast, fit, and powerful most of the time—becoming lumpy, clumsy, and ugly. She was too tall, too hefty, too unfeminine. Jesus, it was like being back in high school.

A tiny leaf had landed in Steph's hair; Rin reached up without asking permission and flicked it away. Even though her fingertips touched the leaf only, Steph froze at the unexpected closeness. But Rin was already stepping back again.

"Right." Rin exhaled irritably. Every shot seemed to frustrate her more. "Up those stairs."

"You're kidding me." The outdoor stairs led to a boarded-up door two storeys high. They were so rusted and rickety Steph doubted they would take her weight.

"You've already kept me waiting for hours because 'walk a straight line' is apparently too hard for a jock to understand. You think I've got time to kid?"

"*Excuse me*?" She was used to sledging on the court—it was only natural your opponents would try to put you off your game—but what was this woman's problem? Weren't they supposed to be working *together*?

Rin rolled her eyes. "Oh, just climb the damn stairs!"

Steph managed five of them, trying to follow Rin's yelled instructions about leaning over the handrail ("I said moody, not constipated!"). But when she felt the sixth stair buckling beneath her, she refused to go further. It was bad enough trying to ignore the crowd of kids who were yelling things from the bus stop nearby. Her season contract didn't cover her for injuries off the court, not to mention this would be an embarrassing accident to explain to people.

"Hey, I'm sorry if your agent didn't tell you how this works!" Rin raised her voice over the wind that was now whistling across the factory grounds. "But this is my shoot, and you've agreed to follow my directions!"

"Well, I'm sorry if she didn't tell *you* how this works." Steph's teeth were starting to chatter from the cold as she clambered down. "But one accident can end my career. So, forget it."

Rin actually fell silent. Was she outraged, or just surprised? At last she said, "Fine, then. You can chuck some stones." Rin emptied a handful of gravel into Steph's palm, then dusted her own hands off and wiped them with sanitiser. "Think you can manage that?"

"Where do you want them?" *I know where I'd toss 'em*, she thought with a lethal glare. *Right into the lens of your fancy camera.*

But Rin pointed up at the highest shattered window of the abandoned factory. "Let's see you hit it."

When Steph managed it easily, Rin raised one tapered eyebrow. She might have even looked faintly impressed. She lifted her camera. "Do it again."

Steph obliged three more times, feeling the dress threatening to rip under her arm. Hitting her mark was easy, but she didn't like it. "You know, I don't think we should be vandalising buildings, especially when there's kids watching. Us players are supposed to be role models."

"Oh, for Chrissake." Rin's better mood hadn't taken long to evaporate. "Fine, you can walk through that pile of garbage if you'd prefer. And make sure to give it a good kick."

Steph stamped over, feeling more and more resentful as the wind screeched around her. Even her ears and nose were frozen, and her fingers were throbbing with cold. God knew what these bloody pictures would look like. She imagined an elegant middle-aged woman leafing through the magazine at the supermarket checkout, catching one glimpse of Steph, and throwing it back in disgust.

As the light worsened and a few spots of rain hit the concrete, Rin's instructions grew frenzied and shrill: "Lift your chin! Your left, not my left! For God's sake, *relax*!"

"Why does it have to look all dirty and ugly?" Steph couldn't help provoking her. "And why can't I smile?"

"What have you got to smile about?" Rin snorted. "You look like a rugby player at a drag night! I'm trying for irony here." She fiddled furiously with the camera. "Ill-fitting frivolity amidst urban decay. I wouldn't expect you to understand."

"What is your *deal*?" Steph's temper was rising fast.

"Oh, apart from freezing my ass off because you can't follow a few simple instructions?" Rin's voice had not been quiet this entire session, but now it seemed to rattle the broken windows.

"I'm doing what you told me to!"

"I said to act natural. You look like Robocop on his way to the prom!"

"Well, excuse me for not being a glamour model catwalk...person." Steph stumbled, then scowled. "But at least I'm good at my actual job." She cheered herself up for a moment by imagining Rin as a very puny opponent who could be sent flying by a well-timed shoulder charge. "You're the one who's meant to be some kind of genius at taking photos—which is not that friggin' important, by the way, even if you think it's better than brain surgery. So if the pictures are turning out crap, whose fault is that?"

Rin lowered the camera. Behind her designer spectacles, her black eyes glinted murderously.

"Maybe this boring, provincial, little desperate-housewives magazine, which can't think of anything better to do with my considerable talents than happy snaps of pathetically closeted B-grade athletes—to print in between cupcake recipes and tampon advertisements! Maybe it's their fault!"

Steph flinched at the "closeted" remark. The stylist had backed away by now; her assistant was hiding in the car. But Steph stepped forward. "You've got no reason to talk to me like that. In fact, you've been an arsehole from the word go. You think I want to be here doing this? If I've made some sacrifices, it's because I love what I do. If you don't even like your job and you think you're too good for it, why don't you get a better one and stop being such a bully?"

Rin's eyes widened, her face a mask of rage. The stylist ducked behind the car, fumbling for her keys as if to make a quick getaway. The wind howled with renewed force, whipping Steph's hair across her face.

Rin ripped the camera from around her neck. Steph got ready to dodge before slowly and with visibly forced calm, Rin lowered the instrument to her side. Holding Steph's gaze, she stepped forward, moving closer until Steph could see the tiny, delicate lines at the corners of her mouth and eyes, like the faintest of brushstrokes across Rin's pale skin.

"Oh, believe me, I wish I could." Rin's voice had contracted to a furious whisper. She pressed her narrow lips together as the camera shook in her hand. "If I'd stayed at *GN* magazine last year, I'd be at the top of my game by now. Do you know I had a whole project lined up with one of their reporters: inside life on a polygamous Mormon compound? Not to mention an exposé on juvenile prisons." She shook her head. "Back then, if anyone had suggested a shoot like this, I would have laughed in their face."

"Why aren't you there now, then?"

Rin exhaled hard through her nose, then slumped and ran a hand over her impeccable hair.

"A little incident with our biggest advertiser. Who went to college with our biggest shareholder. Not everyone agreed with how I handled it."

"What did you do? Tell *him* that his tattoos were 'literally giving you the worst migraine of your life'?"

"No." Rin hesitated. "I threw a bowl of shrimp salad at him."

Steph couldn't help gaping. "For real?"

Rin nodded.

"Why?"

Steph got a hard look in response. "Demanding blow jobs from frightened young interns doesn't play well with me." When Steph stared, Rin curled her lip. "You want to talk bullies? Some of these assholes are worse now than they were in the seventies." She looked away, across the scattered bricks and the puddles rippling with new drops of rain. "My own fault for getting too comfortable inside the capitalist machine. I thought I was in high enough demand that I could make my point and fuck the consequences. But it's true what they say: 'You can always be replaced.'"

She took off her glasses and wiped the rain off them. "By the time those guys were through, I was damn near unemployable."

"Wow." Steph took that in. "All because of a bowl of salad?"

She cocked her head. "Well, there might have been a platter of sushi too. And a basket of zucchini vegan mini-muffins."

"Best use for zucchini muffins I can think of," Steph offered.

Rin gazed upwards. "And a trestle table."

"You did the right thing." Steph's weight shifted from foot to foot. "Well, sort of."

"No." Rin sighed. "A tray of shot glasses would have been way more rock-and-roll. Damn lunchtime launches."

A weary silence fell. The rain was settling in, spattering in fat, cold drops against Steph's face and pooling inside her sparkly shoes.

Rin sighed. "Oh, let's get out of here. The shots we've got will have to do."

"Sorry if the photos are no good," Steph mumbled. She picked up the sodden, grimy train of her dress in one fist and followed Rin to where their cars were parked.

"Oh, you were right." Rin shrugged. "It wasn't your fault."

"Well, I can't do dresses." Ten minutes before, there was no way Steph would have shown weakness in front of this scornful, bad-tempered woman, but now she heard herself say, "I've always looked awful in them. Even when I was a kid. You were kind of right about my high school formal, actually. It was, like, torture."

"Please." She waved a hand. "Naomi Campbell couldn't have done anything with that dress. It looks like someone threw up a blue Slurpee into Dolly Parton's purse."

"Yeah, it—" Steph tripped over her own sentence. "Hang on, you chose it!"

"*Me*?" Rin reeled, then, for the first time that afternoon, actually laughed. Up close, her slightly crooked front teeth made her look younger. "Honey, if you weren't half my age and twice my size, I'd slap you for that. The dress was a deal between the designer and the magazine—nothing to do with me."

"Really?"

"Hey, when I do bad taste, I do it well."

As they reached the car, Rin adjusted her square spectacles, then appraised Steph's top half: her broad, bare shoulders; her large hands; the black rings of her tattoos shimmering as the rain washed the concealer away. Steph looked down at Rin. There were drops of water sliding through her raven hair and beading on her velvet lapels.

"If I had my way," Rin said, "I wouldn't have shot you in that monstrosity. With the body you've got to work with... Well, let's say I wouldn't have hidden it under ten million ugly sequins."

A burst of surprised laughter escaped Steph's lips, and she looked away in embarrassment. But even as she did so, she felt a pleasurable heat rising in her cheeks.

"I don't know about that..." She hesitated, then to her own surprise she added, "But I'm heading to the gym now. If you want..." She glanced down at Rin's camera. "I mean, Evie wouldn't like it. And I guess it's not what the magazine wanted. But..."

The rain was coming harder now. Rin slid into the car without another word and yanked the door shut.

Crestfallen, Steph took a step back before her phone sounded in her bag.

There in 20, it read. *Text me the address.*

Steph had only ever worked out in front of teammates, coaches, and personal trainers. But she'd been competitive right from the beginning, eager to impress, always wanting to be the one who could go faster, who could last longer.

"You come alive in front of an audience," her high school phys. ed. teacher had joked, and Steph, so shy and awkward outside of gym class, had grinned back.

Who knew all it would take to push her to the next level would be a short, cranky, fifty-something photographer in kinky shoes?

The Rin Takahashi who followed Steph into the gym was a different artist to the one who'd pushed her around in the factory lot, barking orders. Once they were in the weights room—with its pounding eighties rock; faded bodybuilding posters; and the smell of leather, sweat, and disinfectant—Rin was transformed.

Gone were the tantrums, the arrogance, the endless complaints. Now Rin watched in near silence through the camera's lens or over its neat black body. Her stance was relaxed, and there was a tiny smile on her face as Steph, now dressed in tight cotton shorts and a singlet, warmed up on the treadmill, then moved to the mat for push-ups and lunges. She stepped around Steph with careful movements and leaned against neighbouring benches and mats, out of her way but always present. Occasionally she would murmur some suggestion—"Turn your face a little?"

Steph felt her skin growing warm, her pulse stirring beneath her drowsy flesh. Her muscles, cold and stiff from those wasted hours outdoors, protested at first, but before long, she felt them lengthening, growing accustomed to the burn. Her heartbeat quickened. The camera blinked and whirred.

"I used to look down on sports photography," said Rin as Steph dropped to the mat for another ten push-ups. "Before I tried it, I mean."

"Oh yeah?" Steph paused in mid-air, feeling the muscles groaning pleasurably along her arms and shoulders. She lifted her face to smile at Rin.

"Yeah. I assumed it was some kind of pathetic wish fulfilment. You know, for the sort of nerdy kids who fantasised about hanging out with the athletes."

"Is that right?" Steph rose to her knees, noting with satisfaction the traces of her own sweat left shining on the mat.

Rin chuckled. "Well, it might be a little bit right, actually."

As Steph led the way to the weights area, she could feel perspiration trickling from her hairline down between her shoulder blades, making her singlet stick to the small of her back. She tugged the soaked fabric away from her skin and caught Rin watching.

"You know," said Rin, "we're almost by ourselves in here, and none of that lot are looking." She pointed to a lone group of men in the far corner, who seemed much more interested in each other's glutes than in Rin and Steph's photography session. "You could take that shirt off."

So Steph did.

In her sturdy black sports bra and tiny shorts, she moved onto the equipment: lat pull-downs, then bench presses. As her body hit its familiar rhythm, she closed her eyes, breathing out with each searing push of her muscles, then inhaling the tang of her own exertion, offset by puffs of chemical sweetness as her deodorant kicked in. She could feel the heat hammering in her temples, the perspiration sliding down between her breasts. She sensed Rin watching her and was determined not to disappoint, pushing herself on and on. The memories of the humiliating fashion shoot were fading fast. This was where Steph belonged, and she would show Rin what discipline looked like.

Only when her body was screaming for release did she let herself move on, over to the bench for a set of bicep curls.

"Happy with these shots?" she asked Rin in between rough breaths, the weight rising and falling in a steady rhythm.

"Not quite," said Rin from where she sat on the next bench. But she was smiling. She lowered her camera and leaned over, reaching around Steph's mighty arm where it was curled to her chest, the dumbbell steady in her hand. She stroked one stray lock back behind Steph's ear.

Rin's fingertips were soft.

"Now I'm happy," Rin said.

That night, stretched out alone on the couch, Steph found her mind drifting back to that gym shoot. Usually she showered and changed as soon as she got home, but somehow tonight she preferred to stay in her shorts and bra that carried the vague scent of her workout and an enticing artificial spiciness that might have been Rin's perfume.

A women's rugby sevens replay was on, but for once, Steph couldn't concentrate. She shut her eyes, recalling how it had felt to impress Rin, a woman who acted like she'd seen it all before. She remembered the non-stop clicking of Rin's camera, capturing every crunch and release of her muscles, every heavy breath and bead of liquid that ran down from her temple.

And she'd done well, hadn't she? Gone harder than ever before? The lingering ache in her limbs, that delicious, well-earned exhaustion told her so. Absently, Steph ran her fingertips down her thick, sleek thighs, relishing the power that lay dormant there and the smooth warmth of her skin.

Her phone beeped. She picked it up to find a text.

Thanks for today. You were impressive.

Steph smiled.

My pleasure.

The phone sounded again.

The pleasure was mutual, then. And if I can persuade our boring editor to take a risk on a photo shoot, thousands of women might get to enjoy you too.

That made Steph laugh out loud.

Not sure about that.

There was a pause before the reply.

Oh, think about it. Bored, pampered rich lady drops off the kids, settles on the sun lounge with a Bloody Mary, opens her magazine—and sees this.

Rin had attached a photo: a close-up of Steph craned over on the bench, her face set in determination, her bicep swollen taut with effort, the weight curled to the level of her chin. Rin had altered the background so it lay in shadow; there was nothing in the picture but Steph herself. Her tattoos bulged, and her bare skin was gleaming.

"Woah," Steph whispered to the empty room and messaged back.

Some trick—looks incredible! WTF did you do?

She could almost hear Rin's odd, curt chuckle in the message.

No tricks. That's what you look like. My job is to weed out the mess and distractions so people can see what's there.

This time, there was only a brief pause.

Imagine how that picture might brighten up some suburban lady's afternoon—or change her life.

And Steph did find herself imagining it: some middle-aged woman with perfect hair, impeccable make-up, and designer sunglasses, wearing the sort of expensive activewear Steph usually despised. She'd be sitting poolside, flipping open a glossy page and expecting to find salad recipes and celebrity gossip—and instead stumbling across that picture. Steph pictured the woman lifting her shades, her eyes widening over the rim of her glass…

How about these?

One picture showed Steph at full tilt on the treadmill, arms pumping, dreadlocks flying. Her face was focused intently on some point in the distance. Her eyes were sharp, her nostrils flaring as she inhaled deeply. The next picture captured her in mid-push-up. The strength in her upper body that she'd worked to build every day since she turned twelve was unmistakable.

Steph stared at it for a long time. Okay, she'd known she was fit, but this…

Suddenly the stupid blue photo shoot dress, the dreadful pictures from her school formal, and a hundred other tiny humiliations throughout her youth were shown for what they were: irrelevant.

Amazing. Never thought I could look so good.

Rin's message shot back.

Why not?

Steph gazed at the photos again and then at a fourth one Rin had sent through. It showed Steph prone on the bench, bare legs braced, elbows bent as she drew the weight slowly and smoothly all the way down to her chest. Sweat was glistening across her bare belly and the tops of her breasts. Her lips were pursed as she exhaled.

Damn. Rin's words repeated inside her head: *Why not?*

Why wouldn't that woman sipping cocktails on her sun lounge pause to take a second look? Why wouldn't she study the contours of Steph's body, the fruits of such hard and dedicated training, and admire the determination on Steph's face? Why wouldn't she run the fingers of her free hand over one bare thigh as she examined the picture, gliding upward until she reached the seam of her shorts, now warmer and damper than usual?

Like Steph was doing now…

Steph slipped her fingers beneath the cotton to stroke the tender flesh at the very top of her thigh, tracing light circles with her middle finger while her thumb kept bumping against her clit. She was swollen and sensitised down there, tingling already.

Her phone flashed again.

And as for this…

Not many women could manage to do pull-ups on the gym's thick door frame, so when Rin had challenged her, how could Steph resist? The photo, taken from below, showed her round, firm arse at an angle she'd never seen before.

"Jesus…" The picture on Steph's phone did battle with the image in her head, of that horny rich woman now ogling this particular photo before sliding one hand, with its ruby-red nails and diamond rings, down beneath the waistband of her tight, white shorts. To soothe the need that throbbed below…

Steph's black cotton panties were shockingly wet. Had she really done that to herself so easily? Through the material, she gave her clit a tentative rub, then gasped at the intensity of her body's pleasure. Unable to wait, she lifted the elastic at her hips and thrust her hand inside.

She dug her first two fingers into her fleshy outer lips, massaging them slowly up and down before pausing to give her hair several firm, quick tugs, just the way she liked it.

Her body responded with a rush of heat that lifted her hips off the couch. She glanced back at her phone, swiping through the pics with her free hand, lingering over the startling beauty of her own face, of her almost-naked body. *Fuck, yes.* She slipped her fingers lower, between her more delicate and frilled inner lips. They were dripping.

Her phone sounded, startling her. Rin again.

You've gone quiet. Having fun?

Steph breathed out hard. How did she know? Or were the pictures really so hot that any woman might do the same? She imagined that haughty middle-aged woman again on her pool lounge, her drink now forgotten beside her. Imagined her licking her painted lips as she breathed faster over Steph's pictures, pausing to finger her nipples through her tight pink top, her hips jolting, her right hand busy between her elegant thighs.

Except now that woman was starting to look like Rin.

The phone wobbled in Steph's hand.

Mind your own business.

She yanked her shorts and underwear down her legs, parted her thighs, and slid a single questing finger up inside.

As if testing her strength against yet another weight, she breathed out slowly while the protective muscles clenched then relaxed to permit her entry. Damn, it felt so good: the roughness, the sponginess, and then her body's firm grip giving way to a hot, delicious friction.

Behind her closed eyes, the sexy socialite definitely looked like Rin now. And although Steph had resented Rin's orders that morning, now the two photo shoots merged in her head, and Steph imagined herself back at the gym, sweat pouring down her and Rin's voice snapping at her: *Harder! More weight! Get up, you're not done yet! Show me what you're made of!*

Her hand pushed and pumped, and she angled her finger upward to hit that sweet spot. Hot pulses of pleasure were reverberating down the backs of her thighs. Her phone flashed again. *Damnit,* she was almost—

Oh, really? So you won't want these, then?

Steph's eyes widened. She'd almost forgotten the outdoor session in the gym's battered old basketball court. The sight of herself in her element, spinning a ball on the tip of one finger to show off, was amazing. Rin had faded the background into a blur of concrete and metal, but every detail of Steph's figure was crystal clear: her joyful grin, the muscles standing out like ropes in her lean thighs, the silver butterfly stud in her left ear. In one picture, her powerful frame was crouched over the ball as she travelled it fast down the court; in another, Rin had captured Steph's figure in flight, both feet off the ground, one long arm stretched all the way to the hoop. God. She was magnificent.

Left-handed, she texted back.

Hell yes, I want them. Incredible.

It was as if Rin had already had her finger poised over the *send* button.

I could do better. Next time I'll go with an Olympian theme. You as the champion, naked in a laurel wreath. Spears and arrows and discus shots. Show off those guns properly. Would you do it?

Steph felt her face crack into a smile. She couldn't believe Rin was being so flirty, or that she was loving it so much. Slowly, she withdrew her slippery finger and strummed the very tip of her clit until it shot sparks right through her.

She texted back.

Naked? Sure you could handle that?

Then she jammed her hips back into the cushions, wriggled her finger inside again, and stepped up the pace, working her pleasure spot until her body was one great raging fire below the waist.

Handle it? Honey, I've already got an ideas board worked up. Maybe a lion skin like Hercules to wear over your shoulders. And young maidens to feed you grapes and rub olive oil into that exquisite body of yours.

Steph's thumb was slipping over every word.

I can see why you've got a bad reputation.

Thank God for predictive text. The base of her hand was hammering against her outer lips, pounding her clit until her whole body sang.

She wondered what Rin was doing right now. Did she have her pants unzipped? Was she naked, even—panting and sighing as she played with herself too? Or was she sitting in some cool rooftop bar, surrounded by musicians and TV stars, calmly sipping a vodka and soda as she teased Steph into madness?

Her next message arrived so fast Steph wondered if she'd been thinking this over in advance.

Or maybe we could go with a wrestling theme? Would you like that? You and some other Amazon tangled up in the sand, naked and oiled up, fighting for glory?

Fuck! Steph groaned out loud. She could picture it, all right—maybe Jill, the short, stocky tough girl on their team, the one with the crew cut, who had to tape over her nipple bars before each game. Steph imagined the two of them puffing and grappling each other for some magazine centrefold, limbs entangling and breasts flattening as they rolled over and over, their fingers clawing into tanned skin. And Rin behind the camera, barking out instructions: "*Grab tighter! Hold her there! That's it, grind that beautiful ass! Jesus, you know what you look like?*"

Steph's orgasm rang in her ears like a goddamned siren. Her muscles were quaking as juices slid down her fingers into the hot, strong palm of her hand.

Weakly, she turned her head to glance at her phone. It had gone quiet again, the screen now a small, black mirror. Then it flashed one more time with a final message from Rin: a single cross. A kiss, maybe, or an *X* to mark the spot.

A month later, an advance copy of the magazine arrived in the mail. As Steph opened the envelope, a letter fell out; it was written in fountain pen on marbled green paper. She hadn't known anyone still sent letters. Was neat handwriting the new punk?

You'll enjoy these, the letter said. (Trust Rin not to bother with question marks or "I hope".) *And thanks. You're a star.*

Steph's fingers itched to flick straight to the pictures, but she wanted to hear from Rin first, from the woman who'd pissed her off, then amazed her, then made her come, all without touching her—except for that one tender brush of her hair.

I'm staying at Women's Life *for now,* Rin wrote. *I figure it's more fun shaking up suburban moms than arguing with twelve-year-old hipster man-babies at the "edgy" publications. And hey, the editor liked your spread. She wants me to do something similar next month with the winner of that fuck-awful reality show* Mile High Club! *See what you've gotten me into?*

Grinning, Steph put down the letter and picked up the magazine. She flicked past famous faces, makeover tips, and psychic advice columns until she saw her own face glowering back at her.

Yes, Rin had kept the dress shots in there. Using some mix of software and imagination, she'd made those original photographs appear to be inside ornate brass frames like something in an art gallery. There was Steph in her blue sparkles, climbing those rickety stairs, looking down in trepidation, slumped miserably against the graffiti-ed wall. But the framed pictures were hung up behind the newer images of Steph pounding away on the treadmill or dribbling the ball expertly between her own legs. The dress pictures became a backdrop to Steph's present-day workout.

Oh, and Rin was good. The pics she'd sent to Steph's phone had been striking enough, but now on a full-sized page, every detail stood out: Steph's smooth, short nails as she grasped the dumbbell, the liquid glinting in the hollow of her throat, and the tension in her body as she held the muddy hem of the blue dress away from her ankles.

One page showed a framed picture of Steph taken through the chain-link fence of the factory yard, tugging glumly at one powder-blue shoulder strap and staring down at her cold, sequined feet. The picture hung on a darkened wall, and beside it, on the door frame, the new Steph was hauling herself into a chin-up. Her back was to the camera, the muscles rolling across her shoulders, her butt high and tight.

Steph traced the page with her fingertips and shook her head. How did Rin do it—see things that other people didn't? And then show them to you so plainly that you couldn't believe you hadn't noticed all along?

And funnily, the dress pictures didn't look so bad. They were grungy and mournful, but not ugly like she'd imagined. And basically harmless, now that they'd been contained in a frame and put in their place.

She turned Rin's letter over.

And, babe, you were right again: my job isn't that important—but neither's yours. Don't make too many more of those sacrifices, okay?

Steph traced one finger over Rin's spidery handwriting. Here was a woman who was not afraid to fail and who made no apologies for who she was. And who could persuade people to see things differently, the way she did. Could Steph do the same?

If you ever feel like giving an interview here at the magazine—something a little more revelatory, yeah? I could swing it with the editor.

A smile played across Steph's lips as she lingered over Rin's final words.

It'd be my absolute fucking pleasure to take your picture again.

EPHEMERA

NADINE FORRESTER WRENCHED OPEN THE front door with a Stanley knife in one hand. A paintbrush was in the other, and she had a murderous look on her face.

"What the bloody hell do you want?"

Bethany jumped. That face... It was so familiar, from coffee table books, documentaries, and the Arts and Lifestyle. But to see it translated into real life was disorienting.

The woman had a ragged mane of dark red curls, their colour maybe no longer natural, held back by a white scarf. Her face—which had once inspired painters, sculptors, designers of album covers, and, rumour had it, at least one Rolling Stone—nowadays was like a medieval castle ravaged by the weather: roughened, stark, a little sunken in places. But its beautiful contours and fierce angles were more striking than ever.

Bethany swallowed, aware of a dryness in her throat. She'd been an art student before she got into media studies (the only career aspiration, she now realised, that paid even worse), and back in her university days, Nadine Forrester had been one of her idols. Bethany had once written six thousand words on how Nadine had redefined Australian art, and she had even petitioned the university to buy one of Nadine's early works to hang in their great hall.

But she hadn't imagined her idol looking so thoroughly pissed off to meet her.

Nadine's loose peasant blouse hung down over a long Indian skirt, and her hands were speckled with dried paint. Her only make-up was a vivid slash of lipstick, fire-engine red. Right now, those lips pressed together in suspicion.

"I'm Bethany Willis from the *Herald.* We spoke on the phone..."

"Oh, Christ, the bloody journo." Nadine slumped. "Was that today?"

"Thursday at one." Bethany smiled, hoping for reciprocation. She got a grimace instead.

"Hey, kid, sorry and everything, but I'm in the middle of something here. I don't suppose you could come by tomorrow?"

"Um, no. My deadline's tonight." Bethany wriggled in discomfort, but, seriously, come on. She might be a fan, but she wasn't a pushover. She had driven two hours to this town, full of tree changers and pot-smoking retirees, then spent another twenty minutes searching for Nadine's unnumbered property, not to mention ruining her tyres and shoes on the muddy, potholed track. She'd rung the doorbell for a small eternity before getting a response. Admittedly, it had been almost fun, like being a proper old-fashioned reporter for once. But still, there was no way she was going to do it all again tomorrow. Not even for Nadine Forrester.

She tried for a positive tone: "And our readers will be really excited to read about that new exhibition you've got coming up. Your agent made it sound so interesting..."

"Her." Nadine rolled her eyes. "She'd sell my toenail clippings in the gift shop if I'd let her." The older woman extended the pause an unnaturally long time, clearly hoping Bethany would be polite and uncomfortable enough to give in and leave.

The wind chimes by the door rippled. A breeze rattled the boughs of the gum trees. Somewhere nearby a magpie sang.

"Oh well," Nadine huffed at last. "Suppose it'd be quicker to talk to you now than listen to her marketing bullshit scolding later. But this isn't convenient."

She swung around and strode off down the corridor, leaving Bethany to close the front door behind them.

Oh wow. Nadine's house was love at first sight: There were polished timber floorboards, sloping beams of red gum, and stone fireplaces in every room. Books and tapestries lined the walls, and huge skylights bathed the rooms in sunshine and drew her eyes upwards to a flawless blue sky. Bethany was starting to have doubts about the house's owner, though.

Glancing around the walls, Bethany noticed how many images of Nadine's own face surrounded her: on psychedelic vintage posters, on framed covers of underground magazines, in photographs taken with George Harrison and Susan Sontag... The sight made Bethany's eyebrows rise. Who filled their home with pictures of themselves? If someone Bethany's age did that, she would look like a narcissistic nutjob. Mind you, if someone Bethany's age dropped out to do paintings and hitchhike around the world nowadays, most likely she wouldn't end up with a house like this to hang her pictures in.

Nadine paused outside a kitchen crowded with pots of herbs, spice racks, and battered cookbooks. "I suppose you'll want photos?" she grumbled.

"Your workspace would be ideal."

With a shrug, Nadine led her out the back door towards a huge converted shed. She hauled open the door, and Bethany blinked at the chemical aroma of paints, varnish, and cleaning agents, at the intense white light.

The studio was a kaleidoscope of colours: half-finished canvases, squeezed-out tubes of paint, jars of coloured water, old palettes smeared with rainbows. A track of rainforest noises played softly in the corner, echoing the rustle of trees and bird calls from outside.

She'd seen Nadine's works hanging in galleries, but here in their natural habitat, the new paintings were startling, almost unbearably vivid: Lost children with features like goblins peered out from behind the trunks and branches of monstrous ghost gums. Sunflowers grimaced and wailed. Centaurs with the heads and torsos of apes did battle with fish-tailed serpents. Angels with reptile faces looked down upon a collapsing earth. The pictures were passionate, nightmarish, playful.

"They're amazing." Bethany touched a hand to her heart, feeling her chest tighten with wonder.

"Yeah, thanks." Nadine jerked her head, beckoning Bethany over to a threadbare, paint-spattered couch, where they sat down. "So. What do you want to know?"

The interview started well enough. Nadine's upcoming exhibition was titled *Ephemera*, and all its pieces were mortal or fleeting in some way. She led Bethany around her studio and let her photograph some of the items. There was a sand mandala engraved with the birthdates of Nadine's ancestors, ready for a wave to wash away. Next to it was a hedge cut with unbelievable delicacy into the shape of a Victorian grandfather clock ("Bloody awful idea, you wouldn't believe the maintenance") and a gigantic dandelion, its tufts of pollen crafted from scrunched and lacquered scraps of newspaper ("Reviews of my work going back to 1976"). She even opened a fridge to reveal a small, exquisite statuette of a naked woman studying her breasts. Bethany frowned over the statuette's fleshy, mottled texture before Nadine explained it was made primarily from blue-veined cheese.

Nadine cackled. "And you just know some pretentious wanker is going to buy that and then have to spend a fortune getting the stink out of his carpets!"

Bethany laughed. They'd had an inauspicious introduction, but maybe everything was going to be all right after all. Nadine was certainly generous in describing her methods, from detail brushes and sea sponges to blowtorches and hedge clippers. As she spoke, she stared openly at Bethany, until Bethany felt a blush rising in her cheeks. Most famous people she'd interviewed had ignored her after the first hello, preferring to watch their own reflection in her sunglasses. She had not expected to find herself being scrutinised by Nadine Forrester, of all people.

But when Bethany asked "What would you say is the greatest inspiration behind your work?", she felt the temperature in the studio drop several degrees.

"No idea what you mean."

"Well, for example, some critics see you as the ultimate postmodern artist, while others claim you're subtly critiquing postmodernism."

"I'm not interested in academic jargon," Nadine snapped. All at once, she looked bored and irritable again. "And I'm not 'post' anything. I'm here now, aren't I?"

"Okay..." Bethany tried to relax her shoulders. "But what about this piece, for instance..." She pointed at the grandfather clock. "Why make it out of a hedge? Why do something so difficult, that needs continuous work?"

"Because I knew it would look good." Nadine waved a hand as if to shoo away such silly questions.

"But what were you actually trying to *convey*?"

"Well, if you can't figure that out, one of us doesn't deserve to be here."

"Let's say I can't figure it out." Bethany struggled to stay pleasant. "How would you sum up the message of that piece?"

"Oh, for Christ's sake!" Nadine folded her arms with a huff. "There isn't one, all right? I'm not making bloody adverts!"

"All right. Let me see..." Bethany's hand trembled a little as she flipped through her list of questions. What was Nadine's problem now? Why was she being so mean? Bethany had been really looking forward to today, and now... She recalled some advice a senior journalist had given her: *Never, ever interview your heroes.*

"So, Nadine...were you surprised when your work started to become successful?"

Nadine's green eyes narrowed. "No."

"What are the greatest influences on your art nowadays?"

She pursed her lips and shrugged. "Nowadays? Cookbooks, mostly. And gardening books. Have you ever really looked at those bloody things? No cake, casserole, or flowerbed has ever looked that good in real life. *That* is hyperreality, and their use of colour is bloody superb."

As she glanced down at her notebook, Bethany realised she was longing to smack Nadine with it. To think she had gone into journalism expecting to uncover scandal, corruption, violence, and state secrets—imagining she was going to change the world! Instead, her working days were mostly one disappointment after another: rewording articles from press syndicates, cribbing press releases, scanning social media for ready-made quotes, and babysitting obnoxious minor celebrities. And it looked like the great Nadine Forrester was just another one of those after all.

Bethany cleared her throat. "So, Nadine, over the years you've become well-known not only for your art but also for the struggles of your personal life. You've battled with drug addiction, been married and divorced four times, and never settled anywhere for long. Your son has gone on record describing you as a distant and difficult mother." Bethany looked up. "Do you ever feel the cost of art is too high?"

"Is this you getting ready with your opening paragraph?" Nadine crossed her arms. "'Despite being a tragic, unnatural failure of a woman, Forrester still managed to do one or two paintings that a couple of men thought were all right'?"

"That wasn't what I meant."

"Please." Nadine snorted. "If a woman had painted the Sistine bloody Chapel, some newspaper would have printed an interview with her childhood pet rabbit whining that she didn't chop his carrots up properly."

"People are interested in personal stories." Bethany was starting to get very sick of Nadine's complaining. "Art isn't made by machines, is it? People want to know the real you."

Nadine stared, then flung an arm behind her that took in the entire studio with a wild sweep. "This is the real me." She fixed Bethany with a glare that was contemptuous but also strangely urgent. "Think about it—I could have worked in a supermarket all my life and still been a drunken old slag who screamed at her family and smoked in bed. You wouldn't have written a bloody article about me then, would you? It's my creations you should pay attention to. It's the fact that I bloody made them at all."

"But you won't explain to me what you mean with them." Bethany's own voice was rising in frustration.

"No one can 'explain' them! You have to experience them." Nadine leapt to her feet and began pacing the room.

"Why are you so resistant to being written about?" Feeling very bold, Bethany added, "Are you really worried I'll get something wrong, or that I'll get something right?"

"I know exactly what you'll write: the same bland, clichéd, name-dropping bullshit you lot have been churning out about me for the last thirty-odd years! Let me guess: I'm an ambitious bitch who's taken over the art world, or a tragic junkie who couldn't keep a man? Or a sell-out or a schizophrenic or a bad mother or a jumped-up groupie who should have stuck to doing lines with Fleetwood Mac?" Nadine smacked the edge of the table. "Well, go on, then! If you're going to write that stuff, why can't you get that sulky look off your face, get on with it, and stop asking me questions you don't really want answers to?"

Bethany stood up. "I've had enough of this." Her cheeks were hot, and her fingers clamped tight around her pen. "If I'm sulking, it's because I asked for this job and I hoped you would turn out to be really awesome. You're not. And because this time next year, the newspaper I work for will have laid off all its staff except the advertisers. And knowing my luck, I'll end up working in a gift shop somewhere, selling novelty mugs with your horrible orange-tattooed-pig-giving-birth painting on them!"

Nadine stared. For a long time. Then she burst out laughing.

"It'll be snow domes, actually. Jesus, you should see the mock-ups." She turned away and lit a cigarette, her shoulders still shaking. "Bloody repulsive. My agent says they'll be 'ironic'. Don't get me wrong, I love tacky souvenirs, but I'm not sure the world is ready for that." She looked back, a smile lingering on her painted lips.

For a moment, Bethany made a point of glowering, then allowed herself a small half-smile in return.

With her eyes closed, Nadine took a deep drag on her cigarette. She seemed to be relishing the rush. For a moment, Bethany could see the girl she'd once been, running wild in Chelsea and New York, scratching out her first crazy, obscene, revolutionary paintings.

Then Nadine opened her eyes and looked Bethany up and down. "Well, far be it from me to stop a young woman making her way. Tell you what, I'll do you a deal: I'll answer any questions you like. Although if you're thinking of asking more about my working 'process', I warn you, it's not that interesting. One per cent inspiration, ninety-nine per cent caffeine and home-grown botanicals."

"And?" Bethany's voice was wary.

"And in return, you can help me with a new piece."

"Um—okay." Bethany's lips parted in surprise. "But I'm not sure how helpful I'll be..."

"Oh, you'll be perfect."

Something in that expression sent a funny little shiver running down Bethany's spine, and then another as Nadine stepped closer.

"Right now, I'm fascinated by change. The passing of time, the things that vanish, and the little scraps that we're left with. There's so much we don't know about people who lived a hundred years ago when a handful of photographs and some medals stood in for a person's whole life. Nowadays we've gone in the opposite direction, haven't we? We're busy burying ourselves under mountains of crappy possessions, and every moment of our lives gets documented—usually in some format which will be obsolete in ten years' time." Frowning, Nadine sucked on her cigarette, then released a slow plume of silvery smoke. "What will be left of us, do you reckon?"

Nadine's voice sounded thoughtful now, her face alight with so much energy it was hard to believe this was the same woman who had grumped and snapped her way through their interview a minute ago. Was this the Nadine who had created these artworks?

"I've used materials and images here that are temporary," Nadine went on. "But *real.* Tangible. Sensory, you know?"

"And by making them into art, you make them last forever," Bethany said.

Nadine raised an eyebrow. "You flatter me, love. But there's one material I haven't explored in this collection." She reached out to run her thumb along Bethany's hairline, tracing the precise shape of Bethany's bun with a nearly inaudible sigh.

As Bethany's eyelids fluttered closed, she breathed in, inhaling the sharp, acrid scent of Nadine's cigarette smoke drifting around her.

"The human body," said Nadine, "would be a real challenge."

Bethany's eyes flew open. "Um…"

"You have the most bloody exquisite skin, you know that?" Nadine was staring at Bethany's face and throat now with an intensity that Bethany found both embarrassing and exciting. "Flawless. Like white magnolia petals. Will you let me paint you?"

The suggestion made Bethany stutter. "You—you want to paint my portrait?"

"No." Nadine took another drag on her cigarette, then stubbed it out. "I want to paint *you.*" Abruptly, she reached out, grasped Bethany's shoulders in surprisingly strong hands, and turned Bethany around.

Bethany wondered if she should protest, but the words died on her lips. Nadine ran her hands over Bethany's shoulders and down her sides, stretching her thin blouse tightly against her, tracing Bethany's ribcage and the ridge of her spine. The process felt intrusive yet impersonal—an artist sizing up a new set of materials.

Was that an insult? But Bethany found herself submitting to Nadine's touch, intensely aware of the warm pressure of each individual fingertip.

"Yes," Nadine said. "Pity you're so petite, but this area would do. Then a photograph to go in my exhibition."

"What?" Bethany's voice came out breathless and squeaky. Nadine's hands were at her waist now, kneading the soft flesh there before tugging Bethany's blouse free from her waistband. Nadine's fingers crept beneath the fabric to probe speculatively over tender skin, sending a current of sensation rippling across Bethany's body.

It was all almost too much. But Nadine gave her most winning smile, one that had captivated people much older and more jaded than Bethany.

"Come on. I told you: you have to *experience* my work. And this would make a hell of a novelty angle for your story..."

"Well..." Suddenly Bethany's clothing felt too tight, too hot. Her palms grew slick; her pulse quickened. She startled herself with her own reply.

"Okay."

Nadine seemed to have forgotten their argument entirely. She was already in her element, rifling through her materials, looking for the right brushes, the best colours. A smile hovered on her lips, and the vivid studio light picked out the golden highlights in her deep red hair. She hummed softly.

Bethany hesitated. How had she ended up agreeing to this? But the thought of getting so close to the art of Nadine Forrester was hard to resist. So was the lingering memory of Nadine's hands on her body.

Nadine called over her shoulder, "Take your shirt off and get comfortable."

Comfortable was not the word Bethany would have used. But when Nadine did not look back, she began unbuttoning her blouse.

"Let me try something." Nadine strode over to hold her palette up against Bethany's skin. Shoulders, arms, and belly were bare now, and Bethany's breasts were hoisted up by a strawberry-pink lace bra. She wondered if Nadine would make some sarcastic comment about the colour or the style—or the way it pushed her plump, tender flesh together and forwards. But Nadine was focused on her paints. When she glanced back at Bethany's exposed skin, it was as if Bethany were just another canvas.

"Hmm, a hint more peach..." She hurried away.

"What are you going to paint?" Bethany wrapped her arms across her chest. Her fingers skimmed all the way up her body, leaving a tingling trail of goosebumps.

"Something exquisite." Nadine winked. "Go ahead, lie down on your stomach."

Moving gingerly, Bethany did as she was told, feeling the sun-warmed couch cushions beneath her naked torso. Her chin came to rest on her folded arms. From this angle, she had a clear view of a small side table ahead and to the right of her with scattered artist's tools—a spatula, a paint-spattered rag, various brushes. Beyond the table, she also had a perfect view out into Nadine's garden.

That garden had been featured in so many magazines, it was a minor celebrity in its own right. Rocky paths lined with ferns wound their way through an artificial bushland of Chinese lanterns, bright, spiny banksia, and fragrant gardenia. A spray of palm trees was visible above the shrubbery, and looming over everything else was a mighty Moreton Bay fig, its oval leaves dark and glossy, its spilled fruit casting seeds across the ground between its snaking roots. Its bark made Bethany think of dinosaur hide.

"What a place," said Bethany.

"It was a junkyard when I bought it," Nadine said. "Nothing but old tires and acres of lantana and weeds. It took years of work to get it looking so natural. In some ways, I think it's my best piece of all. In my spare time, I'm painting views of my garden."

She tapped a canvas on an easel just to the right of the side table. It was half-completed and depicted a spray of white Christmas lilies. Nadine said, "I can't seem to get the finish right, though. The gloss of the petals, that pollen dustiness… I need something to make them glisten the way they do in the sunlight. It's bloody frustrating. And I'd hoped to feature it in this exhibition."

She laid out her materials on the table, then sat down sideways on the couch beside her subject. Bethany sensed the solid shape of Nadine's thigh against her hip and turned to her side, where she could just catch a glimpse of her in her peripheral vision. After a moment, she turned forward again and felt a gentle scrape and tickle at the base of her skull: Nadine was brushing a few fine, loose hairs to one side, tucking them back up into her bun. She rested her hand around the back of Bethany's neck. The warm pressure made it impossible for Bethany to think of anything else.

Ghosting her hand down Bethany's spine, Nadine said, "It's funny, you know. For years, I resisted doing any kind of natural paintings. Flowers, especially. Afraid of being a clichéd woman artist, I suppose, all still lifes and pretty pictures. I wanted so badly to be daring and edgy." She paused, and Bethany felt a pinch between her shoulder blades, then a sudden release of compressed flesh. Nadine had unhooked her bra and was gently spreading the fabric away from Bethany's skin. "Silly, wasn't I?" Nadine murmured. "After all, what's a flower, when you think about it? Just a set of hungry, hermaphroditic genitals."

"You must be fun on Valentine's Day," Bethany managed to say.

Nadine was rubbing the balls of her thumbs across Bethany's ribcage and over her shoulders with little circular caresses. It occurred to Bethany that Nadine must mean to remove the strap-marks from her new favourite surface. Her touch—appreciative yet detached and purposeful—was more intriguing than Bethany wanted to admit. The massaging fingertips slid around Bethany's ribcage, brushing the edges of her breasts. The new and sudden intimacy made Bethany quiver.

"You'll have to stay still if you want this painting to turn out well," Nadine chided her.

"It tickles." Bethany's breath caught in her throat.

"It's going to tickle a lot more." Bethany saw hands picking up an angular flat brush and dipping it in a deep charcoal colour. "It's going to feel wet and cool and slippery at first, and then it will grow sticky and dry and pull at your skin. It'll take discipline, I can tell you that. After a while, you'll be desperate to sit up, wriggle around, scratch whatever itches—it'll drive you absolutely mad—but you can't do it, all right? Not until I say so. Sure you're up for it?"

Bethany sensed she was being mocked, and she pouted in response. "Of course. Just pass me my phone, will you? If we're going to talk for real this time, I'd better hit record."

Once she'd sorted it out, Nadine said, "Ready now?"

When Bethany nodded, she pressed her left hand between Bethany's shoulder blades, pushing down hard to hold her subject in place. Bethany stifled a gasp as the cold tip of the paintbrush licked a slow trail all the way up her spine.

"I'm painting you a plum blossom." Nadine's voice sounded above her. The tone, so abrasive and impatient before, now was slow, lulling. "I have the most beautiful one growing right in the middle of my sculpture garden here. She's my queen."

The brush moved over Bethany's flesh with painstaking care. Nadine was sketching the trunk of the tree, Bethany guessed, with firm sweeps of the brush up and down Bethany's backbone. The cold, slick pressure sliding along that sensitive ridge made Bethany twitch, her back arching against the deft strokes.

"Bloody hell. Hold still, will you?" But Nadine sounded amused as she leaned more of her weight on her left hand. Pinned on her stomach, Bethany struggled to maintain any kind of composure.

"Don't worry about the ingredients, by the way," Nadine added. The brush slithered outward, following the grooves of Bethany's ribs and leaving a fresh trail of gooseflesh in its wake. Nadine must be starting on the tree's branches. "They're body paints. Non-toxic. Most of the ingredients are edible, actually, although I've never had a reason to sample them."

Bethany imagined Nadine's crooked grin.

Shit, she was supposed to be interviewing Nadine about her work. "How important are the ingredients of your art to you?" she managed to ask. But it came out unsteady.

"Extremely," Nadine replied. "I make my work materials from scratch wherever possible. I've even been experimenting with paintbrushes made from my own hair." She plucked a small mop brush from her collection and twitched it in front of Bethany's face, letting her glimpse the dark red filaments trimmed neatly into shape. Then she brushed the soft plume once against Bethany's cheek. "It's about being in touch with the source of what you're creating. Putting your own stamp on things."

The strokes of the brush now moved in an easy rhythm across her back: fleshy swoops and dexterous little flicks which tapered off at the end. A breeze passed over her painted skin, and she felt the shape of Nadine's creation stand out with crisp precision: the wet trails of the tree trunk and branches now snaked out from her shoulders down to her waist. The drying paint prickled, and she breathed deeply to control the urge to thrash around, determined to prove she wasn't the trifling brat Nadine seemed to think she was.

"How's it looking?"

"Excellent, of course." Nadine selected a thin dagger brush and swirled it in reddish purple, which Bethany guessed was for the leaves. Each miniature oval-shaped stroke made Bethany tense with surprise. Such meticulous concentration focused on such tiny patches of her skin—it sensitised her almost unbearably. Her whole body kept contracting into the places the brush touched, her attention focused down to the level of each pore, each fine, trembling hair.

"You've gone quiet," Nadine teased. "Isn't there anything else you'd like to ask me?"

It was all Bethany could do to think of a single question. She knew she would not enjoy listening to her own recording later; her voice sounded distracted, stammering, and breathy by turns as the moist point of Nadine's brush teased her skin.

"A retrospective of your work was showcased at the National Gallery last year," Bethany said with some effort. "Was that a significant moment for you?"

"Galleries!" Nadine laid the dagger brush aside and picked up a pointed round brush. From her delicate dabbing and intricate swirls, it had to be the blossoms now. "Bloody funeral homes, the lot of them. People creeping around, too scared to crack a smile, let alone talk to anyone. Why do they do that? It's not like the paintings get offended." She sighed. "We started out so rock-and-roll, you know? We were going to transform all that elitist art world bollocks. Whatever happened to those old days, eh?"

"You really hate galleries?" The tip of Nadine's brush traced a figure of eight across the sensitive spot on the back of her neck, forcing her to stifle a squeal. Out the corner of her eye, she saw Nadine dip the brush in a darker shade of ruby. She jumped, though, as Nadine began to peck the brush against her skin over and over: dozens of wet, hard spots, like the first spatter of a thunderstorm.

"Well, I quite like the gift shops," Nadine conceded. "Tasteless as can be, of course; they may as well sell Picasso garden gnomes. But what the hell—people have fun in there. They chat and handle things, and they're not afraid to single out stuff they actually love, even if it is on a postcard or an apron." She took a step back. Despite Nadine's flippant words, despite her angle, Bethany felt the intensity of the artist's gaze bearing down on her.

"How is it looking now?" Bethany tried to keep the nervousness out of her voice. The paint lay across her skin in thick, creamy layers.

"Halfway there," said Nadine. "You want a peek?" Without permission, she fished around in Bethany's handbag until she found a compact mirror, which she handed her before crossing the room and returning with a larger mirror that she held up from behind. Bethany peered into the glass and saw her own eyes widen.

Her back had been transformed. It was not so much a tree as the *feeling* of a tree: a trunk like a black, gnarled wrist plunging up out of the earth, its long witch's fingers unfurling. And spilling out of it to float in the air were dozens of gossamer flowers, their ivory petals streaked with pink, punctured with bulbous stamens in a rich, dark shade of plum.

"It's beautiful."

"Oh, we're not done yet. But let me get a work-in-progress shot." Her phone was plucked unceremoniously from underneath her elbow, and Bethany heard Nadine stepping around the couch, lining up photographs. "Now…time for part two."

"What's part two?" Bethany frowned. The tree had looked perfect to her, and there was little room left on her back for anything else.

Then she gave a squeak of alarm as Nadine's fingers skated along the waistband of her skirt until they found the fastening. There was a rough metallic purr as her zipper gave way, then the warm invasion of Nadine's hands underneath the fabric, coaxing it down over her hips. "What are you *doing*?"

"Don't you dare move." Nadine's voice was stern again. "That paint's not dry yet, and if you let it drip or smudge, I'll never forgive you."

"But what—" To her own surprise, though, Bethany remained still. It seemed vital not to disturb the artwork—and not to send Nadine away.

"I told you," said Nadine. "I'm finishing the painting."

Oh, and now her skirt's silky lining and sturdy woollen waistband were gliding down to her calves. The intense sunlight of the studio settled across her bare thighs and warmed them deliciously. She hadn't forgotten how annoyed Nadine's rudeness earlier had made her, but she couldn't deny her fascination with this painting. And she couldn't help feeling pleased that she'd worn her new black underwear, its lycra-blend fabric and lace edging framing her arse and holding it in a tight, pert shape.

Without a word, Nadine ran both hands up Bethany's thighs and underneath the lace, cupping her cheeks. Her palms, roughened here and there with dried paint, radiated heat onto Bethany's bare skin. Then, with extreme care, she worked the knickers down.

"What are you—" Bethany couldn't finish; she was afraid of the excitement in her own voice. The paint across her back was drying into a stiff, taut surface, forcing her to stay still for fear of cracking it. Everything against her nearly naked body felt hypersensitised now: the threadbare cushions beneath her stomach, the loose, satiny fabric of her unfastened bra, the scratch of its lace trim, the pressure of the underwire. Her own weight was pushing her nipples back into her flattened breasts, but even in this constricted position, she could feel them growing hard and tight.

Nadine rolled Bethany's knickers down to her knees, then stepped back. "Well." She made a thrumming sound of unmistakeable satisfaction deep in her throat. "What a pretty surface to work on."

In the mirror, Bethany saw her select a fresh comb brush. *For the grass*, she thought as its shaggy, layered plume began to whisk back and forth over the tops of her buttocks.

"Don't act so surprised," Nadine said. "Don't you know that half of every tree lives underground?"

The arousal that had awoken across Bethany's body during the first half of Nadine's painting session had now concentrated itself in her swollen clit. The tiny muscles twitched, pulsing, desperate to be touched. Her body tensed even as she tried to lie quietly, afraid that a wriggle of her hips would betray the state she was in.

"No need to come over all shy, dear." Nadine replaced the comb brush and selected a fresh one with a pointed round tip that she twisted with sensual relish in a small blob of dark brown paint. "Didn't you have other questions?"

"Um..." A very thin, ice-cold streak—an electric thrill from the small of her back across her right buttock—made Bethany jolt. Was it a root of the tree?

"Do I have to sit on your legs?" Nadine slapped her bare calf. "Keep still. Precision is just as important for the subterranean depths."

"I meant to ask..." Bethany gulped, trying to focus. "As an artist, do you have any regrets?"

"Trying to make me out to be a failure again, Bethany?" Nadine mocked, sending a new line zigzagging its way down Bethany's bare backside. Bethany yelped, then stiffened, struggling to hold her position.

"No, I'm just—curious."

"Curious, eh?" The brush pushed harder this time as Nadine trailed it to the top of Bethany's thigh.

"That...that feels like quite a root system there."

"Of course. What's hidden underneath can be as big and complicated as what's above the surface..."

Nadine started on another line. Then she returned in a calm voice to Bethany's question. "Regrets? Yeah. Not sleeping with Elton John back when I had the chance. That would have made a great story for dinner parties." Her deep smoker's chuckle seemed to reverberate all the way along the brush to the inside of Bethany's thigh, where the tip of a tree root was being inscribed.

"How is it, um, looking?" Bethany's breathing had grown utterly shallow. Whether it was the relentless caress of the brush, the slick, cool paint gradually warming across her bare bottom, or just the knowledge that she was lying here letting the idol of her student days do this to her—whatever this was—Bethany was becoming turned on to an embarrassing level. It was all she could do not to grind her hips into the couch.

Did Nadine mean to do that to her? Or was she just amusing herself, seeing how much indignity Bethany would put up with for a picture and a story? Bethany dug her nails into her palms. Hell, maybe Nadine really did just like painting on an unusual surface. Maybe Bethany was imagining things.

But she didn't imagine the trail of the brush's wet tip, like a melting icicle, trickling right down into the tender cleft between her buttocks. "Oh!" Bethany gasped and reared back, but Nadine swooped down to push Bethany's shoulders against the couch once more.

"Shh, lie still. It's going to look stunning. It's the source of the tree."

Bethany breathed hard. Lifting her gaze to the mirror, she saw Nadine's tall figure above her, one knee thrown over Bethany's hip, the brush poised in mid-air. She wore an expression of ruthless intensity.

"I—I don't know." Bethany's voice came out husky.

Nadine smiled. "It'll be easy, darling. And when I'm finished, it'll be an absolute bloody masterpiece." She licked the tip of the brush, coaxing it into a sharper point. "*You* will be an absolute bloody masterpiece."

Bethany swallowed. Where would that brush go next? "Okay."

"That's the spirit." Nadine transferred her attentions back to Bethany's decorated flesh. "Now, to prevent smudging..." She slipped the digits of her left hand up between Bethany's thighs. Then, slowly and taking great care not to touch the paint, she opened her fingers, spreading Bethany's buttocks and revealing—*oh God*—everything.

Bethany fought not to cry out with embarrassment at how wet she must be. By now, Nadine must be able to see and smell the proof.

"Well." That gravelly chuckle again. "Always nice to meet a genuine fan."

Before Bethany's inhibitions could overcome her, Nadine got to work, extending the dark, winding streaks of paint towards Bethany's most intimate self, snaking in from all directions to tangle and merge into her pubic hair. The brush was moving quickly now, stroke after stroke—it was circling her asshole, teasing her perineum. Bethany pressed the back of her hand to her mouth, trying not to moan out loud. She could feel Nadine's fingers pressing hard into her flesh to keep her open, grappling for purchase as Bethany's wetness escaped her lips and trickled down.

"Oh, control yourself, will you?" Nadine scolded. "You'll wreck the paint!" With a growl of annoyance, the artist dipped her head and blew hard between Bethany's thighs.

If this was an attempt to dry things out, it had the opposite effect.

Three more swift strokes of the brush and Nadine declared, "There—that's done." She laid the brush down, her left hand still extended between Bethany's cheeks. "We'll just let that settle, and it'll be fabulous. Geez, my hand's cramping, though."

Her voice was as laconic as ever, and Bethany ground her teeth at this mockery. Her clit was throbbing, attuned to every "accidental" bump of Nadine's fingers.

"Ah, this'll do." There was the sound of Nadine reaching over to snatch up something. "You don't mind if I borrow this, do you?"

Before Bethany could answer, the object was slipped up between Bethany's thighs and wedged there to hold them apart as Nadine's masterpiece dried.

Her reporter's notebook.

"May as well get a few more pics for your article while we're waiting." There was a soft, repeated clicking as shoulders, back, and arse were photographed from many angles with Bethany's phone. "Perfect, darling. Can't wait to see these in print."

"I might not print them all." The hard edges of the notebook were biting into her inner thighs. What was between them felt alarmingly exposed to the camera's eye.

"Oh, you might change your mind. They look spectacular." Bethany looked back: Nadine was lining up a final shot. She then replaced Bethany's phone by her head. "Now, I might sneak in some work on my Christmas lilies piece while we're letting your paint dry." She paused. "You might be able to help me with that, actually."

"Help you? With what?" Nadine was choosing a fresh mop brush. It was the kind used for large washes, and its rounded head was soft and clean. There was something odd about it... She realised it was the brush she'd been shown earlier, the one made from Nadine's own hair.

"You can help with the patina," Nadine said. "I told you, I've been struggling to find the right mix of polleny texture and deep gloss for the petals. But maybe..."

Bethany cried out loud as Nadine slipped the fuzzy head of the brush right up between Bethany's inner lips. It swirled in a slow circle, gathering up the wetness there.

"Oh, you can't..." Bethany's words faded into a groan of disappointment as the brush withdrew. Nadine began to apply the brush to the canvas, coating the painted petals with Bethany's juices.

"Don't worry, I won't disturb your artwork. I know how to handle my own creations." Nadine must have been satisfied with the effect, because she dipped the brush into its source again, making Bethany draw in another startled breath.

"Lovely," Nadine murmured, spinning back to the canvas. "This speaks to my theme of transience and permanence, by the way. You should make a note of that for your article. Or is your little recording app still running?"

Bethany prayed it wasn't. The thought of listening back to her own murmurs and moans from Nadine flicking the soft, well-coated brush from her aperture all the way up to her straining clit was too much to bear. The strokes continued over and over, now across the canvas, now up and down over Bethany's cunt.

"Transience and permanence," Nadine repeated. "I seek to bring those opposites together in that point when the whole world is put on hold for the sake of a moment's pleasure..." The soaking plumes of the brush rotated around Bethany's clit, and she jerked convulsively. "That ephemeral moment"—Nadine painted the wash of Bethany's arousal across her canvas—"is now preserved forever. Just think of this painting hanging in some gallery with hundreds of people walking past it every day"—she resumed her quest between Bethany's legs—"all debating amongst themselves: 'What did the artist really *mean* by this piece? What was her *message*?'"

"Oh God, I have to..." There was no way Bethany could hold herself still any longer. Her hips surged, lifting off the couch, thrusting backwards towards Nadine's teasing instrument. She was right on the edge.

"Oh, for goodness sake." Nadine yanked the notebook free and tossed it aside. Then she repositioned herself on the couch between Bethany's knees, tugging them as far apart as they would go. She slipped her right hand up to touch Bethany's clit directly at last while her left hand rotated the soft brush head around Bethany's dripping entrance.

The touch of those fingers at long last made Bethany cry out and grip the couch cushions with all her might. Risking another look in the mirror, she saw her own face, taut with the quest for pleasure, while Nadine knelt above her, massaging Bethany's clit in firm, brisk circles.

"Come on, love, don't be stingy now. Give me a little more to work with."

Bethany struggled and sweated, pushing her clit harder against Nadine's dextrous fingers. Every touch sparked off a burst of heat, each one more intense than the last. Bethany was transformed into a mess of incoherent murmurs and helpless little whimpers of pleasure.

"That's it, darling," Nadine muttered. "Give me all you've got. Let me show everyone how exquisite you are...."

Bethany's fingers and toes clawed at the cushions. She felt the paint crackle and split right down the length of her spine as she arched into a desperate, wailing orgasm.

"Mmm," Nadine purred. "Perfect."

Her fingers and brush withdrew at last. She lay dazed on her stomach as Nadine turned away and hummed to herself as she added more layers to her lily painting.

"I—I've damaged the paint." Bethany's voice caught. She raised up the top half of her body and reached behind her with tentative fingers to touch the layers across her back.

"I know you did, you naughty girl." Nadine clicked her tongue. "But, actually, it works. It cracked along the tree trunk, you see, so it gives the bark that extra texture." With one hand, she swatted Bethany's fingers away and then tipped her forward onto her belly again. There were another half a dozen or so final clicks as Nadine took some final, lingering photographs. "All right, you can get dressed now." And with that, Nadine went back to her lilies and her tubes of paint as if nothing unusual had happened at all.

Bethany pulled her clothes back on with shaky fingers. She stared at Nadine, who stood ramrod straight in front of her canvas, puzzling over some detail there with a concentration that shut out everything else. Bethany recalled what it had felt like to be the focus of that attention. Exhilarating—and short-lived.

"What do I do about…this?" Bethany gestured towards her back. It was covered up with her ordinary blouse and skirt now, with no sign of the unique creation underneath.

"It'll clean off easily enough." Nadine shrugged. Then she caught Bethany's look and relented a little. "You've got your photos, darling. You know it was real. It always will be."

Bethany gave her a slow stare, then nodded. When Nadine said nothing more, she picked up her notebook, bag, and phone, and walked towards the exit.

She was opening the door when Nadine called out to her. "Wait a moment."

Nadine selected a detail round brush, the slenderest one in her collection Bethany had yet seen, and dipped it in black pigment. Then she made her slow, sauntering way over to where Bethany stood with one hand still on the door handle.

"Forgot something." Nadine winked. She stepped behind her guest. Then, in one smooth movement, she sank to her knees and yanked up Bethany's skirt.

"What are you—" The words died in Bethany's throat as she felt the point of the brush swirling in a single cursive line up the inside of her thigh. The brush head travelled higher and higher until it nudged the seam of her underwear. Nadine was signing her name.

"There." Nadine blew along the signature until the paint prickled into dryness while Bethany clutched the door frame, her knees wobbling. Then the hem of her skirt hit her thighs again. Nadine straightened up, darted a quick kiss against Bethany's cheek, and pushed her gently out the door.

"Thanks for the interview, Bethany. I've got to admit it was more interesting than I'd expected."

Overwhelmed by a sudden longing, Bethany reached out for Nadine's hand. But Nadine's fingers slipped through hers, leaving only a trace of paint on Bethany's palm, a tiny smear of deep forest-green.

"Now, I know you'll forgive me if I get back to work. I don't have much time, you see..."

Nadine turned in a swirl of loose white clothing and dark red hair. And Bethany, with the artist's signature brushing between her thighs at every step, walked out into the garden and the dazzling sun.

LAST STAND

ESPERANZA WOKE WITH HER HEAD resting on the Colonel's breast. The warmth of her skin through the cotton, the gentle rise and fall, the languorous twist of the Colonel's fingers in her hair might have lulled Esperanza back to sleep. But not today.

She opened her eyes. The Colonel was watching her. Through the arrow-slit window far above them, Esperanza could glimpse the mountain peaks in the distance, blasted with snow, and a condor soaring in search of prey.

The Colonel said, "You should leave. Today. Now, before they come for you."

"No."

Overnight, their bare legs had tangled together, pressing closer with each twitch and slumbering breath. Esperanza's legs were slimmer, shapely, and covered with fine, downy hair; the Colonel's were sturdy and muscular from a lifetime of training and long marches. The Colonel's shaved calf felt smooth and raspy by turns as Esperanza rubbed her foot up and down it.

"Beloved." The Colonel's rich alto voice was hushed; you never knew who might be listening. "For your safety, please, think. Once they take me into that courtroom, I can't help you anymore."

"I've done my thinking." Esperanza pulled back the sheet. The morning sun struck the Colonel's dark skin and made it gleam. The sheets were white and worn, the covers made from some scratchy grey fabric that made Esperanza think of horse blankets. This bluestone compound had been a monastery before the war, before the army of the Covenant had seized it, looted the temple, and housed their fighters in these cells.

Now the monk's old bedclothes were rumpled, hanging halfway off the mattress and scented with Esperanza's hair oil and the pungent traces of both women's slickness and sweat. Last night had been passionate; Esperanza had come gasping, her fingers clawing for purchase in the Colonel's close-shorn hair, but her sobs of pleasure had been silent as always. They had to be silent in here.

"There's still time to get you out." The Colonel's voice was growing firmer now, a familiar note of command creeping in.

Usually that tone caused Esperanza a shiver of pleasure, but this morning, she turned her back. "I still have things to do." Clad only in her nightshirt, she padded barefoot across the room to adjust the pillow and blanket on the camp bed against the opposite wall, yanking out the wrinkles and tightening the corners. This was where she, Esperanza, must pretend to sleep.

"You may not get a chance later. Right now, they won't be thinking about you. It's bigger game they're after. But they will not forget what you are to me."

"I can handle myself." Esperanza filled the basin with water from the pitcher. A few icy drops spattered across the floor, making her flinch. At their last headquarters up in the mountains, the water had frozen solid every night and bats had hung from the rafters.

The Colonel rose from the bed in one graceful movement. She stripped off her loose nightshirt and stood naked on the flagstones. Her body was tall and hard with muscles, her calves, biceps, and buttocks jutting like rocks, her belly flat, the tendons in her forearms standing out. Her skin was still unlined after five decades, but it was nicked with old scars—twenty-four of them. Esperanza knew every one.

The Colonel scooped the chilly water over her face and throat, then sponged her body clean. She did not flinch at the cold droplets that hit her bare feet. She worked on rubbing herself dry with the rough little square of a towel while Esperanza moved back across the room to make their bed. When Esperanza looked up from her work, the Colonel was standing very still, inspecting her own reflection in the shard of glass Esperanza had tacked to the wall months ago.

"I never asked where you got this." The Colonel touched its jagged edge. "The monks weren't permitted such vanities, you know."

"I found it." Esperanza tugged and smoothed the Colonel's bedclothes until they lay flat enough to roll a coin over. Every now and then, she paused to pick off one of her own longer hairs. The Colonel had always been adamant that no traces be left behind. "Maybe it used to be part of the altar display once. You know, before the war."

The Colonel nodded absently. Over her shoulder, in the glass's reflection, Esperanza could see the water still trickling down from the Colonel's hairline. Her eyes were wide. Right above the mirror, where the women could not fail to see it, hung a black banner. It was tattered around the edges, but in its centre was a ring of silver swords: the crest of the Covenant.

Every morning the Colonel must look at that above her own face.

There was a sudden pounding at the door. The wood vibrated; the iron knocker rattled. Esperanza's heart clenched.

"Hurry up in there! You think we've got all day?" She recognised the voice: that guard with the lazy eye who used to leer at her every day on her way to the kitchens.

"She needs more time!" Esperanza hollered back, fighting to keep the fear from her voice.

"To do what? Get you pregnant?" The guard gave a lecherous chuckle. "Sorry, pretty one, but she doesn't have what it takes!"

Esperanza heard his colleague mutter, "Don't talk like that; she was the old duke's niece, remember? And she fought at Ambush Bay." This won a snort of contempt.

"Who cares? That freak thinks she can steal our women and act like a man? Today she'll hang like one."

He must have kicked the door; it shook again. Esperanza grabbed the nearest thing to hand—a small wooden stool—and raised it as she shouted back, "We know the law! You're not allowed in here!" She heard a muffled argument between the two men.

"Half an hour," the other guard said through the door. "Be ready then."

Esperanza waited until the tramp of their boots had receded down the hall, before she slowly lowered the chair. Her heart was hammering.

"You must leave." The Colonel swung around. "I don't want you to be here when it happens."

"You think I would leave you to face them alone?"

"It's not your decision." The Colonel stood with her feet planted firmly, her shoulders thrown back. Unlike most women, she did not fold her body inward as if to hide her nakedness. Gooseflesh stood out across her skin, but she held herself without shivering, upright as a statue. Esperanza thought her glorious.

"I'll not put you in danger." The Colonel paused. "And you shouldn't be exposed to their ridicule, their cruelty. You know what they'll say…"

The Colonel's attachment to her young page had been tolerated in the past; people had shrugged and mumbled that it was better than pregnancies in the ranks and jealous quarrels amongst the men. Blind eyes had been turned.

But that was wartime, when the Colonel's brilliant strategic mind and fearless soldiery—not to mention her family fortune—had been necessary to the victory of the Covenant. As soon as the peace had descended, the whispers had begun: accusations of hermaphroditism and whoredom, the suggestion that the Colonel's military prowess was the sign not of a hero, but of a freak.

And in the midst of those accusations, how easy it had been for more dangerous suspicions to take root. How easy it had been for some to believe the Colonel guilty not only of unnatural deeds, but of treason.

That word caused Esperanza a cold shudder. She could not forget the painful look she had glimpsed on the Colonel's face a week before, after that weedy adviser to the First Guardian had turned up at her door to read out the charges against her. Esperanza had watched from the corner of the room, her face tightening with rage. He had not bothered to hold back a smirk as he spoke.

Grave accusations… Conduct unbecoming… Calling into question…

The Colonel had remained stony and impassive under interrogation. She would not dignify their lies by engaging with them. Only afterwards, when he and his guards had left and they were alone, could she bring herself to look at Esperanza. Neither of them spoke, but the stricken expression on her lover's face had cut Esperanza to the bone.

"You did it all for them." Esperanza's face had grown tight with anger. "Risked your neck for how many years—and this is how they repay you?"

The Colonel had almost smiled. "Nothing makes people resent you more than a debt of gratitude."

From habit, it seemed, the Colonel glanced down at her bed now, checking as she did every morning that it had been made to her standards. In spite of herself, Esperanza smiled at this familiar gesture. The Colonel's dedication to neatness and order had always bordered on the fanatical. It showed in her clean hair and scrubbed nails, her fastidious table manners, and her refusal to brook any breach of the rules, be it in a chess game, a fencing bout, or a battle.

Esperanza suspected it was this rigorous side to the Colonel, her stubborn honesty, which had landed her in trouble. Had the Colonel objected to some outrage committed by her own side, some act of violence or corruption? Had she refused to back the right promotion or grease the right palm? Either the Colonel had never been told her offence or had chosen not to tell Esperanza. The Guardians of the Covenant made grand promises and noble speeches, but Esperanza had seen them up close and recognised them for what they were: a bunch of old men, moaning about their bad teeth, gout, and flea bites, and gloating over their money.

"Enough." The Colonel shook her head, as if to drag herself back to the here and now. "There's no time to lose." She twisted the gold ring on her little finger, yanking it down over the knuckle. Then she crossed the room, seized Esperanza's hand, and folded her fingers around the circle of gold. Esperanza had seen it before. It was an heirloom, engraved with the Colonel's family crest. "The guards out there are no heroes. They would look the other way for less than this." She held Esperanza's gaze, and her voice dropped to a desperate whisper. "Get yourself out of here, beloved. I won't let them destroy you too."

Esperanza looked down at the gold ring in her hand, at the promise of safe passage and freedom it represented. She could walk out of this chamber now, disappear into the city, and start again on her own. She'd done it before.

The Colonel spoke quietly. "There's nothing you can do for me now."

"That's not true." With a slow, deliberate movement, Esperanza laid the gold ring down on the table and turned her back on it. She said, "I can help you dress."

With extreme care, Esperanza laid the items out on the bed: the tunic, underwear, and breeches; the weapons belt and scabbard; the richly embossed scarlet coat. She scrutinised each garment for loose threads, scuff marks, or stains—her brushes, sponges, and tweezers at the ready. This was her ritual each morning, but today every movement, every particle of the fabric before her seemed to stand out with unnatural clarity.

Finding nothing out of order, she folded and refolded the garments, poring over the seams, buttons, and edging, pulling hard at the impeccable collars and cuffs until they stood out with edges sharp enough to leave a crease in her fingertip.

"You're an artist." The Colonel stood as if on parade.

"I used to be a street rat," said Esperanza. "A refugee. Before you took me in."

"Don't stay because you're grateful, beloved." Tears glittered in the Colonel's dark eyes. "I couldn't bear that."

Esperanza straightened up, held her gaze. "That's not why. Now, sit down."

The Colonel did as she was told on the edge of the bed. Esperanza scrambled up to kneel behind her, gazing with longing at her Colonel's bare skin. She resisted the urge to run her hands over it, knowing that was not her task now. Instead, she cupped the back of the Colonel's head, relishing the feel of the short black hair—half an inch long, dense and crisp. The Colonel kept it that length so that no enemy could seize a hold. It scarcely needed tending, but Esperanza picked up the ivory comb anyhow and scratched her way gently over the Colonel's skull, just the way she liked it. She took her time so the Colonel would feel each ticklish scrape of the comb's teeth over her tender scalp.

When she laid the comb down, Esperanza could not help running her thumb along the soft shell of the Colonel's ear, the neat brown lobe unmarked by jewellery or piercing. *Perfect*, Esperanza thought. How could anyone look at such beauty and want to harm it?

She reached over to the far end of the bed, took up the wide bandage, and began the morning's ritual of winding it around the Colonel's chest. She took care not to touch the vulnerable flesh beneath, the small pointed breasts that flattened out with each careful pass of the binder around the Colonel's body. The Colonel had never sought to deceive anyone as to her true nature, but insisted that she looked and felt better this way when moving through the outside world. A world that could be a savage place for a woman, as Esperanza knew.

The Colonel had never seemed easy with Esperanza touching those breasts of hers, but some nights Esperanza had felt them rubbing along her bare back as the Colonel took her from behind, rock-hard nipples scraping up and down Esperanza's shoulder blades. It felt so good that Esperanza had to cram the pillow into her mouth to keep from screaming. But it was when the Colonel had first instructed her on how to apply the binder, bandaging up the private, tender parts of her that included her heart, that Esperanza had known she was truly trusted.

The Colonel held up her arms, and Esperanza slipped the loose white tunic over her head, covering and obscuring the female curves and the adjustments that kept them in check. To a casual observer, the Colonel's silhouette might look almost indistinguishable from that of her male comrades.

Esperanza could tell the difference, though. She'd spotted it right from that first moment she'd seen her.

She slid down to kneel in front of the Colonel and helped her to pull on her breeches, working the skin-tight fabric inch by inch up her firm calves, over her knees, then up her thick-muscled thighs. Esperanza recalled the first time she'd noticed the Colonel's figure. Esperanza had been a mere hanger-on back then, an apprentice, still struggling to convince the Colonel she was up to the job. One afternoon, she had been stationed in the great hall, where the Colonel was training with her elderly fencing master, her powerful legs on display in her breeches and high leather boots. The Colonel's face had been taut, her eyes narrowed with terrifying focus as she lunged and parried, the sweat glinting in the hollow of her throat. Her coiled stillness and sudden, lethal movements were snake-like. Mesmerising.

Oh yes, Esperanza had mouthed to herself.

All she had wanted to do then was trace her way up those powerful thighs with her tongue—which was what she did now before a light tug of her braids signalled her to stop. Reluctantly she turned her attention back to the breeches, easing them along the Colonel's legs and up over her raised hips.

She took her time with the fly buttons. She drew them together as slowly as she could, working her nose through the gap to nuzzle the thinner material of the Colonel's underwear, savouring the feel of the thick curls and the dark, wild scent. Esperanza thought of the mornings she had buried her face there for minutes at a time, running her lips and nipping teeth along the underwear's seam before nudging the fabric to one side with her snuffling nose and extending her tongue to dance over the other woman's clit—swollen, plum-coloured, and glistening.

Such an appetite you have, the Colonel had told her the first time, her eyes wide, her breath shaky.

Some mornings, if the Colonel was in a certain mood, she would get the cane out then, bend its springy length double between her strong hands, then turn it loose against Esperanza's raised and proffered backside. Esperanza would grip the Colonel's open thighs and lick her harder, faster, her breath coming in moans against her cunt with each flick of the cane. The switching impact to her buttocks tickled, then stung, then seared, making her knees scrape and strain against the stone floor and that delicious heat pulse between her legs.

How reassured Esperanza had felt by that carefully measured pain, the white-hot stripes that faded to a more manageable throbbing in the quiet moments between blows. The Colonel had taught her what she was capable of withstanding, never going too far. The sparks of sensation, and the knowledge that someone cared enough to deliver them, had awoken Esperanza after years of numbness, squalor, and drab loneliness. She had grown up assuming chaos and cruelty were the only things you could depend upon, but in her sternness, the Colonel had taught Esperanza what it was to feel safe. And the blissful cool afterwards, as the Colonel massaged ointment into Esperanza's stinging skin, her leg pumping skilfully between the younger woman's thighs, had transported Esperanza to a level of pleasure she had not known was possible.

It had brought her happiness too, which was an even more dangerous thing around here.

Forcing back her tears, Esperanza withdrew and reached for the Colonel's boots. They were knee-high and made from chocolate leather, polished every evening by Esperanza to a mirror gloss. That was her last task at night before joining the Colonel in her bed.

As she slid them on and grappled with the fastenings, Esperanza felt a sob threatening to break from her chest. The Colonel reached down and drew Esperanza's chin up, to look at her. There was no point in asking what was wrong. "Why?" Esperanza whispered, her chest on fire from holding everything in. "Why should we lose all this?" All the Colonel had done, all her life, was serve, follow orders, and lead her fighters. And all she'd sought in return were these quiet hours. Now a tribunal of scabby old men were about to erase that service from the record.

Erase her from the record.

The Colonel stroked her hair. "I can take it from here. You can still leave. You should leave."

Esperanza's chin jutted out. "No."

For a moment, they stared at each other. Then the Colonel's gaze slid down Esperanza's body in her thin nightshirt and then to her own well-shod feet. Some emotion rippled behind her calm expression, then was quickly repressed. When her face became a neutral mask again, the Colonel lifted her right foot.

"This won't do," she said, turning the boot from side to side. "I can't see myself in here. It's gone dull. You can do better than that."

Esperanza began to rise, to reach for her cleaning rags, but a slight shake of the head told her that was not the Colonel's intention. Esperanza sank back onto her haunches, took her nightshirt's hem, and rubbed it in a tentative circle over the boot's toe. The Colonel's nod and knowing smile were almost imperceptible, but it was all Esperanza needed.

Moving swiftly—how much time did they have?—she hauled her nightshirt up over her head. Kneeling naked, she drew the Colonel's foot into her lap, balled the fabric up in her fist, and began to rub vigorously.

She started at the top, just below the Colonel's knee, and worked her way gradually downwards using firm, circular motions, her left hand clamped around the Colonel's ankle to hold her in place. Esperanza lowered her head to concentrate as she scrubbed each little brass button, her bare breasts swaying with the exertion. The smell of the animal hide rose to tickle her nostrils, mingling with her own body's sweat and musk.

Esperanza's rhythmic movements took her down over the Colonel's calf muscle where it bulged against the restrictive leather. Unable to resist, Esperanza bent her head and swept her tongue up the Colonel's instep, savouring the sharp, illicit taste and winning a growl from above.

With light but unmistakable movements, the Colonel began to shift her foot, coaxing her way between Esperanza's thighs, letting her feel the smooth, hard sole and neat stitching against her tender flesh. Esperanza yielded at once, shuffling forward on her knees, her thighs parting open. Sleek leather brushed against her sex lips, growing warmer with each pass.

Esperanza opened her thighs as wide as they would go, giving the polished hide complete access to her throbbing clit. She was painting the leather with her body's juices. One of Esperanza's arms wrapped around the Colonel's waist, pulling their bodies closer, while her other hand locked around the calf muscle, positioning her just right. Esperanza's tight brown nipples scrubbed up and down the Colonel's leg, sending bolts of sensation through her. Panting, she buried her face in her lover's lap.

Part of her felt ashamed to be behaving like some desperate hussy when they were facing destruction. It shouldn't feel so good, so easy. But her body was pouring out its need, jerking to an irresistible rhythm. The Colonel wove her fingers down to the roots of Esperanza's hair, pushing her face deeper into her groin. Her foot worked to and fro now with expert movements, massaging Esperanza's lips and clit with the dripping leather. Esperanza's legs began to quiver, an exquisite fluttering between her thighs building to spasm after spasm as her fingers dug into flesh, her hips thrusting, her groans muffled in the Colonel's strong thighs. The first time she'd felt like this, in the Colonel's bed, she'd cried out with amazement as much as delight. She had not known being alive could feel like that. And having felt it, she would not lose it again.

The waves receded to ripples, and Esperanza sensed the muscles in the Colonel's belly tightening. The Colonel bent over her, and the soft touch of lips pressed onto the back of her head. A long moment passed before Esperanza drew back and used her nightshirt to wipe the slippery new sheen from those boots.

She rose to her feet. She held out the Colonel's red coat and held it out, the silk lining catching the light. The Colonel stood and slipped her arms through it. Then Esperanza gave the garment one last inspection, scrutinising it for loose hairs or dust and running her fingertips over the gold stitching. She leaned her forehead against the Colonel's shoulder, drawing in the scent of clean wool one last time. The epaulettes, embroidered with the emblem of the Covenant, felt stiff and abrasive against her skin. The Colonel had worn this uniform and others like it since childhood. Some nights, the Colonel had worn nothing else, the vivid red draped over her bare skin and Esperanza spread across her lap or pressed against the wall as they fucked.

"I'll miss this." Esperanza touched the garment one last time.

The Colonel's face tightened. "You shouldn't. You know why the army chose that colour? To hide the bloodstains."

Esperanza shut her eyes a moment. Blindly, she groped for the Colonel's hand. "Is that why you didn't try harder to fight their charges?" she asked.

Was the Colonel tired of it all, Esperanza wondered? Weary and ashamed of those long years spent killing for a cause she no longer had faith in? Sick of scouring her hands clean, stifling her nightmares, keeping her own counsel about what she had seen and done? "Do you think you deserve this?"

For once, the Colonel couldn't meet Esperanza's eye. "Don't you?" she whispered.

"No." Esperanza stood there until the Colonel was forced to look back at her. "And I never will."

With a shaky sigh, she lifted one hand to caress the side of Esperanza's face. "You're not going to leave." Her tone was tender, resigned, that of a good soldier who knows when she has been defeated. "Are you?"

Esperanza managed a crooked smile. "Not without you."

With practised movements, she buckled the Colonel's weapons belt around her hips, fingering the supple leather straps that had once delighted them both. Then she took the sword from its place on the wall and slid it into the decorative scabbard. It was a ceremonial item, this weapon, for formal occasions only. Esperanza buffed the blade to a silvery sheen every day, but it was blunt.

Unlike the short, rough dagger that lay concealed in the false bottom of the trunk, beneath Esperanza's own tunic and leggings.

She dressed herself in a few hasty movements, then waited until the Colonel's back was turned and she was busy tucking her helmet beneath her arm. Esperanza drew out the dagger and strapped it to her wrist, ensuring it was hidden beneath the loose fabric. The Colonel would not have consented to this, to Esperanza placing herself in mortal danger.

Which was why Esperanza had not told her.

Esperanza caught a glimpse of herself in the mirror and pulled her shoulders back.

No doubt the Colonel would play by the rules at the tribunal today. She would be gallant and stoical in the face of the old men and jealous comrades. Maybe she would accept exile or prison without protest. Maybe she would walk to the gallows with the same graceful, erect stride that carried her now to the door of their little stone room.

But Esperanza would not accept it. What the Colonel didn't know was that Esperanza had made her own plans for today, had doled out her own bribes, had called in her own favours. She had stashed lookouts, horses, and swords where they could be of use. She was no politician, but she understood a few things: Like which locals would agree to start a disturbance three streets away at just the right time. Like which guards could be persuaded to leave their post for a few precious moments. Or which group of women would be outside the gates with spare veils and coverings, ready to hide a stranger in their midst as they bustled by on the road leading out of the city.

"I've done my thinking," Esperanza said under her breath.

That was the thing about having been a street rat, a beggar, an outcast, and surviving to become the page and beloved of the Covenant's finest soldier. Esperanza would never again believe that a thing she wanted was impossible. Nor would she ever stop fighting.

It might still end in catastrophe, of course. But she forced herself not to dwell on that. She looked out the arrow-slit window instead, to the mountain crags outlined against the clearing sky. Beyond them were lands where the power of the Covenant had not reached, places where a runaway might begin again. Possibilities those old men could not destroy.

Esperanza pulled on her boots. She held the heavy oak door open and followed the Colonel out of the room, leaving it ajar behind them.

ABOUT JESS LEA

Jess Lea lives in Melbourne, Australia, where she started out as an academic before working in the community sector. She loves vintage crime fiction, the writings of funny women, and lesbian books of all sorts. Jess can be found writing in cafes, in parks, and in her pyjamas at home when she should be at work.

CONNECT WITH JESS

E-Mail: JessLeaContact@gmail.com

Twitter: @JessLeaMusings

OTHER BOOKS FROM YLVA PUBLISHING

www.ylva-publishing.com

DON'T BE SHY

Astrid Ohletz & Jae (Eds.)

ISBN: 978-3-95533-538-0 (mobi), 978-3-95533-539-7 (epub)
Length: 139,000 words (350 pages)

From kinky phone sex to unexpected, steamy encounters with the new neighbor. Fun with a love swing and unexpected relaxation techniques. This anthology has it all.

Twenty-five authors of lesbian fiction bring you short stories that focus on the sensual, red-hot delights of sex between women and the celebration of the female form in all its diverse hedonism.

Are you in the mood for something spicy?

HEART'S SURRENDER

Emma Weimann

ISBN: 978-3-95533-183-2
Length: 305 pages (63,000 words)

Neither Samantha Freedman nor Gillian Jennings are looking for a relationship when they begin a no-strings-attached affair. But soon simple attraction turns into something more. What happens when the worlds of a handywoman and a pampered housewife collide? Can nights of hot, erotic fun lead to love, or will these two very different women go their separate ways?

NIGHTS OF SILK AND SAPPHIRE

Amber Jacobs

ISBN: 978-3-95533-511-3
Length: 309 pages (113,000 words)

Abducted from a land of wealth and privilege, Dae is chained to a slaver's caravan crossing the vast Jaharri desert. It is a strange world of blistering sun, rolling dunes, and wind-carved plains, ruled by the Scion Zafirah Al'Intisar, a powerful and mysterious woman with seductive eyes of sapphire blue.

When Zafirah liberates the caravan the rescue Dae prayed for is not as it seems; Zafirah's carnal appetite is legendary. Dae is taken into Zafirah's harem, a decadent world of excess and sexual freedom. At first, Dae struggles with desires she has never before experienced, but as love and lust collide these two women slowly forge a bond as one learns to listen to her heart, and the other to the call of her awakening body.

THE CLUB

A.L. Brooks

ISBN: 978-3-95533-654-7
Length: 227 pages (72,000 words)

Welcome to The Club—leave your inhibitions and your everyday cares at the door, and indulge yourself in an evening of anonymous, no-strings, woman-on-woman action. For many visitors to The Club, this is exactly what they are looking for, and what they get. For others, however, the emotions run high, and one night of sex changes their lives in ways they couldn't have imagined.

The Taste of Her
© 2018 by Jess Lea

ISBN (paperback): 978-3-96324-009-6

Published by Ylva Publishing, legal entity of Ylva Verlag, e.Kfr.

Ylva Verlag, e.Kfr.
Owner: Astrid Ohletz
Am Kirschgarten 2
65830 Kriftel
Germany

www.ylva-publishing.com

First edition: 2018

No part of this book may be reproduced, scanned, or distributed in any printed or electronic form without permission. Please do not participate in or encourage piracy of copyrighted materials in violation of the author's rights. Thank you for respecting the hard work of this author.

This is a work of fiction. Names, characters, places, and incidents either are a product of the author's imagination or are used fictitiously, and any resemblance to locales, events, business establishments, or actual persons—living or dead—is entirely coincidental.

Credits
Edited by Michelle Aguilar and Amanda Jean
Cover Design by Streetlight Graphics

CPSIA information can be obtained
at www.ICGtesting.com
Printed in the USA
LVHW111329120221
679171LV00024B/147

9 783963 240096